Acclaim for R

Make You Feel My Love

"Robin Lee Hatcher never disappoints! I loved both eras of this dual timeline story, each with characters you will grow to genuinely care for. The beautiful overarching umbrella for both generations' stories is redemption from the pain of past betrayals. Another keeper from one of my favorite authors!"

—Deborah Raney, author of *Bridges* and the Chandler Sisters Novels series

"What a delight to step back in time with the charming community of Chickadee Creek! Robin Lee Hatcher is one of my favorite storytellers, and I loved both the past and present threads in her latest novel as the main characters partnered together to overcome their difficult pasts and find genuine hope in God. With endearing characters and elements of suspense, this heartwarming romance was pure joy to read."

—Melanie Dobson, award-winning author of *The Curator's Daughter* and *Catching the Wind*

"More than a century apart two young women flee home, determined to forge new lives in remote Chickadee Creek, where they pray their abusers will never find them. Robin Lee Hatcher weaves together two generational love stories of the Chandler family, both rich in the courage required to relinquish fear and to discover the freedom in trusting God beyond the pain of betrayal. *Make You Feel My Love* blossoms as a novel of faith, love, and hope amidst the brave and sometimes faltering steps of newly found faith. An uplifting read with great characters, Hatcher's fans will love this."

—Cathy Gohlke, Christy Award–winning author of *Night Bird Calling* and *The Medallion*

Cross My Heart

"In *Cross My Heart*, book two of her Legacy of Faith series, author Robin Lee Hatcher continues to delve into the powerful influence of a spiritual family heritage. She weaves together two touching stories that examine life choices and their consequences. Utilizing a dual-time plot set against World War II and present day, Hatcher writes with realism and compassion about how hope and healing can grow from our deepest wounds."

—Beth K. Vogt, Christy Award–winning author

"Hatcher *(Who I Am with You)* continues her chronicle of the Henning family in the powerful second installment of her Legacy of Faith series . . . This touching story of forgiveness and redemption will appeal to fans of Colleen Coble."

—*Publishers Weekly*

"Robin Lee Hatcher tells the story of two people dealing with addiction in their lives in *Cross My Heart* . . . This is a good romance that deals with some very tough issues that happen all the time now."

—*Parkersburg News & Sentinel*

"As usual, Hatcher is an auto-buy for all library collections."

—*Library Journal*

Who I Am with You

"In this seamless time-slip novel, Hatcher provides inspiration in each character's growing relationship with the Lord and prompts readers to reflect on their own journey. This story of loss and redemption is sure to win the hearts of contemporary and historic romance fans alike."

—*Hope by the Book*

"This [is] a lovely story of love and loss and forgiveness."

—*The Parkersburg News & Sentinel*

"Bestselling inspirational romance star Hatcher weaves a story of love and identity lost and found . . . The characters are authentic, the butterflies of anticipation are persistent, and the protagonists' deferred attraction is thrillingly palpable; you cannot help but hold your breath until they realize it too."

—*Booklist* review

"Hatcher's moving novel is rich in healing and hope and realistically portrays the tough introspection that sometimes comes with being hurt."

—*Publishers Weekly*

"Tender and heartwarming, Robin Lee Hatcher's *Who I Am with You* is a faith-filled story about the power of forgiveness, second chances, and unconditional love. A true delight for lovers of romantic inspirational fiction, this story will not only make you swoon, it will remind you of God's goodness and grace."

—Courtney Walsh, *New York Times* and *USA TODAY* bestselling author

You're Gonna Love Me

"Whenever I want to fall in love again, I pick up a Robin Lee Hatcher novel."

—Francine Rivers, *New York Times* bestselling author

"Hatcher's richly layered novels pull me in like a warm embrace, and I never want to leave . . . Highly recommended!"

—Colleen Coble, *USA TODAY* bestselling author

"A heart-warming story of love, acceptance, and challenge. Highly recommended."

—*CBA Market*

"*You'll Think of Me* is like a vacation to a small town in Idaho where the present collides with the past and it's not clear which will win. The shadows of the past threaten to trap Brooklyn in the past. Can she break free into the freedom to love and find love? The story kept me coming back for just one more page. A perfect read for those who love a romance that is much more as it explores important themes."

—Cara Putman, award-winning author of
Shadowed by Grace and *Beyond Justice*

Make You Feel My Love

Also by Robin Lee Hatcher

You're Gonna Love Me
You'll Think of Me
The Heart's Pursuit
A Promise Kept
A Bride for All Seasons
Heart of Gold
Loving Libby
Return to Me
The Perfect Life
Wagered Heart
Whispers from Yesterday
The Forgiving Hour
The Shepherd's Voice

Legacy of Faith Series
Who I Am with You
Cross My Heart
How Sweet It Is

**Kings Meadow
Romance Series**
Love Without End
Whenever You Come Around
Keeper of the Stars

**Where the Heart
Lives Series**
Belonging
Betrayal
Beloved

**The Sisters of Bethlehem
Springs Series**
A Vote of Confidence
Fit to Be Tied
A Matter of Character

Coming to America Series
Dear Lady
Patterns of Love
In His Arms
Promised to Me

Stories
I Hope You Dance, included
in *Kiss the Bride* and *How
to Make a Wedding*
Autumn's Angel, included
in *A Bride for All Seasons*
*Love Letter to the
Editor*, included in *Four
Weddings and a Kiss*

Make You Feel My Love

ROBIN LEE HATCHER

THOMAS NELSON

Since 1798

Make You Feel My Love

Published in Nashville, Tennessee, by Thomas Nelson. Thomas Nelson is a registered trademark of HarperCollins Christian Publishing, Inc.

Thomas Nelson titles may be purchased in bulk for educational, business, fundraising, or sales promotional use. For information, please email SpecialMarkets@ThomasNelson.com.

Scripture quotations are taken from the New American Standard Bible® (NASB). Copyright © 1960, 1962, 1963, 1968, 1971, 1972, 1973, 1975, 1977, 1995 by The Lockman Foundation. Used by permission. www.lockman.org.

Publisher's Note: This novel is a work of fiction. Names, characters, places, and incidents are either products of the author's imagination or used fictitiously. All characters are fictional, and any similarity to people living or dead is purely coincidental.

Library of Congress Cataloging-in-Publication Data

Names: Hatcher, Robin Lee, author.
Title: Make you feel my love / Robin Lee Hatcher.
Description: Nashville, Tennessee : Thomas Nelson, [2021] | Summary: "One broken woman. One lost man. And the long-buried secrets tying them together"--Provided by publisher.
Identifiers: LCCN 2021005175 (print) | LCCN 2021005176 (ebook) | ISBN 9780785241409 (trade paper) | ISBN 9780785241386 (epub) | ISBN 9780785241393 (downloadable audio)
Subjects: GSAFD: Christian fiction. | Love stories.
Classification: LCC PS3558.A73574 M35 2021 (print) | LCC PS3558.A73574 (ebook) | DDC 813/.54--dc23
LC record available at https://lccn.loc.gov/2021005175
LC ebook record available at https://lccn.loc.gov/2021005176

Printed in the United States of America

21 22 23 24 25   LSC   10 9 8 7 6 5 4 3 2 1

To Sue, Katie, Larissa, Susan, Pat, Sara, and Mia,
the ladies of the Larkspur Kennel Club (unofficial
but so delightful). All of you and all of our four-legged
pals brighten my life as well as our neighborhood.

Chapter 1

The door complained loudly as it swung open before Chelsea Spencer. To a stranger, the gloomy interior of Rosemary & Time might resemble something out of a horror film, shadows and strange shapes abounding. But the antique store was as familiar and welcoming to her now as it had been when she was a child.

Many things used to frighten her. Some things still did. But not this place.

She located the light switch and flipped it on. Shadows went into hiding, and the strange shapes of moments before became familiar shelves full of books and old dolls, displays of costume jewelry, ancient furniture, knickknacks and bobs of all sorts, and plenty more. There was also a musty odor, thick layers of dust, evidence of small rodents escaping the elements, and dense spiderwebs in the corners.

"Aunt Rosemary," she whispered. "How did it get like this?"

Outside, rain began to fall from the slate-gray heavens, and a gust of wind rattled the old building. Chelsea turned to close the door, shutting out the storm.

In her memories, the shop on Alexander Street was a quaint place, with lots of wonderful nooks and crannies where a girl could curl up with a good book and get lost for hours in some imaginary world. In her memories, the shop smelled of apples and cinnamon and was bathed in golden sunlight. Had she remembered it wrong, or had it changed that much since she was a girl of eight?

Oh, that wonderful summer in Chickadee Creek with her warmhearted great-aunt, the sister of Chelsea's maternal grandfather. Sometimes she wondered if that season had been real or if she'd only dreamed it.

Drawing a slow, deep breath, she moved farther into the shop, running her fingers over the dusty display tables and counters. Many hours of cleanup, repairs, and reorganization awaited her. Days of it. More like weeks. But perhaps that was a good thing. Physical labor was what she needed. Labor that would leave her too weary to think—or feel. That would be ideal.

The door flew open, banging against the wall. She squealed as she spun around, halfway expecting to see . . . to see . . . *him*. But it was only the growing storm, blowing rain into the shop. She hurried to shut the door again, this time making certain it was securely latched. Making sure she was safely inside. Making sure nothing—and no one—could get in.

The terror hit her then, as it so often did, out of nowhere. As powerful as a punch in her solar plexus, the panic almost took her to her knees. Instead, she leaned on a display case as tears welled in her eyes.

"Oh, God," she breathed out. "I'm afraid, and I'm so tired of being afraid. Help me get beyond it."

Liam Chandler stood at the front window of the house, watching the hundred-feet-tall lodge pole pines sway from side to side. Rain, driven before the wind, ran in sheets down the glass.

Jacob loved to be here when it stormed like this.

Liam closed his eyes for a few moments. In those weeks immediately following his brother's funeral, he hadn't welcomed reminders of Jacob. He'd pushed every thought of him away. They'd made him angry. They'd hurt. They'd made him want to lash out. They'd made him feel guilty for being alive.

But that had begun to change. Slowly. Little by little. Over the months, he'd started to write down random memories of Jacob in a journal. Writing about his brother, about himself, about their family, had begun to heal something inside of him. Eventually he might even figure out why things were the way they were in his family.

"What about your career?" In his mind he heard the phone message his mom had left for him yesterday. *"Are you going to throw it all away?"*

He clenched his jaw as he looked out at the storm again.

All his life, he'd wondered why he didn't measure up in his mom's eyes, why he hadn't been as good as Jacob. Jacob, her favorite son. Years ago, when Liam had talked about going to California to try to break into the movies, his mom had scoffed and told him not to waste his time. She'd told him he needed a sensible career, like his father's. Now things were different. Perhaps it was because Jacob was gone, because Liam was all she had left. Or maybe she wasn't as indifferent as he'd believed her to be.

Still, going back to Hollywood held little appeal for Liam at the moment. Was what he did in front of the cameras really a career? As far as he could tell, it wasn't talent that had garnered him attention from directors, producers, fans, and eventually *People* magazine and the tabloids. It was his looks, and he'd had nothing to do with those. Inheriting good genes wasn't a talent.

But Jacob? His brother had been at the front of every line when they were passing out talent. His voice had been the kind that could make the angels weep. He'd been proficient on half a dozen musical instruments. If he heard a hummed melody once, he'd been able to create a symphony from it on the keyboard. Jacob Chandler had been destined for greatness—before the Big C came calling.

Drawing a deep breath, Liam turned his back to the storm. Lamplight warmed the large, rustic room in which he stood. The rustic part was intentional. The house itself was less than five years old. Liam had it built after the premiere of his first major movie, one in which he'd had more than a minor role. He'd intended to use the house for hunting trips and short getaways, not for a permanent residence. His thinking had changed about that. The quiet of the forest appealed to him. And it wasn't as if he was completely isolated. Chickadee Creek was only a few miles away. Although only a single lane, the dirt road that connected him to the small town was maintained throughout the year. He had power, a landline, and even cable service that included the internet. The builder had told him that only the electricity and landline would have been available to him as little as two years before the house was built. Cell service remained spotty in these mountains, but that wasn't a negative in Liam's mind. Without his smartphone—he refused to connect it to the Wi-Fi in his home—the world left him mostly alone. Almost no one had his landline number. Just the way he wanted it.

As if to belie his thoughts, the phone rang. Amused by the timing, he shook his head as he went to answer it. "Hello."

"Mr. Chandler? This is Grace Witherstone at the mercantile. We've got that order you placed last week."

"Great. I'll be in to get it after the worst of the storm passes."

"It's supposed to hang around awhile. You might want to wait until tomorrow. Unless you want to get drowned while you're loadin' everything into your truck."

He glanced toward the window. "Yeah, you may be right. Won't hurt for me to wait another day."

"I see you got a case of paper. You writin' a book or somethin'? Maybe about our little town or the Chandler family history?"

"I'm not a writer, Mrs. Witherstone. Just want the paper for printing when the need arises."

"Well, if you decide to write about Chickadee Creek, you might be interested in knowing Rosemary Townsend is comin' back to town."

Liam sank onto the sofa. If he'd learned anything in the months he'd lived in these mountains, it was that the owner of the town's general store liked to talk. There was usually a nice mix of gossip and history included in Grace's soliloquies. Having nothing better to do on this stormy day—and preferring not to think any more about his brother and their mom for now—he might as well listen. "Who's Rosemary Townsend?"

"She owns the antique store on Alexander. She closed it down over a year ago, even before she took a really bad fall and busted up her leg. But she's recovering from surgery now. Guess she feels a whole lot better, because she's plannin' on opening up the shop again. Anyways, she knows the history of Chickadee Creek better'n anybody hereabouts. She's got bunches of old books and newspapers too. So if you were needin' to do research, she'd be the person to talk to. Especially if you want to know more about your own people. There's been Chandlers in these parts for a hundred and fifty years."

The woman paused. Liam assumed she needed to take a breath.

"Rosemary's from one of Chickadee Creek's longtime families too. Same as the Chandlers, although the Townsends stuck around and your folks kinda came and went, even though they kept hold of most of their property. The Townsends don't go back as far as the gold-rush days, but they was here startin' before the first world war."

"Gold rush, huh?" He knew the history of the area, but he figured he should say something to let her know he listened.

"Land sakes. Don't they teach such things in schools no more?"

"Sorry. I guess I didn't pay enough attention in history class. Tell me about it."

"The Boise Basin was what founded Idaho, pretty much. More gold come out of these mountains than the California 49er or the Klondike rushes. Maybe put together, though I can't say for sure on that. Anyways, Idaho City was bigger than Portland at the height of the rush. Biggest city in the northwest for quite a spell."

Liam nodded, as if the woman on the other end of the line could see him.

"By the time Rosemary's people came to these parts, the rush was long over and big companies were mining the land in other ways. Not sure what the Townsends did back then. All I've ever known was Rosemary's antique shop. Guess I'll have to ask her what they did. Or maybe I'll ask her niece. A great-niece, actually. She's come to stay with Rosemary and help out while she continues her recovery."

"Do you know her great-niece?"

"Not really. She visited for a summer when she was a little thing. Maybe eight or nine. Lots of freckles and red hair. That's what I remember most. Quiet little thing. Quiet as a church mouse. Wonder if she's still like that. Time'll tell."

"Time will tell," he echoed softly.

"Well, looks like I've got a customer come in despite the storm. Gotta go. I'll see you tomorrow. Good talking to you."

"You, too, Mrs. Witherstone. See you tomorrow." Liam grinned as he set the phone in its cradle. Next time he'd better show he knew more than he'd let on, or Grace Witherstone would have him run out of town on a rail.

Cora

APRIL 1895

NEW YORK CITY

Cora Anderson moved toward the ballroom of the McKenzie mansion, her satin gown swooshing against the marble floor. Her gloved fingers rested in the crook of her father's arm. She felt the weight of her mother's diamond necklace against her breastbone, but it wasn't as heavy as the weight upon her heart.

Her role tonight, she knew all too well, was to convince a man to marry her. But not just any man. It must be the man her father had chosen as the most advantageous for the family.

Aaron Anderson, her father, had made his fortune in the years immediately after the Civil War. An ambitious young man, he'd soon been able to build a fashionable residence on a fashionable avenue in New York City. A year later, he'd married above his station. Ever since that momentous occasion, he'd sought acceptance into the upper echelons of society. Sought it and failed. He was tolerated but not embraced. It was now his only surviving child's duty to achieve what he hadn't been able to realize on his own.

Cora and her father stopped inside the ballroom doorway and watched the couples whirling around the dance floor to the strains of a waltz. When the music came to an end, the buzz of conversations increased. Men escorted their dance partners to the side of the floor. Young women checked their dance cards or waved fans before their faces. Shy smiles were exchanged, as were calculated looks.

It was like an elaborate marionette performance, Cora thought as she observed it all. There were invisible hands controlling every movement in the room. Some were clueless of what went unspoken, but she wasn't one of them. She was all too aware of her father's manipulations and what the end result would look like.

As if summoned by the thought, Duncan Abernathy broke away from a group of men and strode in her direction. Her father patted her hand, signaling that he'd also seen the man's approach.

"Miss Anderson," Duncan said as he stopped and bowed.

"Good evening, Mr. Anderson." It was more nod than bow this time. "It's good to see you both."

Duncan Abernathy came from old money. His family had become shipping tycoons several generations back. Later, the Abernathys expanded into the railroad industry, managing to multiply their wealth even during economic downturns.

From what Cora could tell, Duncan held no interest in ships or railroads. He would rather spend the money his forefathers had made than make any of his own. He liked fast horses and trips to the Atlantic shore and to Europe. He liked dancing and gambling. He liked champagne and fine wines and rich foods. He liked to be seen with a beautiful woman on his arm. More than anything else, he liked to talk about himself.

She disliked him intensely.

"I believe this next dance is ours," he said, holding out a hand.

She placed her fingers onto his palm and felt his hand close around them, like a noose tightening around her throat.

APRIL 1895

The gardens behind the Anderson mansion were in full bloom on the day Cora's father sat down at his desk to hammer out the details of the marriage contract. Cora and his wife knew, since he'd made no secret of it, that he would be settling a very large sum on Duncan Abernathy as soon as Duncan and Cora married. The bridegroom, in turn, had promised to make doors open for the senior Andersons throughout New York City and along the entire eastern seaboard.

Aaron Anderson thought it a brilliant exchange.

Cora Anderson thought it a prison sentence.

The years of her life spread out before her—predictable, boring, unchanging, lonely, unescapable. All the polite tea parties. All of the fancy dress balls. The travel that took her only to places she had been before to see the people she already knew. She would be tied to a man who thought quite highly of himself but who had nothing interesting to say. When he had an affair—as he most surely would—he would be relatively discreet. Rules were rules in their society, after all. But it wouldn't occur to him that his wife might mind when he took a mistress. Cora would be little more to him than an attractive ornament on his arm. She would be expected to bear his children and to see that they were raised well. But she wouldn't be expected to have a thought of her own. Definitely not a thought that differed from his.

"We will announce the engagement at a dinner party," her mother said.

Cora turned from perusing the gardens.

"In two weeks, I think."

At the age of forty-five, Beatrice Anderson remained a striking woman. Her golden-brown hair was free of gray, her face unlined, and her waist still narrow despite giving birth to three children in quick succession.

Of those three children born to Beatrice and Aaron Anderson, only Cora had lived to adulthood. The two Anderson sons had died, one as an infant, the other at the age of three. Cora, the youngest of the children, didn't remember either of her brothers. Perhaps that was why her unhappiness with the life she led also made her feel guilty.

"Cora, do sit down. Your fidgeting is making me nervous."

Cora obeyed her mother, moving to a sofa and settling onto it.

"Now, as I was saying, we'll have a dinner party in two weeks to announce your engagement to Duncan. Perhaps forty people." She pursed her lips. "I suppose I must wait to see who the Abernathys want to invite before I make up my own list."

"Aren't your friends important enough, Mother?"

"Whatever do you mean?"

"Nothing." Eyes lowered, Cora plucked at a loose thread on the sofa.

"Straighten your shoulders, dear. A slouch is so unattractive on a woman."

It doesn't look good on a man either.

"Perhaps we should go to Paris to buy your wedding gown. Unless, of course, the engagement is to be less than a year. Has Duncan given any indication of his preference?"

"No." She supposed he would like to marry sooner rather than later. The way he spent money, he could surely use an infusion into his bank account.

"I was nineteen when I married your father. Three years younger than you are. I was so happy to leave my parents' home and begin life as a married woman." Her mother's voice trailed away on a wistful note.

But why was her mother wistful? Did she regret the life she'd led? She showed no true affection for her husband and little devotion to her daughter. She cared most about how things appeared. Had she ever desired to walk a different path?

Cora rose from the sofa and returned to the window, as if hoping the colorful gardens could change the directions of her thoughts. It didn't work.

Am I as passionless as Mother?

It took only a second to answer her own question. *No!*

Cora wasn't passionless. There were many things she cared about, many things that interested her. However, she'd spent most of her life hiding her true feelings. She'd been trained to keep her opinions to herself. She'd been sent to school but not with an actual education as the goal. No, it had been so she could rub shoulders with young women of quality—and, with luck, to meet some of their eligible brothers.

She closed her eyes and drew in a deep breath.

If she could do anything in life, if there were no restrictions upon her as a woman, she would become a concert violinist. Nothing stirred her soul like music, especially the music of a violin. But it wasn't considered seemly for a woman to perform on a stage. Her father would rather see her dead.

She looked out the window again as she wiped a tear from her cheek.

Liam's Journal

The storm yesterday made me think a lot about Jacob. I remember one summer when we were up here in the old cabin we used to have. I was about six, I think, because the Jacob I can see in my head was still really little. There was a storm that day too.

Mom and Dad were fighting. I can't remember anything they said, but I remember that Jacob and I wanted to get away from them. So we went up into the attic. Dad didn't know that if I stood on the top bunk and used the bunkbed ladder, we could get up there, but we could.

There were small windows at each end of the attic. Not sure why anybody would build a place like that since it wasn't really a room. Jacob and I could stand up straight, but Dad couldn't have, if he ever tried. Except for dust and cobwebs, the attic was empty. I suppose because it'd be too much work to put anything up there.

Jacob and I sat by one of the windows, watching the rain run down the glass in sheets and the wind bend the trees way over. There was lots of rolling thunder. One of them cracked right over our heads. It was scary and exciting at the same time. Jacob clung to me tight. Now that I think back on it, he was probably scared to death. He probably wanted to go back to our room but was too afraid to go on his own.

I loved Jacob. Always did. Always will. I admit that sometimes I was jealous of the way Mom preferred him to me. I never understood why that was. Still don't understand it. But I never held it against Jacob. It wasn't his fault he was so likable. Besides, he was my kid brother, and I loved him. Like that song from the soundtrack of <u>Rambo III</u> (one of Dad's favorites), I could always say, "He ain't heavy. He's my brother." Because that's how I felt about him.

Liam's Journal

Chickadee Creek is a quaint place. (That's what Grandma called it back when I was a kid. "Quaint." You don't hear that word often these days.) People are friendly, although I can't say I've given them much of a chance to prove it to me personally since I came up here this winter. The only person I really know is Mrs. Witherstone at the general store, and I've never met anybody who likes to talk more than she does. Definitely friendly.

The old family cabin wasn't in town. It wasn't too far from where I built my vacation house. So we didn't mix with folks back then either. Jacob and I ran all over these mountains. Rode our bikes along back roads and trails. We climbed trees like a couple of monkeys. We explored up around the remains of the old dredger. "Hooligans" is what Grandma called us. Another of her funny words.

One Christmas vacation we came up to stay. I think I was maybe ten and Jacob nine. There was a big snowstorm. Bigger than anything we'd seen in Boise. So Jacob and I took an old garbage can lid to use as a sled since nobody thought to bring sleds with us. There was this hill not too far from the cabin. It went down at a really steep degree, then made an abrupt turn up again. Formed a near perfect *V*. What we didn't realize, being stupid kids, was that when we hit that *V*-shaped bottom, the lid was going to come to a sudden and complete stop. We weren't going to simply start up the other side.

Don't know why we both didn't end up with broken necks. We flew down that hill until we hit bottom. Wham! I flew off one way, and Jacob flew off another. Knocked the breath out of us both. I'm pretty sure that's when I discovered what it meant to "see stars." I don't know how long we lay there, just trying to breathe normal. Finally, I was able to get out, "Jacob, you okay?" He answered, "Yeah," in a squeaky little voice. It was quite a while longer before we had the strength to get up and walk home.

We never did tell Mom or Dad about that. Not even after we grew up.

Chapter 2

*L*ight crept around the edge of the bedroom curtains. Not full daylight, but enough to disturb Chelsea's sleep. With a groan, she rolled onto her other side and pulled a pillow over her head. Too late. She was awake now. Staying in bed and pretending otherwise was useless.

She pushed the pillow away, opened her eyes, and sat up. The clock on the nightstand read 5:32 a.m. A ridiculous time to get up, in her opinion. It was suitable for farmers with cows to milk, maybe, and those irritatingly cheerful morning people—the ones she tried to avoid at all costs. But it wasn't suitable for her.

Still, nothing she tried made sleep possible.

Grumbling, she got out of bed and went into the bathroom. The lengthy shower did little to improve her mood. She remained grumpy as she went down the stairs to make her first cup of coffee.

Seated at the kitchen table a short while later, she sipped the creamer-laced beverage, her gaze moving around the room. The cupboards had no doors. Plates, cups, and glasses sat stacked or placed in neat rows on the two shelves. There weren't enough dishes to host a large dinner party, but there were enough for a few guests on special occasions. Of course, there wouldn't be many for Rosemary Townsend to entertain in this small community, even if she wanted to.

Chelsea rose and carried her coffee mug out to the deck that wrapped around two sides of the house. The wood beneath her bare feet was wet from the previous night's storm, and a chill permeated the air. According to the weatherman, the cool temperatures wouldn't linger. Warmer weather would follow on the heels of the storm.

Settling onto a deck chair, she looked across the winding road to the building that housed Rosemary & Time. It appeared less ominous than it had yesterday. Less ominous, but also in dire need of repairs. A broken window on the second story had been mended with duct tape. A shutter on the window to the left of it had lost a bracket and hung crooked, giving the building a crazy-eyed appearance. Another good windstorm might blow the thing off. The whole place needed a coat of fresh paint. And that was only the outside. She already knew what awaited her on the inside. It was overwhelming when she thought about it.

She took a deep breath and released it. Aunt Rosemary would have to hire someone for any major jobs, and painting the outside of the antique store was definitely a major one. Plus, Chelsea wasn't particularly handy when it came to household repairs. She was willing to work hard and was able to follow instructions, but her expertise ended with changing light bulbs and swapping out batteries in smoke alarms. Heaven only knew what other updates were needed before the shop could reopen.

"But I can clean and reorganize," she said aloud. "I'm good at that."

The rumble of an engine drew her gaze up the road. Sounds carried a long distance in the forest, so it was hard to tell how soon the vehicle would come into view around the bend. In this instance, it wasn't long.

Although the truck with its SuperCrew cab was a newer model, the shiny black paint job was covered with a layer of dirt. Yesterday's storm hadn't dumped enough rain to wash it clean. The driver looked her way as he passed by Aunt Rosemary's house. She didn't know anybody in Chickadee Creek, but she waved anyway. She wanted to show that she belonged there and wasn't trespassing.

That was probably my excitement for the day.

She drained the last of the coffee from the mug, then stood. It was time to get to work. She had three more days before Aunt Rosemary would be released from the rehab center in Boise and return to Chickadee Creek. Chelsea wanted to surprise her great-aunt with how much she'd accomplished in only a few days' time.

She carried the empty mug to the kitchen and set it in the sink. A slice of toast would do for breakfast. When she'd hastily left Spokane, she hadn't brought much food with her. Just a loaf of bread, a jar of peanut butter, and a few apples. Later, she would make a trip to the store to stock up on groceries. Aunt Rosemary had said to tell the woman at the mercantile to charge it to her account.

A smile tipped the corners of her mouth. How many places were left in this country where somebody had an account at a market? Couldn't be many. Only in places the size of Chickadee Creek. And places like Hadley Station where she'd grown up. Places where the woman at the grocery store would call a kid's mom if they bought too much candy. Places where everybody knew your name and what family you belonged to.

Which meant the guy who'd driven by in the black truck already knew who she was and why she was in town.

"There you be," Grace Witherstone said the moment Liam stepped through the mercantile doors.

He glanced around the store. No other customers. Which meant he would be listening to Grace for a while. There wouldn't be anything or anyone to distract her.

"That was some storm we had yesterday, but we coulda used more rain than blow. Tree come down behind my place. Lucky we all still have power. Never know when a tree's gonna fall on them wires."

He made a sound in his throat to show that he listened.

"I hear tell that development closer to the highway's got buried utilities. That's gotta help when the weather turns."

Liam looked around again. "Maybe I could get my order."

"Oh, sure. Listen to me. Yakkin' your head off. The boxes are right over there in that corner." She pointed.

He moved in the indicated direction.

"I heard Rosemary's great-niece got here yesterday."

"Rosemary?"

"The woman I told you about on the phone. Rosemary Townsend. The one who owns the antique store."

He thought of the young woman he'd passed on the way to the mercantile. She'd sat on a deck, her ginger hair resplendent in the morning sun. Only now did he realize the antique shop was across the road from where she'd sat. Rosemary's great-niece? Probably. Hadn't Grace mentioned that the little girl who'd come to stay years ago had freckles and red hair?

"When my help comes in this afternoon, I'm headin' over to see her. Want to know what day Rosemary's expected back." The woman grinned. "And I want to see what that girl's made of. No small job, trying to reopen the antique shop. It's a mess. Rosemary has her own way of doing things, but I sure as shootin' wouldn't call her organized. But there's plenty of interesting stuff inside that shop, that's for sure."

Liam lifted two boxes, one stacked on top of the other. "I'll have to go to the shop when it reopens. Have a look around."

"You sure should." Grace picked up a third box. "And make sure you talk to Rosemary when you get the chance. Like I said, nobody knows the history of Chickadee Creek better than she does."

Liam hid a smile as he headed out to the truck. If the conversations of the past two days were any indication, Grace Witherstone wouldn't be content until he met Rosemary Townsend. And since this town was where he meant to stay for the immediate future, he might as well get to know the locals. Up until recently, he'd kept himself isolated. It was time for him to change that.

After setting the boxes in the bed of his truck, he turned toward the woman, who had followed him out. "I promise I'll make it a point to meet Mrs. Townsend."

"It's Miss Townsend." Grace set the box she carried next to the others in the truck bed. "Rosemary never married—although she was engaged, I hear tell, when she was real young. I've seen pictures of her back then. My, oh, my. She was a beauty." She laughed softly. "Rosemary could've been in films. Movie-star pretty, she was."

"I'll get those last two boxes," he said, then strode back into the store.

Liam didn't know if Grace knew he was an actor or if she'd seen any of his films. Despite her love for gossip, if she did know, she'd never let on to him, and he'd found it a refreshing change to be treated just like anybody else in this small town. All too often, all someone wanted to talk about when they met him was his acting. What was it like in Hollywood? Who did he know? Was this actress or that one as beautiful as she looked on the screen?

Grace didn't follow him into the store, and by the time he returned, she was talking to another customer who'd arrived in Liam's absence. With all of the boxes now in the back of his truck, he closed the tailgate, gave a quick wave to Grace, and climbed into the cab.

It was strange, he thought as he drove toward home, that he desired anonymity. He'd worked hard to improve his acting skills, and he'd wanted the fame that came with success in Hollywood. He'd wanted the recognition. His lucky break had come several years back, leading to roles in some major motion pictures. Small roles led to bigger ones. His latest movie had released on Thanksgiving of the previous year. There'd been rumors of possible supporting-actor award nominations for him, although they hadn't panned out. Rarely did for that kind of film. Not that he'd paid attention to any of the hoopla at the time. Jacob had been in a bad way by then.

After his brother's death, after the funeral and helping his parents with all of the details of tying up a life cut too short,

Liam had come to Chickadee Creek. To get away. To get his head on straight. To grieve. The few townsfolk he'd interacted with over the winter months seemed willing to leave him alone. Again, he couldn't be sure if they didn't know what he did for a living or if they just didn't care.

Maybe I don't care either. He let the words play in his mind for a few seconds, testing their veracity—and not for the first time. Did he care? Didn't he care? *God, what is it I'm supposed to do? What's next for me?*

As he approached the antique store, he saw the young woman from the front porch crossing the road ahead of him, carrying a pail and a ladder. She was a slip of a thing and looked even slighter as she carried the ladder. He slowed the truck. She wore a sleeveless top and jean shorts suitable for the summer heat. Her ginger-colored hair had been down around her shoulders when he drove into town. Now it was smoothed back and captured in a ponytail. She glanced toward the truck and hurried the last few steps across the road, stopping on the boardwalk outside the entrance to the shop, where she leaned the ladder against the wall.

Liam was tempted to say something to her through his open window, then thought better of it. She was busy, and he needed to get back to his own place. He pressed gently down on the accelerator and drove on.

Still, he couldn't quite shake the image of Rosemary Townsend's great-niece carrying that ladder. Maybe it was her hair. He had a weakness for women with red hair. All shades of it. From the palest strawberry blonde to the darkest auburn. It didn't hurt that Hollywood had more than a few of them. Jessica Chastain, Emma Stone, and Bryce Dallas Howard were just three of the redheads he'd worked with on films, and if he was honest, he'd had a crush on each of them in turn. Not that they'd noticed him much. They were way out of his league, even if they'd been available. None of them were.

But the memories made him smile. He had lots of good memories from his years of working in the film industry. So why wasn't he ready to go back to it? That was just one of the hard questions he needed to answer.

He hoped he'd be able to do that while staying in Chickadee Creek.

Chapter 3

*M*erciful heavens!" Aunt Rosemary stood framed in the doorway of the shop, her eyes large and round. "I don't believe what you've accomplished in so little time." Leaning on her cane, she stepped inside the building.

Chelsea smiled, warmed by her great-aunt's praise. She'd worked hard over the past three days, but there was a lot more still to be done. Dusting and mopping had made the shop look better on the surface. Reorganization would take much longer. Still, it felt good to have her efforts noted. Praise had been a rare thing throughout her life.

Aunt Rosemary tried to hide a grimace, but Chelsea saw it. She moved forward to take the older woman by the arm. "Let's get you back to the house and settled into your bed."

"Not in bed. I've had my fill of beds."

"But you're still recovering," Chelsea protested. "You need lots of rest."

"I've completed my rehab and been sent home. I'm not starting off my freedom by being shut in my bedroom."

Chelsea bit back more words of concern and instead steered her great-aunt out of the antique shop and across the road to her house. She didn't attempt to argue further. Aunt Rosemary was able to decide where to sit, and an oversize recliner with a view of the road and the shop beyond was her choice.

"Are you hungry?" Chelsea asked. "Or maybe you'd like a glass of iced tea? I made a fresh pitcher this morning."

"Iced tea would be lovely. And after you pour us each a glass, you can sit down and we'll have a nice chat. There's a great deal of catching up for us to do."

Chelsea felt a twinge of guilt as she walked to the kitchen. She should have come to visit her great-aunt long before this. Long before her help was needed. She should have come to see Aunt Rosemary the moment she'd been free of her father's control.

As she took the pitcher of tea from the refrigerator, she wondered—not for the first time—how much Grandpa John had told his sister. She also wondered if he'd arranged Chelsea's stay for Aunt Rosemary's sake or if his main goal had been to help Chelsea get away from an untenable situation.

From the living room, Aunt Rosemary said, "By my recollection, it's been at least a decade since I saw you."

"Eleven years," Chelsea answered in a raised voice. "I'd just graduated from high school."

"And you'd won a scholarship to college. I remember that."

Her chest tightened at the reminder. She'd been so excited when informed about the scholarship, but the excitement hadn't lasted long. Her dad had refused to let her go to college. He'd already been against high school, believing education was wasted on a girl. Her job was to stay home and help her mother with the younger kids until a man came along who wanted to marry her. And nobody in Hadley Station, the tiny northern Idaho town named for her father, ever went against Hadley Spencer's wishes. Nobody. Certainly not his children. Her dad hadn't been one to spoil the child by sparing the rod—or, in his case, the belt and buckle.

She pressed the palms of her hands onto the counter and closed her eyes, forcing herself to take slow, deep breaths. She thought she'd come to terms with memories of her father, but her troubled relationship with her ex-boyfriend, Tom Goodson, had shattered the fragile peace she'd found and reopened old wounds. A shudder ran through her.

Jesus, take away these memories. Please.

"Did you find everything you need?" Aunt Rosemary called.

"Yes." She opened her eyes. "Thanks. I've got it." She filled the tall glasses, set them on a tray beside two long-handled spoons, sliced lemons on a saucer, and the sugar bowl. Then she carried it all to the living room where she set the tray on a side table next to her great-aunt's chair.

"Oh, my. That looks good."

"Didn't they have iced tea at the rehab center?"

"Tea, yes. But not anything that looked this pretty and inviting."

"Presentation matters." Chelsea settled onto a nearby sofa. "It's something you taught me."

"I taught you that?"

"The summer I stayed with you."

Aunt Rosemary reached out a hand and pressed it against Chelsea's cheek. "And you've remembered all these years."

You were the only one who ever tried to teach me about pretty things. She might have said the words aloud if not for the enormous lump in her throat.

Aunt Rosemary added both sugar and lemon to her tea, then

stirred, the spoon making soft clinking sounds as it hit the sides of the glass.

Chelsea left her tea untouched.

"Well, tell me how you are," her great-aunt said as she placed the spoon back onto the tray.

She drew in a deep breath and released it. "I'm fine."

Aunt Rosemary sent her a look that said she expected much more than that.

Chelsea had never been one to talk about herself. As a child, that was because there hadn't been others, outside of her own family, to talk to. And her family already knew everything there was to know. Later, staying silent had been the prudent and safer thing to do. Silence was a hard habit to break.

"Tell me about your mother, then."

"Mom's okay. She's been seeing a man she met where she works. I wasn't sure she would ever do that after . . . after Dad died. She was so . . . worn down."

"And what about you, dear?"

Chelsea stared into the glass of iced tea in her hands. "How much did Grandpa tell you?"

"About that man? What's his name? Tom?"

She nodded.

"Enough to know you're better off here with me than staying in Spokane where he can bother you."

Chelsea offered a tight smile. "Anyone would be better off here with you, Aunt Rosemary."

"I love that you think so, dear." Aunt Rosemary leaned forward and reached out to touch the back of Chelsea's hand. "But now, tell me truly, how *are* you?"

"I'm better," she answered after a short silence. "It's been hard, the whole experience. Dad. Tom. So much confusion. But God's taught me a lot through it all. About myself. About Him."

This time, Aunt Rosemary smiled. "Tell me about that. Tell me how you came to know Jesus."

Some of the tension drained from Chelsea's shoulders. "I wasn't looking for God. I had my fill of religion because of Dad. Dad and his rules. Seemed to me religion just messed up the whole world. So I don't know how Jesus found His way into my heart. But one day, He did."

"I believe it happened because so many people were praying for you and your family."

"Yes." Chelsea smiled through unshed tears. "I'm sure that's the reason. I was prayed into the kingdom." She drew a deep breath. "Once I knew the Lord, once I understood His love for me, once I knew I was important enough for Him to die on a cross for my salvation, it changed me. It gave me the courage to do what I couldn't do before."

"Oh, you precious thing," Aunt Rosemary whispered.

Chelsea blinked back the tears. "Finding His love was worth everything else. Truly, it was."

"If you've learned that lesson while still young in your faith walk, you're already far ahead of many of us." Aunt Rosemary sipped her tea, allowing silence to fall over the room.

Chelsea looked out the window. She didn't *feel* especially far along in her faith walk—or in any other area of her life, for that matter—but her great-aunt's words were encouraging.

"I'm thankful you came to stay with me, Chelsea."

"And I'm thankful you wanted me to come, Aunt Rosemary."

"God is good."

"Yes," she whispered in response. "He is good."

Liam ran a brush through Chipper's coat, muttering when he found another knot on the dog's haunches. "I should've got a short-haired dog."

As if understanding, Chipper turned his head and licked Liam's face. A good swipe right across the lips.

Liam drew back, laughing. "Okay. I give up. I'm going to find a groomer. Surely there's somebody who does that in these hills." He tossed aside the brush.

The dog understood the grooming session was over and shot off the deck. He raced around the circular driveway, the way he always did after a bath and brushing.

Liam stood and moved to the deck railing, his thoughts going back to when the dog had been a pup. Out for a walk in the Boise neighborhood one late afternoon, needing a breath of air before returning to watch his brother try to hide his illness, Liam had come across a family giving away puppies. The young mother was a black-and-white border collie. The family didn't know about the male that sired the litter. Only that puppies weren't supposed to happen before they got their female spayed.

Chipper—twelve weeks old at the time and solid black except for one completely white ear and a white tip on his tail— scampered over to where Liam stood, sat with his rump rolled to one side, and whimpered up at him, as if to say, "Take me home." Liam almost cried, right where he stood, surrounded by strangers. And he wasn't the kind of man who cried easily. He told himself he was taking the puppy to show to Jacob and hopefully make his brother smile. But in truth, Liam had needed Chipper for himself. He'd needed the love and comfort the little guy gave him, especially through the dark days that were still to come.

Everyone, including Jacob, knew by then that the cancer was terminal, but Liam kept insisting his brother would make a comeback, that a miracle would happen and he would beat the disease, once and for all. It hadn't happened that way. Jacob had fought as hard as his failing body would allow. Maybe too hard. He'd suffered for many months before the end came at last.

The sound of a vehicle drew Liam's gaze away from the dog and toward the road. Through the trees, he saw a light-blue sedan make the turn into his driveway. He wondered if the driver was lost. Not many cars came out this direction, and most of the locals favored trucks, Jeeps, or SUVs.

"Chipper, come." He moved toward the top of his steps and waited.

The dog glanced toward the approaching vehicle, then did as his master commanded, joining Liam on the deck and sitting at his left side.

Sunlight glinted off the windshield as the car came to a stop, and Liam shaded his eyes with a hand against the brightness. Dust rolled on ahead of the car, the cloud drifting into the trees where the driveway curved away.

Liam frowned. Just as he was losing patience, waiting to see who was in the vehicle, the door opened. The driver's shoes touched the ground. Large, shiny black shoes, stirring up more dust. Then the driver stood.

"Kurt?" Liam blinked, not believing his eyes.

"Glad you still recognize me," his agent said, a wry grin pulling the corners of his mouth.

Kurt Knight was a giant of a man, over six feet four with broad shoulders and a gravelly, baritone voice. There was something about his appearance that made him look more like a laidback country singer than a cutthroat Hollywood agent. But looks were deceiving. Kurt was a man at the top of his game, and his many years in the business proved his staying power.

Liam came down the steps. "What're you doing here?"

"What do you think? I came to talk some sense into you."

The two men shook hands and clasped upper arms in greeting. Then Liam motioned for Kurt to follow him onto the deck. Stopping beside some chairs in the shade, he asked, "Would you like something to drink?"

"Got anything about eighty proof?"

"No. Your choice is Diet Coke or sparkling water in lime, lemon, or watermelon."

"Watermelon?" Kurt wrinkled his nose in disgust. "You've gotta be kidding me."

Liam shrugged.

"Not even a light beer?"

"What can I say? I don't keep liquor in the house. Not my thing."

It wasn't necessary to tell Kurt that he didn't drink alcohol or keep it around. Kurt knew. Kurt knew just about everything there was to know about Liam Chandler, both public and private. He might know more about Liam than Liam knew about himself.

"Okay," Kurt said in a begrudging tone. "I'll go with the sparkling water. But not the watermelon. Thanks." He looked behind him, took a step back, and sank onto the chair.

Liam gave his head a shake as he headed into the house. In the kitchen, he got two large plastic tumblers, added ice, then poured lime-flavored water into each of them. By the time he returned, a glass in each hand, he discovered Chipper making friends with their guest.

Kurt looked up. "A dog, huh?"

"Yeah." He set the drinks on the table between the two chairs.

"Too lonely up here?"

"Got him while I was still in Boise."

The look in Kurt's eyes softened. "Ah."

Liam sat on the nearby chair, picked up one of the tumblers again, and took a drink before setting the glass down a second time.

Kurt looked around the acres of tall pines while continuing to scratch Chipper behind one ear. "Sure is quiet here."

"I know. Sometimes the chipmunks start chattering, and the blue jays can get noisy." He stared up at the closest tree. "Had a persistent woodpecker last week that I considered shooting." He pointed to the spot on the tree where he'd last seen the bird. "But mostly, it's quiet and all I hear is the breeze in the pines."

"And it hasn't driven you crazy yet."

"No." He looked at Kurt. "It hasn't driven me crazy."

Silence stretched between them for a lengthy spell, and Liam was content to leave it that way.

Finally, Kurt cleared his throat. "Liam, directors and producers are still asking when you'll be ready to make another movie. What can I tell them?"

"That I'm not ready yet." *Maybe I'll never be ready*, he added silently.

"They won't ask forever, you know. Eventually they'll find

another guy for those same parts. If you let it go too long, you'll be an also-ran instead of a new leading man."

"I understand." Liam leaned forward, resting his forearms on his thighs. "But I'm not ready to go back to work. Or to Los Angeles. This is where I need to be."

"I know it's been rough. I understand you've got to get through the grief. But you could—"

"Sorry, Kurt," Liam interrupted. "This is how it's got to be for now."

"You're making a mistake."

"Maybe. Maybe not."

Kurt picked up his glass and drank some of the water. "All right. I won't pressure you. Now, how about you give me a tour of this place. I had to pass on your invitation when you were coming up to hunt a few years back."

"I remember." Liam stood. "Come on in, and I'll show you around. I've got a guest room all ready if you can stay."

"I was hoping you'd ask. It'll give me more time to try to change your mind."

"So much for not pressuring me."

Kurt laughed as he put down his glass and got up from the chair. "Guilty as charged."

Oddly enough, Liam didn't mind.

Cora

MAY 1895

The farcical musical performed on the stage that night would not have met with her mother's approval, but Cora adored it.

She laughed along with the rest of the audience throughout the production. It was the first evening she'd spent with Duncan since the announcement of their engagement that hadn't bored her to tears.

"Would you like to meet a few of the performers?" Duncan offered his arm, the final applause having faded and a loud buzz of conversations now filling the theater.

"Could we?"

Like her mother, her father would heartily disapprove of the idea, which made the prospect all the more enticing.

Duncan guided her from their private box and toward a back staircase. A tall man, dressed more like a dockworker than a gentleman out for a night on Broadway, held the door open for them. Cora didn't know if she should be alarmed or excited by the dark staircase leading them to a place unknown, especially with that coarse-looking man following right behind her. She supposed she was a little of both.

They descended the stairs into the bowels of the theater. Down there, it was a beehive of activity. Women—some rather scantily dressed—sat before mirrors removing makeup or fixing their hair. Men of all ages and sizes carried equipment and props and even pieces of scenery, some going one way, some another.

Duncan leaned close to her ear. "This was the troupe's last night in New York. They're leaving for Chicago in a couple of days, taking the show on the road."

Cora nodded to indicate she'd heard him.

"This way." He tugged on her arm. "I want to introduce you to the producer of the show."

Charles Bowen was a squat man with a balding pate and pale

eyes that stared at Cora from behind a pair of round spectacles. He looked to be about her father's age.

"Good heavens," he said as he bowed over her hand. "If you aren't a vision of loveliness." His gaze shot to Duncan. "However did you get her to agree to marry you?"

I agreed because my father demands it, Cora answered in her head. *Duncan proposed for the money.*

Some of her pleasure with the evening vanished.

Ignoring Mr. Bowen's question, Duncan asked one of his own. "Is Bridgette still here? I'm sure Miss Anderson would like to meet her too."

Bridgette? Cora glanced around, beginning to understand. This wasn't Duncan's first visit to this theater or to this busy basement. He knew the pretty actress who'd sung a number of risqué songs throughout the production. He knew her by her first name. And even with his fiancée on his arm, he didn't want to leave without speaking to her.

Cora waited to feel upset. She didn't. Not truly. Her heart was no more invested in Duncan Abernathy than his was in her. After they were married, they would likely keep separate bedrooms and mostly separate lives. He would trouble her little, especially after she gave birth to a son. Other children might follow, but giving him an heir was of paramount importance. After that, what she did and how she kept herself busy wouldn't concern him.

Cora understood more about the nature of reproduction than her mother would like. Not that she'd had any experience with men beyond the perfunctory kisses she'd exchanged with Duncan. But she had a habit of listening as the servants talked, and between what she'd overheard and a glance through some medical books in a friend's father's library, she'd pieced together enough to know what a married relationship held in store. She was not impressed with the mechanics, especially with a man like Duncan.

"Oooh, Mr. Abernathy. You came to see our little show." Bridgette Chevrolet approached, clad in a satin robe. Her lush brown hair tumbled free over one shoulder. "Mr. Bowen said you might come tonight."

Cora didn't believe her French accent was real, not even for a moment. Nor was her surprise at seeing Duncan below stage.

"Yes." Duncan cleared his throat. "May I introduce Miss Anderson?"

"But of course. Your fiancée. What a pleasure it is to meet you, Miss Anderson."

"And you, Miss Chevrolet," Cora replied. "You have a lovely singing voice."

"Oooh, you liked it. Thank you so very much." A small frown pinched the space between her brows. "You are ever so much prettier."

Prettier than what? Cora wondered. She glanced at Duncan. His attention remained locked on Bridgette Chevrolet. Cora's instincts told her that he'd talked about her with the actress on more than one occasion, and his words hadn't been complimentary of the woman he planned to marry.

If things were different, she might have been disturbed, insulted. But if she were to talk to someone in confidence about Duncan, her words wouldn't be complimentary either.

And yet they planned to marry in a few months' time.

Am I truly going to chain myself, my entire future, to a man I don't love and can't respect?

Heart starting to race, she said, "Duncan, I believe it's time you take me home."

He looked at her. "What about our reservation at—"

"No. I'd rather go home."

Duncan glanced at the actress. "I . . . You'll have to excuse us, Miss Chevrolet. Miss Anderson seems to be unwell."

Not unwell. Unsettled. Unhappy. In need of a way out.

Preston

MAY 1895

Preston Chandler stepped from the train car onto the Boise station platform. Once out of the way of other departing passengers, he stopped and looked around. It felt slightly strange to stand on solid ground. He'd grown used to the rocking and swaying of the car, and it took him a short while to feel his land legs again. Once he did, he collected his bag and hired a hack to take him from the railroad station to the hotel.

"How long will you be with us?" the desk clerk inquired as he looked at Preston's signature in the guest register.

"I'm not sure. Four or five days, I believe."

"Very good, sir."

Preston suppressed a grin. He was still getting used to the small courtesies extended to a man of means.

The clerk held out his room key. "Do you require assistance with your luggage, sir?"

"No. Thank you. I can manage. But I am hungry. Any recommendations on where I should eat?"

"Yes, sir." The clerk glanced around, then leaned forward,

adding in a low voice, "Breakfast is all right in the hotel restaurant, but you're better off elsewhere for dinner."

"Good to know. Appreciate it."

The clerk gave the names of a couple of restaurants, followed by easy instructions on how to find them both. Preston thanked him again before heading up the stairs to the second floor. He found his room at the far end of a long hallway. It was clean and spacious with a comfortable bed. Everything was altogether better than the many rooms he'd stayed in throughout his life.

After a quick wash, he put on a clean shirt and headed out again. One of the recommended restaurants was only a few blocks away. An easy walk, and he was ready for a bit of exercise.

As he left the hotel, a trolley car rolled noisily past him, the tracks running down the center of the street. Businessmen in suits and vests, cowboys in Levi's and boots, women in long skirts and big hats rode the trolley and strolled along the sidewalks. Large buildings made of stone boasted of Boise's promise.

From his research, he knew that what was now the capital city of Idaho had been established over thirty years before as a lowly supply town for the gold and silver mines in the mountains to the north and south. Now, with most of the mines played out—or at least long past their prime—it was Boise City that thrived while the gold-rush towns dwindled to mere ghosts. If things didn't work out for Preston as planned, maybe he would come back to Boise for a new start.

He gave himself a mental shake. He had no intention of failing. His circumstances had changed for the better, and he meant for that to continue.

Seeing the restaurant sign, he paused on the sidewalk, then crossed the street, avoiding several wagons going in opposite directions. One day, he was certain, a man would have to dodge motor carriages instead of horse and buggies, but that time hadn't arrived yet.

Delicious scents greeted him as he entered the restaurant. He was shown to a small square table covered with a pristine white tablecloth. Gas lamps on the walls bathed the large room in a golden glow, the light reflecting off the table service and china plates.

He scanned the menu the waiter handed him, then ordered the fried trout with Creole sauce and julienne potatoes. "I'll have some of the Edam cheese and water crackers while I wait. And coffee too."

"Yes, sir. I'll bring them at once." The waiter walked away.

Preston looked toward the window and the busy street beyond. First thing tomorrow he would pay a visit to the Boise City National Bank and make certain the transfer of his funds had been completed. He'd seen the three-story Romanesque bank structure with its sandstone facade on his way from the railroad station to the hotel, so he wouldn't need to ask for directions. Afterward, he would drop into the office of his recently retained lawyer, a man who'd been recommended to him by a trusted friend. Once done with the final legalities of his inheritance, he would be free to explore a little more of Boise before heading north into the mountains.

— *Liam's Journal* —

Jacob was too sick to go see <u>Destination: North Star</u> in the theater when it released, but I managed to get a copy to play for him at home. His bed was in the living room by then. No way could he climb the stairs, and it made it easier for the nurses who came to tend him 24/7 and the guests who dropped by to be with him for short bits of time.

But that night, when we watched my new movie, it was just the family: Mom, Dad, Jacob, and me. When the film was over, everybody said the things they were supposed to say. Exciting movie. Lots of action. Funny in the right spots.

After Mom and Dad went to bed, I stayed up with Jacob, and we talked for a long time. He told me the parts he really liked about the movie. But then he asked me why I always chose those roles. "Don't you want to go deeper?" is how he put it.

Deeper. He meant give up outer-space movies and adventure films for something about a family coming apart at the edges. Something that made the audience tear up. A weeper, our grandma called them.

I wasn't surprised. Jacob had that kind of nature. He was more emotional than me. He was a deep thinker too. Really deep. He liked to look at people and situations and figure out what was going on, deep down.

In fact, he was the one who told me how unhappy Dad was. On all my visits back home after I moved to LA, I hadn't noticed Dad was unhappy. And after I came up to Idaho to be with Jacob, I guess I figured Dad was sad about him. But Jacob said no way. Dad's been unhappy for years. Since we were little kids. That's one reason he works all the time. He doesn't want to come home.

I wasn't sure I believed Jacob when he told me, but after Dad moved out of the house a couple of weeks after the funeral, I knew my brother was right all along.

I've tried talking to both Mom and Dad about what's going on between them. Dad always says I need to ask Mom. Mom says she can't talk about it. Maybe she would've told Jacob if he'd asked her. Maybe he did ask her before he died. Maybe he knew and chose not to tell me. I don't know.

Families are strange. People who love each other and hurt each other at the same time. I'm pretty sure Mom loved me. Loves me. But she's said a lot of things that hurt me too. I got thicker skin as I got older, but I was always aware of the comparison, the way she preferred to be with Jacob over me. The way she wanted to protect him but left me to fend for myself.

Can't say that I blame her. Jacob was special. He loved people. He loved life. He loved God. Long before I came to a place of knowing Christ, Jacob opened his heart wide to Him. Jacob was good to everybody. Didn't matter if he was talking to the mayor of a city or a homeless guy on the street, Jacob treated them with the same kindness and respect. He listened to them. He listened to me. Really listened.

Wish I could say I'm like that, too, but I'm not. In school, I was usually off somewhere, trying to impress a girl or a teacher. Trying to impress a producer or director in recent years.

What's that say about me? Nothing good.

Chapter 4

*H*earing a sound, Liam turned from the stove to see Kurt stop at the bottom of the stairs. Unlike Liam, who wore baggy shorts and a T-shirt that had seen better days, his agent looked as if he were heading to a business meeting at one of the studios. Even his shoes were shiny again; not a speck of yesterday's dust remained on them.

Liam held up the spatula in his hand. "Breakfast?"

"You bet." Kurt moved into the kitchen, stopping at one of the barstools at the raised counter.

"Coffee's ready." Liam motioned with his head in the direction of the coffee maker.

"Even better."

Liam returned his attention to the egg mixture in the frying pan, quickly adding the cheese, diced ham, and bell peppers to one side before folding the omelet over and then, when ready, sliding it onto the waiting plate. "Your timing was perfect, as it usually is." He carried the plate to the counter and set it in front of Kurt. A moment later, he added a fork and napkin next to the plate.

"I never pictured you as domesticated." Kurt chuckled, the

deep sound seeming to echo in the large kitchen. "A delicious dinner last night. Now omelets for breakfast."

"I don't know about domesticated, but I enjoy cooking. It relaxes me. Of course, it's more fun when I cook for somebody who'll appreciate it." Liam pointed at his friend's plate. "Dig in before it gets cold." He turned back to the stove to prepare his own omelet.

"Wish I could stick around a little longer," Kurt said.

"You're welcome to stay as long as you want."

"Can't. I've got some important meetings on Monday."

Liam looked over his shoulder. "You could stay one more night. We can take a drive, and I'll show you the area. We could even go up to Galena Summit. Amazing views of the Sawtooth Valley from there."

"Tempting, but I already booked my return flight. It's early this afternoon. I'll have to head down to Boise soon." He checked his watch. "Another hour or so."

Liam let it drop. If Kurt left soon, he would have less time to try to make Liam change his mind. And Kurt would try again. He hadn't come all this way to fail.

His own omelet ready, Liam slid it onto a second plate and went to sit at the counter. The two men were silent while they ate. For a short while, the only sound in the kitchen was the clink of forks on plates. But once the plates were clean and the coffee mugs refilled, Kurt turned a serious gaze on Liam.

"One of my meetings on Monday is about a movie that's meant for you. A starring role, and you're the director's first choice."

Before he could help it, Liam asked, "Who's the director?"

Kurt leaned forward and softly said the name of the top-tier director as if it were some national secret that had to be protected.

Excitement blossomed in Liam's chest. Who wouldn't be excited? Every actor in Hollywood wanted to work with Grayson Wentworth. The guy was a genius. He excelled at everything—action movies, rom-coms, science fiction, drama. What he touched turned to the proverbial gold.

But being flattered wasn't enough to pull Liam back into that world before he was ready, and he checked himself before he let Kurt see his involuntary reaction. It wasn't time to go back. He knew it wasn't. And more important, God hadn't released him to return. He wished he could explain that to Kurt, but his agent had a way of blocking any God talk, as he called it. In fact, his frequent advice was for Liam to believe whatever he wanted but to keep it to himself. Hollywood wasn't interested in his Christian faith. Neither was Kurt Knight.

Liam had followed his agent's counsel for years. His faith remained a private matter. Nobody's business but his own. Only he felt less comfortable with that decision of late. What kind of disciple never spoke about the teacher he followed?

"Well?" Kurt's voice had a sharper edge to it now. "Aren't you going to say anything? A Grayson Wentworth film and your chance to star in it."

Liam stood, grabbed his empty plate as well as Kurt's, and carried them to the sink. He drew a breath before he turned, leaning his backside against the counter. "That would be amazing, Kurt. Really. I would love to work with him. Wentworth is the best of the best. Maybe I'll get to work with him in the future. But I can't commit to anything right now." He was starting to feel as frustrated as Kurt looked.

"You're killing me, Liam."

"I know, and I'm sorry. I wish I could say something different, but I can't. We've been over it more than once. Look, Kurt. You've done great things for me and my career. You've hung in there with me through the ups and down, and I appreciate it more than you know. I'd like to make things easier for you now. I would. But I can't."

How was he supposed to explain that still, small voice in his heart to a man who didn't believe in the God behind that still, small voice? There weren't enough words, and there wasn't enough time.

"I'm not ready to go back to work," Liam added. "I'm not ready to leave Idaho. I need to be here for now. I've got a lot to . . . work through. It's more than just grief, but there's plenty of that too."

He looked toward the large window in the great room. Outside, morning sunlight beamed down through the tall trees, golden shafts breaking through the greens and browns of the pines.

A few moments later, the scrape of stool legs upon the floor drew Liam's gaze back to his friend and agent. Kurt stood beside the counter, shaking his head slowly. "All right. I give up. I won't hassle you anymore. I'll tell him . . . I'll tell Wentworth something. Maybe he wants you enough to be willing to wait awhile longer."

Aunt Rosemary flipped over the sign in the window of the door. "I've heard it's called a soft opening," she said as she drew back.

Chelsea had tried to convince her great-aunt to wait a few

weeks before reopening Rosemary & Time. In her mind, they were nowhere close to ready for customers. But she'd learned it was pointless to argue with the woman. Rosemary Townsend was seventy-five and still recovering from surgery, but she knew what she wanted.

Using her cane, Aunt Rosemary moved to a wingback chair set near the large front window of the shop. She dropped onto it with a sigh, then leaned forward and pulled the matching padded stool closer and placed her injured leg on it.

"Don't mind me if I nod off every now and then." She tossed a smile in Chelsea's direction. "And if you need to ask me something, just wake me up. I'll drift off again if I need to."

Chelsea returned the smile. "Okay."

Aunt Rosemary sighed again, settled deeper into the chair, and closed her eyes.

Chelsea watched the older woman for a short while, then turned and went up the stairs, carrying her laptop beneath one arm. Today she planned to reorganize some of the books on the second-story shelves. She didn't know much about antique books. How did a person tell what was old and valuable instead of simply old and worn? She supposed she needn't worry. Most of the books in this shop would be simply old with no added value because of their age. But if something unusual popped up, she hoped to be able to find its true value. Hence the laptop.

Cobwebs and dust had been cleaned away from the shelves where she planned to begin. Now she would remove books from the cases, sort them as items to keep and items to get rid of as quickly as possible, even if they sold them for only a nickel or a dime. Paperbacks, she assumed, were the least valuable. She would go through them first.

As she pulled a step stool up to a bookcase, memories of another July morning drifted into her thoughts. She'd been with Aunt Rosemary for the better part of six weeks by that time, and she'd explored every nook and cranny of the shop and a good deal of the town and surrounding forest. Within Rosemary & Time, she'd climbed ladders and used step stools and tucked herself away in unusual hiding spots. But on that particular day, she'd taken a book to the window seat at the back of the second story. With the window open, she'd been able to hear the water splashing over the stones that lined the bed of the creek. It had been a comforting melody, and the book she'd chosen had carried her away to a delightful fantasyland.

In books, even when bad things happened, better things seemed to follow. The boys and girls in the stories could somehow slay the dragon or save the wounded animal or solve the mystery. Good saved the day, and villains were banished forever.

So different from the real world. So different from the true story she'd lived.

"How'd you turn out so worthless?"

"Stop that sniveling. Do you know how ugly you look when you do that?"

"What am I doing with you? I must be crazy to waste my time here."

Chelsea covered her ears with the heels of her hands, trying to shut out the voices from the past. Eyes closed, she reminded herself that she was not only fearfully and wonderfully made but also a child of the King. The opposite of ugly and worthless.

O LORD, *You have searched me and known me . . . You have enclosed me behind and before, and laid Your hand upon me . . . How precious also are Your thoughts to me, O God! How vast is the sum of them!*

After a while, the cruel voices faded into silence, and Chelsea drew in a slow, deep breath. As she let it out, the bell above the entrance chimed, drawing her gaze down toward the door. She expected to see one of her great-aunt's friends. Instead she saw a tall, handsome man pause on the landing, his gaze stopping on Aunt Rosemary who, as she'd warned she might do, was napping.

Chelsea shook off the last remnants of her troubled memories as she stepped off the stool and moved to the railing. "Hello. May I help you?"

The man looked up and smiled.

And what a smile! Her heart did a strange little dance in her chest in response to it. He looked a bit familiar. Did she know him? No, she would remember if they'd met. She was sure of that.

"Hello, there." His voice was warm and soothing, his eyes a deep chocolate brown. "Grace over at the mercantile told me I should talk to Miss Townsend." He motioned with his head. When he continued, he lowered his voice to a near whisper. "But if that's her, I don't want to disturb."

"What's that?" Aunt Rosemary straightened. "Were you talking to me, young man?"

He smiled at Chelsea a second time, then turned toward Aunt Rosemary. "Miss Townsend, my name's Liam. I live a few miles outside of Chickadee Creek."

"I know who you are. You're the young Chandler boy. And I know the house. I remember when it was built, five or six years back. The huge log house where the mining office used to be."

Liam took a couple of steps toward her great-aunt. "Yes, that's right."

"You know, young man, there was a Chandler in Chickadee Creek before there was a town. Owen Chandler was one of the few who made a real fortune here."

"So I understand."

"And Chandlers have owned a good share of the land in these parts ever since."

He nodded.

"So. A Chandler's come back to stay. That's good." Aunt Rosemary motioned to a straight-backed chair against the opposite wall. "Drag that over here and sit down so we can get acquainted."

"Yes, ma'am." He obeyed at once.

Chelsea thought she should go back to work, but something kept her at the railing, staring down at her great-aunt and the visitor. Liam Chandler. Why did his name sound familiar too?

Aunt Rosemary leaned forward enough to pat his knee. "What brought you to Chickadee Creek? We don't get many young folk moving in. Way more move away, like most of your family. Not a lot to offer in these parts, except for the beauty of God's nature. We've got plenty of that."

"I know. My brother and I came up here in the summer as kids. My parents had an old cabin that was in the family for years."

Chelsea pressed her lips together. Could she possibly have met him the summer she'd stayed with her great-aunt? He didn't look to be much older than she was. Maybe four or five years, tops. Was that why he looked familiar, why she felt like she knew his name? Had he come into the antique shop back then?

Aunt Rosemary looked up and saw her watching them. "Chelsea, come down and join us."

50

Caught eavesdropping, she felt heat rise in her cheeks. She quickly shook her head.

"Come on now." Her great-aunt motioned with her hand. "There's nothing so important up there that it can't wait while we have a good visit with a neighbor."

Liam's Journal

Her name was Nanci. Nanci with an *i*. That's what I think of first when I think of her. She made sure everybody knew how to spell her name.

She was the prettiest girl in the ninth grade. No doubt about it. She was in the same homeroom as Jacob, and he had it bad for her. But he was shy, and he couldn't seem to get her to notice him. So he came to me for advice. I was fifteen, in high school, and full of myself. I figured I could help him ask her out on a date.

Then I saw her at a football game, and all I could think was I hadn't understood just how pretty she might be. She was the first redhead I ever fell for. Dark auburn. She wore it long and loose. And she had big brown eyes. Enormous. Almost like a caricature.

I gave Jacob advice. It was good advice too. But I made sure I was always in the picture somewhere when Nanci was around. Unlike my brother, I wasn't shy. I was confident with girls, and I was good with a line too. I knew how to say all of the right things at the right time. (I was an actor even then.) I made sure Nanci noticed me. Jacob didn't stand much of a chance.

I'm ashamed now, writing it in this journal. Seeing what it says about me.

But if Jacob knew what I did, that I intentionally made Nanci want me instead of him, he never let on. Ever.

I wish we'd talked about it after we grew up. Wish we'd talked about it as adults and best friends. Did it matter to him or was it forgotten, along with a lot of things that don't get remembered from our childhoods?

Members of a family remember different things about their lives in that family. And when we remember the same things, we remember them differently. I've learned that. No wonder eyewitness accounts are unreliable.

He was tall and wearing a red knit cap.

No, he was short and wearing a black skullcap.

No, it was a woman in a baggy T-shirt and yoga pants.

?

Funny thing, I don't have a clue what happened to Nanci. She and I went out a few times, but it wasn't like we became a thing. We didn't even break up. We simply drifted on, made other friends. Both of us. It was over before the football season ended.

Did Jacob know that too? Did he care? Did he think about her for years after?

Something I know now that I didn't know a year ago: even when somebody's dying and you know it, you still think you've got time. Time to say the things you want to say. Plenty of time to remember and discuss and share. But you don't. It doesn't go on forever. Nothing does. You run out of time, and there are things you wished you'd asked. Things you wished you'd let them say. I wish I'd talked to Jacob about Nanci and asked him to forgive me.

Something else I know now: when you see somebody you love fighting for breath, struggling against the pain, you stupidly think it'll be a relief when they aren't suffering any longer. And maybe there's a fraction of that. But mostly, after they're gone, you feel the emptiness in your life. You wish them back, despite the suffering. You think if you could have another day or another hour with them, then it would be worth it.

But I'm never going to have another hour with Jacob this side of heaven. Never.

That hurts.

Chapter 5

*L*iam watched as Chelsea left the second story of the shop and came down the stairs. As on the day he'd seen her crossing the road, she wore a sleeveless top—this one a pale pink—and a pair of denim shorts. Her ginger hair was woven into a single braid that fell over one shoulder. She was thin, like a lot of the women in LA, but for some reason, a protective feeling rose in him, as if he wanted to rescue Chelsea before she blew away in a stiff wind.

He gave himself a mental shake. The feeling was probably a leftover from the months he'd watched Jacob wasting away.

"This is my brother's granddaughter," Rosemary said. "Chelsea Spencer. Like you, she's new to Chickadee Creek. Come to help me while I recover with this bum leg, but I hope she'll stay a long time beyond that."

A sweet smile played across Chelsea's mouth at her great-aunt's words.

Liam found himself hoping she would stay in town a long time too. At least as long as he stayed. "A pleasure to meet you."

"You too." Her green eyes narrowed. "Have we met before?"

He shook his head, pretending he didn't understand why he

looked familiar to her. "I don't believe so. But I passed you on the road earlier this week. You were toting a ladder and pail over to this shop."

"No. That's not it."

Kurt Knight might be right. Maybe Liam was already on his way to being forgotten, less than a year after his last movie. He hadn't done interviews around the film's release because of Jacob's failing health. And over these last eight months, few had mentioned him in the trades or on talk shows. Perhaps he'd had his fifteen minutes of fame. And if he didn't mean to return to Hollywood, if he didn't want to resume his film career, why did any of that matter?

"Liam?" Rosemary's voice drew his attention back to the older woman.

"Yes, ma'am."

She shook her head. "That's quite enough of that 'ma'am' business. I can see you're a respectful young man, which I appreciate, but please call me Rosemary. Everyone in Chickadee Creek does." Without waiting for a reply, she looked at her great-niece again. "Chelsea, get a chair and join us. As nice as everybody was at the hospital and rehab center, I confess I'm starved for real conversation."

Had he been crazy to stop in at the antique store after saying goodbye to his agent? Liam wasn't researching the history of Chickadee Creek, despite what Grace Witherstone seemed to think, and he wasn't in the market for antiques. So what was he doing there? Maybe he'd been starved for some real conversation too.

"Tell us why you've come to stay in our little village," Rosemary said.

He cleared his throat. It was okay, he'd learned, to edit his responses while still telling the truth. He'd also learned that he didn't owe his private business to the world, despite what many people seemed to think about celebrities. Or even semicelebrities, like him.

Rosemary laughed softly. "Don't be afraid to tell me to mind my own business, if that's what you want."

It seemed she'd read his mind. Not that he would have put it in those words. But for some reason, her frankness made him more willing to talk about himself.

He leaned back in his chair. "When I had my house built five years ago, my intent was to come to the area for hunting or a brief getaway every now and then. I was living and working in southern California at the time, so it seemed likely that's all it would be. Just a vacation place. Then my family needed me to come to Boise for a while, and when . . . when the crisis was over"—this was the well-edited part—"I decided to come up to Chickadee Creek for . . . for a rest. The longer I've stayed, the more I've liked it."

"And there's nothing in California waiting for you?" Rosemary's eyes were watchful.

"You mean work?" He smiled wryly, thinking of Kurt's visit. "I'm not sure. Possibly, when I'm ready."

"And what is it that you do?"

He swallowed. There was no avoiding it. "I . . . work in the film industry."

Chelsea sucked in a breath of air. "Liam Chandler," she said softly.

His gaze shifted to her.

She pointed at him. "You were in that movie with Chris

Pratt. *Destination: North Star.* I saw it on Christmas Day. That was *you.*"

He shrugged.

"You're a movie star?" Rosemary drew back, her eyes wide. "Well, mercy me. I never."

He wasn't sure what to say to that.

A soft chime sounded, and Chelsea reached into her pocket to remove her phone. She read something on the screen. Her complexion paled, and an emotion flickered across her face. Dread? Fear? Worry? Then she stood. "Sorry. I need to see to this." She hurried away, disappearing through a doorway at the back of the shop.

"Oh, dear," Rosemary whispered.

Although he wondered what was wrong, he decided this would be a good time for him to leave. He didn't want to answer more questions about his films, and he suspected the conversation might veer in that direction if he stayed.

He stood. "It was a real pleasure to meet you, Rosemary. I hope you make a swift and full recovery." He motioned toward her leg as he said it.

"Thank you," she answered, but her gaze remained on the door at the back of the shop, a deep frown furrowing her forehead.

Sitting in the dim light of the small office in the back of the antique shop, Chelsea stared at the message from her sister Evelyn.

Tom still looking for you. Wants you to call him.

Chelsea had mailed a note to her ex-boyfriend, telling him once and for all that it was over, that she never wanted to see him again. Nothing he could do would change her mind. She'd hoped he would take her words to heart and leave her be. She should have known better. Tom was too much like her father. Once he thought of something—or someone—as "his," he wouldn't let go lightly.

But he doesn't know where I am. No one except Grandpa John knows I'm here with Aunt Rosemary, and Tom's never met Grandpa. I'm safe here. Tom can't find me.

Still, another chill passed through her, knowing Tom had contacted her sister. He would probably contact each of her siblings and their mother too. And frustrated in his efforts, he would grow angrier . . . and dangerous.

I'm a long way from Hadley Station. I'm a long way from Spokane. He won't find me in Chickadee Creek. He's never even heard me mention Aunt Rosemary.

Chelsea had destroyed her old mobile phone, and she'd turned off location services when she received her new one from a different service provider. Only Evelyn had her new number, and Evelyn would never betray Chelsea. Not ever.

She imagined Tom standing on the boardwalk outside of Rosemary & Time, and a shudder made her teeth rattle.

Fear not. That's what the Bible told her. She wasn't to live in fear. She could look at the world as it was. She could see and recognize reality. She could know Tom Goodson was a volatile man, a man to be avoided, someone never to be trusted. But she wasn't to live in fear. God told her to be smart, not afraid. He wanted her to turn to Him in trust.

But how? It was a balancing act that too often eluded her.

Jesus, take my fear. I lay it at your feet. Make me as wise as a serpent and as gentle as a dove.

She sat still, eyes closed, and waited for the dread to drain from her heart. It didn't happen right away. But after a long while, she seemed to hear Grandpa John whispering in her ear: *"Courage is being scared to death but saddling up anyway.' You know who said that? The Duke. Always appreciated that man's common sense."*

"'Saddle up anyway.'" Chelsea took a deep breath and released it. "Keep moving forward. Take one step at a time. Do the next right thing." Another deep breath and she was ready to brave the world beyond this small office.

When she opened the door, she saw that her great-aunt was alone at the front of the store.

"Mr. Chandler left?"

Aunt Rosemary ignored the question, instead asking one of her own. "Are you all right?"

"I'm fine."

"Are you sure, dear?"

"Don't worry about me, Aunt Rosemary. I'm saddling up anyway."

Her great-aunt smiled for the briefest of moments, obviously recognizing one of her brother's favorite quotes.

Chelsea leaned down and kissed Aunt Rosemary's cheek. "I'd better get back to my sorting. Can I get you anything before I head upstairs?"

"No, dear. I don't need a thing. I'll go back to my napping." She closed her eyes. "Imagine. We had a movie star sitting in our shop this morning. Who'd've thunk it?"

"Who'd've thunk it?" The oddly phrased question made Chelsea smile, and the lingering fears about Tom scurried away.

She turned and headed up to the second floor, where the work awaited her.

Preston

MAY 1895

The town of Chickadee Creek had never risen to the size or status of Idaho City, once the largest city in the entire northwest. But the gold—found in the creek that cut through the area and in the surrounding mountains—had brought many hopeful miners to the region. Following after those miners had come families, some of whom had put down roots and stayed after the rush was over.

A distant cousin of Preston's had been among the few miners who struck it rich in the 1860s. Owen Chandler was also one of the men who stayed in Chickadee Creek. He used his money to buy land. Lots of land. He built a big house in the town and filled it with fine furnishings. At the age of fifty, he married a woman who was half his age and fathered six children, not a one of whom lived beyond the age of four. His wife passed away before her fortieth birthday, many said from a broken heart, and Owen had lived out the rest of his life alone in that big house.

A big house along with the remainder of Owen's fortune that now belonged to Preston Chandler.

Preston stood in the parlor of the Chandler mansion. Opening the drapes had revealed a thick layer of dust over everything in the room. The furnishings were ornate and somewhat worn, and he guessed the many knickknacks had been purchased by Owen's late wife. He would have to decide what to keep and what to give away or throw out. But that could wait. For now, he wanted to see the rest of the house.

The ground floor—in addition to the front hall, reception area, and parlor—had an expansive library, a dining room that could fit more people than he knew around its table, a spacious kitchen, and a laundry room. There were stairways at both the front and the back of the house. He took the back stairs up to the second story, where he found a bathroom and four bedchambers, all of them with built-in closets.

The largest of the bedchambers sat at the front of the house. A door opened from that room onto a small balcony that overlooked the road leading into the center of town. Preston stepped through the opening and looked around. Mostly he saw trees, but there was a nice view of the creek for which the town was named. The air was crisp, and the breeze blowing through the pines created a soft melody of sorts.

"Hey! You, there."

He stepped closer to the railing.

"What you doing there? That there house is off limits." The man on the road glowered at Preston. "If you was from around here, you'd know that. Now git out before I go for the deputy."

"I'm sorry, sir. No need for the deputy. I'm the owner of this house."

"That right?" The glower faded slightly. "Ain't no owner. Owner's dead."

"The prior owner is deceased. That's true. But I am Preston Chandler, the new owner."

"Chandler, huh. Relative?"

"A cousin."

"Huh."

He fought back a smile, enjoying the encounter perhaps more than he should. For some reason, he believed he and the man below would become friends, given a bit of time.

"Well, I reckon you can prove it if'n you need to."

The fellow turned and went on his way.

Preston stared after the departing stranger. Would everyone in Chickadee Creek meet him with similar suspicion? He hoped not. He intended to put down roots in this town, to call it home. He planned to build on his newfound fortune. He had ideas for mining the remaining gold from the land. And then there was the timber. With Boise City growing as it was, there was need for more and more lumber. He would need many employees as he expanded into other businesses. He wanted to get off on the right foot with the citizens of this little town.

He swiveled on his heel and went back inside. For the second time, his gaze swept the room.

There was as much dust in this bedchamber as everywhere else in the house. Preston was used to taking care of himself, but he wouldn't want to tackle the care and cleaning of this big house on his own. He had other work to do. So it seemed to him that the first thing he needed to do was hire a housekeeper.

His stomach growled.

"And a cook," he said aloud.

He believed the man on the road would even now be spreading the news that Owen Chandler's relative had arrived in Chickadee Creek. Maybe some enterprising woman had already decided to apply for a job with him. Most townsfolk would know the condition the house was in and assume he needed help.

"And they would be right."

The two main roads that made up Chickadee Creek were

not straight, the way the streets were in Boise City. These meandered, one of them running parallel to the creek, the other slicing across it. Thus, the homes and buildings were a bit at odds with each other, one facing a little this way, the next a little that. They weren't built close together either. There was plenty of space between most of them. On his way to the Chandler mansion from the boardinghouse, he'd passed a church and a small schoolhouse, two saloons, a smithy, a doctor's office, a restaurant, and a post office. There was more of the town than he'd seen thus far, but he didn't bother to explore it after leaving his new home. Instead, he went straight to the Chickadee Creek General Store.

The rail-thin man behind the counter on the right side of the deep but narrow building had gray hair and a short beard. A pair of wire-rimmed glasses perched on his nose. He peered over them as Preston approached.

"Afternoon, sir," Preston said.

"Afternoon."

"I'm new in town." He held out his hand. "Preston Chandler."

"Chandler?" Bushy gray brows arched as he shook the proffered hand.

Preston nodded. "Yes."

"Well, I'll be." Now his eyes narrowed. "You plannin' to stay?"

"Yes, I am. And as you can imagine, Mr.—" He broke off, waiting for a name.

"Harris. Alexander Harris."

"Pleased to meet you, Mr. Harris. As I was saying, the Chandler house isn't in the best of shape at the moment. It needs a thorough cleaning and someone who's able to keep it that way once it's done. I was hoping you might be able to recommend someone."

"To clean your house one time?"

"Actually, I'd like someone permanent, if possible. A housekeeper who could oversee any other employees I decide to hire."

Alexander Harris rubbed his chin. "Well . . ." He lifted his eyes toward the ceiling, as if he might find the answer there. After a short while, he looked at Preston again. "I suppose the Widow Mason might be interested. Her daughter up and got married a couple months back, so she's got nobody at home to look after. Good, respectable woman, she is. Yes, sir. I reckon she might be the woman you're lookin' for."

"And where might I find the Widow Mason?"

"As a matter of fact, she's crossin' the street right now. I see her through the windows there." He pointed.

Preston turned in time to see the door open and a woman in a large black hat enter the store. She was older than him, but not as old as the name "Widow Mason" led him to expect. He'd guess her to be less than fifty years of age, perhaps not much more than forty.

"Miz Mason," Alexander said, "this here gentleman is wanting to talk to you."

The woman stopped and gave Preston a curious look. Then she turned back to the storekeeper and held out a slip of paper. "I need a few things, Mr. Harris, if it wouldn't be too much trouble."

"Not at all. Not at all." Alexander bustled away.

The Widow Mason turned toward Preston once again.

"Ma'am." He touched the brim of his hat. "I'm Preston Chandler."

"It's a pleasure to meet you, Mr. Chandler." She stood straight, shoulders back, head lifted. She was a tiny thing. Not even five feet tall and weighing in at under a hundred pounds, he was sure. But there was strength in her eyes and possibly steel in her backbone.

He cleared his throat. "I'm in need of a housekeeper for the Chandler place, and Mr. Harris thought you might be interested in the position."

"Oh, he did, did he?" She glanced over her shoulder. When her gaze returned to Preston, she said, "I might be."

He released a breath and smiled. "That's very good news."

"Shall we go have a look and see if we might come to an arrangement?"

"Now?"

She raised an eyebrow. "Now's as good a time as any."

No nonsense. He liked that about her.

"Yes. Of course." He glanced behind him. "Thanks for your help, Mr. Harris."

"Weren't no trouble at all," the proprietor called. "Miz Mason, I'll have your things ready when you come back."

MAY 1895

Cora awoke with a start, still clutching the violin case close to her chest. It took a moment to realize the rocking of the passenger car had ceased. The train must have stopped at another station. She wasn't sure how long they'd been there.

She straightened on the seat. Her eyes felt gritty, and she longed for a basin of cool water so she could splash her face and wash away the travel grime. She wouldn't mind something to eat, either, but she was afraid to get off the train. She didn't want to be seen. Not until she was farther away from New York City. Her father had friends in many places. Cities like Atlanta and Chicago and San Francisco. She wanted to go where he couldn't find her, where he wouldn't think to look for her.

How far away is that? Where is that place?

Tucked in a purse beneath her corset was the majority of the money she'd managed to bring with her. And sewn into the lining of her traveling skirt was the jewelry given to her by Grandmother Ruth. God bless her maid, Millie, for helping with those tricks. Neither would have occurred to her. She'd never had to worry about pickpockets and thieves. For that matter, she'd never given a thought to money. Whenever she traveled, there'd been servants to care for her and her father's wealth to protect her.

She glanced out the window.

Things were going to be different from now on. She would have to be wise. She would have to think for herself. There wouldn't be a man making the decisions for her or planning in advance. Which was what she wanted. Which was why she was on this train headed west.

She'd left the diamond ring Duncan gave her on the dresser in her bedchamber, along with a simple note of goodbye. He wouldn't, she was certain, be upset when he read it. Perhaps he would mind the loss of the income he'd counted on, but he wouldn't miss her. He would simply find another daughter of a wealthy man, another woman to ignore while he carried on his affairs.

I'm on my own. Her heart fluttered wildly. She was both happy and terrified by the thought.

She imagined her father opening the letter she'd left for him and Mother. The tops of his ears would turn bright red, and his eyes would bulge as his mouth flattened into a thin line. His fury would be almost uncontrollable.

Poor Mother.

Cora closed her eyes, feeling a moment of shame. Father would vent his anger on Mother. Could Cora have done something to warn her, to shield her? No. There was nothing she could have done. If her mother had had the least inkling of what Cora intended to do, she would have gone straight to her husband with the information. That was the sort of wife she was. It wouldn't have occurred to her to do anything that displeased him or contradicted his wishes.

Opening her eyes again, Cora saw a middle-aged woman enter the passenger car, holding the handle of a carpetbag with both hands. She looked even more tired than Cora felt. Cora offered a brief smile of encouragement.

"May I join you?" the woman asked.

"Of course." She drew her feet back to make room.

The woman put her bag on the seat and slid it up close to the window. Then she sat beside it. "Gracious. The car is warm, isn't it?"

"Yes. It is."

"I'm Mabel Johnson."

"A pleasure. My name is Co—" She stopped. Should she give her real name or make one up? And why hadn't she thought of this before? But now it was too late. She couldn't think of a different name. "Cora Anderson," she finished, thankful that the woman didn't seem to notice her hesitation.

"Are you traveling alone?" Mabel looked down the aisle, as if expecting to see someone returning to sit beside Cora.

"Yes, I'm alone."

"I hate traveling alone. The hours pass so slowly without someone to talk to."

Cora hid a smile. She suspected Mabel Johnson had no trouble meeting others, then filling the silence. Not if their own meeting was any indication. "Where are you going, Mrs. Johnson?"

"It's Miss Johnson, and I'm headed home to Denver. Are you going that far?"

She wasn't sure, but she nodded.

"Have you been to Denver before?"

"No, I haven't. But I've heard that the Rocky Mountains are spectacular."

"Yes, indeed, they are. One of God's masterpieces. Wait until you see them."

Cora heard the conductor calling for all to get aboard and felt some tension leave her shoulders. She'd made it through another station. "I look forward to it."

"Are you a teacher?"

"A teacher?"

Mabel's gaze went to the violin case. "I thought perhaps you give music lessons."

"No." She smiled. "But I love to play."

"If you aren't going to teach, are you going out West to get married?"

Cora shook her head. "No." Somehow she contained a shudder.

Mabel leaned slightly forward as if to encourage Cora to say more.

But what could she say? She didn't know where she was going, let alone what she would do once she got there. Oh, she should have thought this through. All she'd wanted to do was escape. She hadn't considered what she might find on the other end of her race to freedom. Panic tightened her throat.

The train jerked, then began to *chug* forward. Thankfully, Mabel Johnson seemed to leave her curiosity at the station. She ceased to ask questions and instead launched into a story about her sister who was a teacher in a small town in the mountains of Colorado.

Cora was thankful for the distraction. For a little while, she could push away her more troubled thoughts.

Chapter 6

For the difficult months of Jacob's decline, Liam had remained connected to his church in California via streamed services, devotional podcasts, and a Facebook group. The habit stayed with him after his retreat to Chickadee Creek. It seemed enough as he wrestled with his emotions—the grief, the anger, the odd feeling of betrayal at being left brotherless.

But for some reason, when he awakened on Sunday morning, he knew he wanted to sit in a church with other followers of Christ. Grace Witherstone had invited him to visit the town's small community church almost every time he'd been in the mercantile. Today, he decided to take her up on it. His church in Los Angeles was a megachurch. The one he'd seen in Chickadee Creek probably wouldn't hold more than two hundred people. Three hundred if they were packed in like sardines. Quite a change from a sanctuary that held thousands in a single service, but one he was suddenly looking forward to.

He showered and dressed, then fixed himself a quick breakfast. Afterward, while sipping a second cup of coffee, he watched Chipper race through the trees, chasing birds and other small forest creatures.

"All right, boy," he called at last. "I'll be late if I don't go now."

The dog came to him at once and, at his master's hand signal, trotted inside.

"Be good." Liam grabbed his truck keys off the table inside the doorway. "I'll be back in a couple of hours."

Chipper lay down with a groan, head resting on paws. His eyes called Liam a traitor for leaving him on his own.

The drive into town took mere minutes, and before he knew it, he was pulling into the gravel parking lot beside the church. Other cars and trucks were there before him. A few people on the main road walked in the direction of the white clapboard building. He pulled the keys from the ignition and got out of the truck. As he neared the entrance, he saw Grace from the general store standing on the stoop, greeting others as they arrived. She grinned widely when she saw him.

"Mr. Chandler, as I live and breathe!" she exclaimed. "You came at last."

He returned her smile. "Yes, ma'am. Here I am."

"Can't tell you how pleased I am to see you." She took his hand and drew him into the vestibule. "Reverend Oswald, look who's here. This is Liam Chandler."

The pastor, who stood near the entrance to the sanctuary, smiled and nodded. "Welcome, Mr. Chandler. We're glad you've joined us."

"Thanks. It's good to be here."

Grace excused herself and moved into the sanctuary.

"I've been meaning to—" The reverend's words were cut short by several chords played on the organ. He glanced toward the front of the church. "Sorry. That's my wife's way of telling me

I'd best take my place." His gaze returned to Liam. "But I hope we'll have a chance to talk soon."

"I'd like that," Liam answered, realizing the words were true.

All of these months, he'd basically isolated himself, wanting to be alone with his grief and anger. Pretty much the only people he'd met in this mountain community were Grace Witherstone at the mercantile and Fred Bishop at the gas station. And as of yesterday, Rosemary Townsend and her great-niece at the antique store. Remembering Chelsea brought a smile to his lips as he made his way to the back row of padded chairs.

Just as he found his place, the congregation rose to sing. The words of the worship song were displayed on a screen above the altar area, but it was one he knew well, so he didn't need to read the lyrics. Halfway through the second chorus, he closed his eyes and mouth and listened to the other voices filling the small sanctuary. This was why God had drawn him there this morning, he thought. He could sing along with others while streaming a church service, but it wasn't the same as being in their midst, as hearing other voices raised in a song of praise.

Not forsaking our own assembling together, as is the habit of some . . .

The snippet of Scripture was distinct in his mind and heart, and he knew beyond doubt that the Holy Spirit had spoken the words to him. Conviction tightened his chest. It was one thing to withdraw from his work in California while he sought to find his way after Jacob's death. It was another entirely to withdraw from the body of Christ.

He recalled something a youth pastor had said many years before: *"You can be a Christian without going to church, but you won't be a healthy one."*

He opened his eyes to look at those in the rows ahead of him. *Sorry, Lord,* he mouthed before joining the singing once again.

Grace Fellowship, Chelsea's church on the outskirts of Spokane, was surrounded by subdivisions full of couples and families. Even so, the congregation wasn't large. That was one reason she'd chosen it after moving away from Hadley Station. She didn't like crowds or tight spaces. They made her anxious. A small gathering of believers was much more to her liking.

Chickadee Creek Community Church reminded Chelsea somewhat of Grace Fellowship. A simple wooden cross, draped with a length of purple fabric, hung high above the altar area. Colorful banners bearing words from the Bible dotted the walls between the windows on either side of the sanctuary. Simple. Warm. Friendly. Exactly what she needed.

While the pastor preached, Chelsea's gaze went to the landscape beyond the nearby window. Late-morning sunlight filtered down through the pines and danced upon the water in the creek. Beyond the gurgling stream and tall trees sat an open meadow full of wheat-colored grass turned gold by the sun. The scene was as soothing as the pastor's voice, and Chelsea said a silent prayer of thanks to God. For bringing her to this small town. For Grandpa John sending her. For Aunt Rosemary wanting her. For a time of peace when she might regroup and find her way again.

The congregation rose to sing another worship song. Then the pastor spoke a final prayer, and the service was over. People rose from their chairs. They clustered in small groups in the aisles, hardly moving. Conversations started all around, voices rising to be heard above the others.

Chelsea glanced over her shoulder. Could she and her great-aunt escape before too many introductions ensued? Her head still swam with the names of the people she'd met on the way in.

Before she could bring her gaze back to Aunt Rosemary, she saw a familiar face. Liam Chandler was shaking hands with an elderly man on the opposite side of the sanctuary.

"Well, look who's here," Aunt Rosemary said. "It's our new friend. The movie star."

Liam turned in that moment, and their gazes met. He smiled.

How had she not recognized him the first moment he entered the antique shop? He looked every bit the handsome hero that he was on film, even in his casual attire.

She thought of a school friend, Shelby Webster. Chelsea's father hadn't allowed his children to spend much time away from their home. He'd begrudgingly allowed them to attend school, but going over to anybody's house was forbidden. Still, Chelsea had managed to see, just the one time, the movie star and musician posters on Shelby's bedroom walls. "Aren't they dreamy?" her friend had asked with a giggle.

Dreamy, indeed. Chelsea couldn't help wondering how many teenaged girls had posters of Liam Chandler on their bedroom walls.

Embarrassed by her thoughts, she turned toward Aunt Rosemary. "It's time I got you home."

"Yes. I'm feeling a bit tired. It'll be good to put my leg up."

As soon as the two of them stepped into the aisle, Chelsea took hold of her great-aunt's free arm and they made their way out of the sanctuary. It was a slow process. Those people who hadn't spoken to Aunt Rosemary before the service all seemed to want to do so now. But somehow Chelsea kept them moving toward the doorway, one determined step after another.

It was outside, on the front stoop of the church, where they met up with Liam again.

"Good morning," he said, still smiling, his chocolate-brown eyes moving from Rosemary to Chelsea and back again.

Something fluttered in Chelsea's stomach, but it wasn't a sensation she welcomed.

"Oh, Liam. So nice to see you here." Rosemary released a deep sigh. "Would you mind letting me lean on you while Chelsea goes for the car? I'm not sure I can make it across that gravel lot again."

"Of course I don't mind." Concern crossed his face as he looked a second time at Chelsea.

She released her great-aunt's arm. "I'll hurry."

Once she knew Liam had a steadying hold on Aunt Rosemary, Chelsea hastened to where she'd left the car earlier. Her great-aunt hadn't allowed her to park by the handicapped signs. "I don't have one of those permit thingies," she'd said, "and I don't intend to get one. Not even a temporary one. I'm not handicapped. I'm simply recovering from surgery."

Now Chelsea wished she'd insisted on parking closer to the church entrance. There wasn't a police officer around who would ticket Rosemary Townsend for parking in a handicapped spot, nor would anyone complain. Everyone in Chickadee Creek knew about her fall, about the multiple breaks in her leg and the surgery that followed. She was a beloved figure in the small mountain town.

It took only moments to back out of the spot and pull to

the front of the church, but worry for her great-aunt made it seem longer. Once Chelsea stopped the car, Liam opened the passenger door and helped Aunt Rosemary sit on the seat, then pivot into place, taking extra care not to bump her bad leg in the process.

"Thank you, my boy." Aunt Rosemary patted Liam's arm. "I don't know why I suddenly felt so weak. It's silly, really."

"Not silly," Liam answered. "You go home and rest."

Aunt Rosemary brightened. "Why don't you come have Sunday dinner with us?"

Before Chelsea could object to the invitation, Liam declined. "Thanks, but I can't today. Maybe another time." He looked across the car at Chelsea but still spoke to her great-aunt. "Now you'd better rest."

"Yes." Aunt Rosemary sighed. "I suppose I'd better."

Thank you, Chelsea mouthed.

He responded with the slightest of nods before stepping back from the car and straightening, then closing the door.

"What a thoughtful young man," Aunt Rosemary said.

"Yes."

It was easy enough to agree. Liam Chandler appeared to be very kind, very thoughtful. But Chelsea knew appearances were often deceptive, and as she drove away, she warned herself not to be fooled again by a handsome man full of charm.

Liam's Journal

Last night I dreamed about Jacob's funeral. I was there at the grave-side service with everybody else. The last goodbye. The ground was covered with a thin layer of snow, and the wind was bitter.

Same as it was in real life. Only there were differences too.

Dad's secretary was there, and he kept turning and whispering things to her, and she took notes. Dad, always working.

Mom wore dark glasses, but I heard her crying. I put a hand on her shoulder to try to comfort her. She shrugged it off.

All of a sudden, I stood on the opposite side of the casket. Alone. And I looked across at Mom and Dad, and I realized how far apart we were. How far apart I was from them and how far apart they were from each other. The perfect Chandler family was a charade. Like one of my movies, we all had parts to play, but none of it was real. Smoke and mirrors. That's all.

I woke up with that thought clear in my mind. The only real thing was Jacob, and he's gone now.

Liam's Journal

I went into Chickadee Creek to attend church. I thought I was getting on all right watching the service from my church in LA on YouTube. But when I got up on Sunday morning, I knew I wanted to actually sit in church with other people. To be in the presence of others as I listened to a sermon, to get to worship with them. It was good too. Small but good.

Rosemary Townsend from the antique store and her great-niece, Chelsea, were there. The older woman got to feeling a bit weak when it was over, and I helped get her into her car. Nice lady.

But I keep thinking about Chelsea the most. Spencer is her last name. (I had to ask somebody at church what her last name was after they drove off because I'd forgotten.) I don't know why I keep thinking about her. Maybe it's that red hair of hers. I'm a sucker for redheads. She's cute too. But there's something else. She seems kind of fragile, and yet at the same time I see strength.

Maybe what I like most is that, even once she put my name with my face and mentioned my latest movie, there wasn't that look in her eyes. That hungry look some girls get. Just about every female in Los Angeles is a wannabe actress, and too often I feel like they want me to be a stepping-stone. And I'm not even a major film star. I'm better known than I was a few years ago. But still not the first guy hired on a film.

That's not what too many girls my age see when we meet. No wonder so many Hollywood marriages (if they even bother to marry) don't last. So much is just the surface stuff. The women I've gone out with in recent years—I don't think any of them wanted to know <u>me</u>. Nobody cared where I came from or about my brother once I learned he had cancer. Okay, that was as much my fault as anybody else's. You get used to wearing that facade, and letting it down isn't easy.

I'd like something real.

Jacob wanted me to be real.

Can I make that happen?

Chapter 7

*D*ust motes hung in the still air of the second-floor storage room. Sunlight filtered through an uncovered window that was in need of a good cleaning. Stacks of boxes lined the walls, and miscellaneous objects filled the floor in the center of the room.

Chelsea stood in the doorway, reminding herself of something Grandpa John liked to ask: *How do you eat an elephant?*

"One bite at a time," she answered aloud. "And I sure hope you're right, Grandpa." She stepped into the room and set the caddy of cleaning supplies on a wooden crate.

Chelsea didn't mind hard work. She was used to it. At four, her assigned chore had been to collect eggs from the chicken coop. By the age of six, she was tasked with fixing breakfast for her two younger sisters and one brother. By ten, she was an expert at chopping wood and starting a fire in the fireplace. The Spencers hadn't lived entirely off the grid, but it had been close. Hadley Station was a town of about six hundred residents. Tucked away in the forests of Idaho's panhandle, it was easily cut off from the rest of the world by winter snows and spring runoffs. Chelsea's dad had loved to remind his children that they must be able to take care of themselves in every instance. Failure to perform brought punishment. Swift and harsh.

A shudder passed through Chelsea, and she felt the walls closing in, threatening to trap her. The light grew dim, and her breathing grew shallow. She moved across the room as quickly as the cluttered floor permitted. There, she opened the window, leaned forward until sunlight touched her face, and breathed in the pine-scented air, eyes now closed.

Oh, how she hated these unexpected moments of terror. They made her feel weak. But she wasn't weak. Small of stature, yes. Too thin, according to her kid sister, Frances, yes. But not weak.

I will rather boast about my weaknesses, a voice seemed to whisper in her heart, *so that the power of Christ may dwell in me.*

"Boast in my weaknesses." She opened her eyes. Then, looking up through the pines at the blue sky, she added, "Your power is perfected in my weakness."

The darkness—along with threatening memories—scurried away, and she released a long sigh.

Her panic attacks weren't always this cooperative. Sometimes they seemed to last an eternity. But at least the attacks happened less frequently than they once had. Her faith in Jesus had changed the grip they'd had on her. She counted that among her many blessings.

"I'm better now. I'm free now. God is with me."

She turned from the window and pinned her gaze on the nearest corner of the room. She would start there. One bite at a time, like her grandfather had taught her. Drawing another deep breath, she reached for a box on top of a stack, set it on the floor, and opened the lid.

Chelsea lost track of time as she sorted, then saved or discarded. It was the growling of her stomach that finally made her realize how long she'd worked in this room alone. And while she could probably go for another hour or two without eating, she needed to stop long enough to fix lunch for her great-aunt. Hopefully, Aunt Rosemary had followed her instructions and stayed in her chair.

As she pushed up from the floor, Chelsea saw something poking from behind a painted chest of drawers. It surprised her that she hadn't noticed it before; the object was black while the dresser was blue. She stepped closer and tried to pull the odd-shaped item free. It didn't budge. Curious, she tugged the dresser away from the wall. This time when she tried, the object slid into view.

Her breath caught. It was a violin case. Was it just a case, or could there be a violin inside? She reached for the latch to learn the answer.

The case wasn't empty, and the instrument inside looked wonderful to her. The brown varnish dull, but wonderful all the same. She didn't know much about violins. She'd only had a few lessons when she was twelve before her father learned of it and forbade her to continue. But her love for violin music had never left her, which made the instrument in the case perfect in her eyes. Perhaps her father's edicts had increased her love. Her favorite country music always included a fiddle. Her favorite classical music always featured a violin.

Heart suddenly racing, she closed the lid and held the case against her chest. No one else was going to buy this violin. She was certain Aunt Rosemary would agree to let her buy it, even if she had to make payments. She had to ask, and she meant to do so right now.

Clutching the violin case tightly, she hurried out of the storage room and down the stairs. At the door, she paused only long enough to flip the sign from *Open* to *Closed* before leaving the shop. At the edge of the boardwalk, she stopped once more to look left and right. Then she ran across the road and up the driveway.

"Aunt Rosemary!" she called as she entered the house. "Aunt Rosemary, look what I found."

"My goodness. What is it, child?" Her great-aunt set aside a book and leaned forward on the chair.

Chelsea dropped to her knees on the floor, setting the case in front of her. "It was in the upstairs storage room." She flicked the latches and opened the lid of the case. "And this was inside." Almost reverently, she drew out the violin. "Isn't it beautiful?"

"Exquisite."

"How did it come to be there? How *long* has it been there?"

"I haven't a clue, dear. I've never seen it before. I promise I would remember it if I had."

Chelsea dragged her gaze from the violin to her great-aunt. "You have no idea? So you don't know who it belonged to before it came to the shop?"

"No, dear. I don't. Someone else must have been managing the store when it was brought in. If I'd known about it, it've gone up for sale right away. Where did you say you found it?"

"In that upstairs storage room on the northeast side. It was behind the blue chest of drawers."

"Heavens. It could have been in there for thirty years or more. Forty, even. That dresser's been in that room almost as long as I've owned the place. Piece of junk and ugly as sin. I never even put a price tag on it. Just used it to put stuff in."

"Aunt Rosemary, I would like to buy it. Not the dresser. The violin. I don't know what you would ask for it, but I'd still like to buy it from—"

"It's yours, my girl. You found it. You can have it." Her great-aunt pressed the violin toward Chelsea.

"It might take a while for me to pay it off."

Aunt Rosemary huffed. "I don't mean for you to buy it. It's my gift to you."

"But if it's a professional violin, it could be worth a couple of thousand dollars." Even as she raised that objection, she pulled the violin the rest of the way to her chest.

"Chelsea Spencer, do you see me going without anything I need? I have this good old house. Got electricity and a nice fireplace. I've even got cable TV and the internet, though I can't say I do much with either. I've got a reliable vehicle. I've got lots of friends. And I've got you taking care of me and spoiling me like I've never been spoiled before. Not to mention all the work you've put in over at that shop. Why, you've near worked yourself to death." She pointed at the violin. "Nothing I could get for that pretty thing in your hands would give me more pleasure than I've already got from giving it to you."

Tears welled in Chelsea's eyes. She wanted to tell her great-aunt how much she loved her, but the words caught in her throat. Obvious signs of affection had been discouraged in the Spencer household. Chelsea loved her mother, her sisters, and her brother, but the words were rarely spoken between them. Silence was a hard habit to break. And the last time she'd tried to break it, she'd paid for it dearly.

Chelsea stood and went to a nearby chair. "I took a few violin lessons when I was in school."

"You did? Well, then. It seems that violin was meant to be yours. You'll have to entertain me sometime."

She laughed softly. "I said a *few* lessons. I can't play at all. I've forgotten the little bit I learned."

"It'll come back fast enough. Seems to me I heard about a lady who gives lessons hereabouts. Up the highway in one of those fancy mountain subdivisions. I'll have to ask Grace about it. She'll know for certain." Aunt Rosemary's forehead crinkled. "You know, I think that's where I heard about the teacher. From Grace. There's a poster on the announcement board just inside the door of the general store."

"I came here to help you, Aunt Rosemary. Not to spend my time learning to play the violin."

Her great-aunt released another huff. "As if you won't have plenty of time to do both." She pointed toward the kitchen. "Go get the phone book out of that drawer. The top drawer on the left. We need to find a music shop that can take a look at the violin. Give it a polish and some new strings and whatever else it needs. I'll cover the cost."

"Aunt Rosemary—"

"Shush, girl. Don't argue with me. I'm an old woman recovering from surgery. You don't want me to get overwrought or anything."

Chelsea recognized the kindhearted manipulation for what it was, and she laughed again as she set the violin gently into its case and went to do her great-aunt's bidding.

It didn't take long to find several listings under "Musical Instruments—Repairs." Of course, the phone book was about a decade old, so they couldn't be sure all of them were still in business. Before placing any calls, Chelsea used her phone to look up reviews online, wanting to be sure she took the violin to the best place available. After talking to a man at the store with the top ratings, she told him to expect her soon and ended the call.

"Go today," Aunt Rosemary said. "There's still plenty of time. You can be there and back long before dinnertime."

"I don't know. I can go another day. I haven't even made your lunch yet."

"Don't be silly."

"And I'd need to shower first."

"So go shower. Now. Can't you tell I'm as excited as you are about getting that violin looked over and ready for you to learn to play?"

Chelsea couldn't deny the excited pounding of her own heart. "All right. If you're sure."

"Go. Scoot. On your way."

Once out of the mountains, the GPS on Chelsea's phone guided her to the music store without a problem. Intense heat accompanied her short walk from the car into the cool air of the shop. A smiling salesman came to ask if he could show her something in particular, and she gave him the name of the man she'd spoken to earlier. The salesman then led her through a collection of pianos to the back of the store.

Another man arrived on the opposite side of the counter. He, too, wore a smile. "How may I help you?"

"I'm Chelsea Spencer." She set the case on the counter. "I spoke with George Frost on the phone earlier today."

His smile grew. "I'm George Frost. A pleasure to meet you,

Miss Spencer." His gaze lowered to the case. "Let's see what we have here, shall we?"

She loosened the clasps and opened the case, revealing the violin.

"Mmm." George looked at the instrument for a long while before removing it. Then he carried it to a nearby work counter with plenty of light. "Mmm."

Did that sound he made mean it was going to cost a small fortune to get the violin in shape? Was it beyond repair? Perhaps being left to sit like that had ruined it.

"Miss Spencer, may I ask how long you've had this violin?"

"My great-aunt just gave it to me. It's been in her antique shop in Chickadee Creek for years. She couldn't say how long for sure. Perhaps more than thirty. It was in a storage room with a lot of junk."

He looked over at her as if to assess the veracity of her words. "And before your great-aunt? Who owned it then?"

She shook her head. "I don't know."

"I see." His gaze returned to the violin.

"Can it be repaired?"

"Yes, Miss Spencer. It can be repaired. It's a fine violin. Very fine."

"Will it—" She broke off, swallowed, then began again. "Will it be terribly expensive?"

He looked at her again. "No. I don't think it will be terribly expensive. And I assure you, we will treat it with the utmost care while it's with us." He left the violin and case and moved to a computer. "Let me get you a receipt. But first, I'll need your contact information." As he spoke, he slid a pad of paper toward her. On the paper were spaces for her name, address, and phone number.

"Of course." She picked up a pen and wrote down the requested information.

When she was done, George Frost looked at the paper and entered everything into the computer. "I noticed there is a tear in the lining of the case. Would you like us to repair it as well?"

"Yes. Thank you. Whatever's needed." Her pulse quickened. Was she being unfair to Aunt Rosemary? She'd told Chelsea not to worry about the cost, that it was part of her gift. Still . . .

George Frost put the printed receipt on the counter. "May I ask you: do you play the violin?"

"No. But I've wanted to learn ever since I was in junior high. Now that I have my own violin, I plan to take lessons. I'm not too old to learn. At least I hope not."

"Extraordinary," he said softly, turning once more toward the instrument on the worktable.

Chelsea took a couple of steps back while folding the receipt and slipping it into the back pocket of her shorts.

"We'll call you before we do any actual work," George Frost said as he moved toward the violin.

Chelsea had the feeling he'd already forgotten her.

Cora

OCTOBER 1895

An autumn chill entered the stagecoach as the horses climbed higher into the mountains. Cora, the lone passenger, held tightly to a strap, hoping to keep herself from being thrown to the floor or to the opposite side of the coach. If traveling by rail seemed wearisome, traveling by coach seemed deadly.

Maybe I should go home?

She'd had the same thought many times over the past five months since first boarding a train in New York. Months that tested her in ways she hadn't anticipated. Months that made her long for the life of privilege she'd taken for granted. It shamed her when she remembered how little she'd noticed the service of others. The baths drawn for her. The bed made for her. The clothes laid out for her. The maid, Millie, who brought her breakfast in bed and helped dress her hair.

A wheel dropped into a rut, jerking the coach sideways, then rocking it back again. Cora's shoulder smacked into the side of the compartment, and she cried out in alarm. Although the window was covered, she'd peeked beyond the leather curtain earlier and knew they traveled a treacherous road with a sharp drop-off on one side. Would she die in these mountains before reaching her destination?

Chickadee Creek, Idaho. That's where she was headed. At last. After spending the past five months in Colorado with Mabel Johnson—the stranger on the train who had turned into her mentor and dearest friend—Cora had obtained her teaching certificate. And now, thanks to Mabel's niece who lived in Idaho, Cora had obtained a position in Chickadee Creek. Even knowing it was true, it still seemed impossible. Not so long ago, she'd had no hope of anything but living out her life with a man she didn't love and who didn't love her. Now she was going to make a life of her own choosing.

As a schoolgirl, Cora had loved her studies, but she hadn't given any thought to what those studies might do for her. She'd certainly never thought they might lead to her becoming a teacher herself. Women of her class weren't supposed to work.

Young women like Cora Anderson were supposed to marry well and have babies, to hostess fashionable dinner parties and attend operas, to travel to Europe, to play the piano or the flute or the violin, to do needlepoint, to paint pictures.

Cora had attended many dinner parties and more than a few operas in recent years. She'd traveled to Europe with her parents twice. She was accomplished on the violin and loved to paint with watercolors. She abhorred needlepoint work but—this thought made her smile wryly—learning to use a needle and thread had helped with the mending she now needed to do.

She glanced down at the hem of her gown. The patch might not be obvious to everyone, but it seemed all too noticeable to her. A year ago, she might have had Millie give the dress away rather than mend it. How frivolous of her. How ungrateful for what she'd had.

"God will look out for you, Cora." Mabel Johnson's words whispered in her memory. *"Trust Him always. Seek His face. He will show you the way."*

Cora hadn't known, of course, when she'd seen a weary fellow traveler getting onto the train five months before, that they were destined to become friends, let alone that Mabel would take her under her wing and become a guiding force in her life.

Mabel knew a lost soul when she saw one.

The memory was bittersweet. It had been hard to leave Colorado, to say goodbye to Mabel. Necessary but hard. Harder even than leaving her childhood home and her own mother. And that realization made her sad. Sad for herself. Sad for her mother. Maybe even sad for her father.

The coach slowed and banked to the left. The driver shouted something at the horses. Cora dared to lift the edge of the leather curtain. The last time she'd looked outside, the hillsides had been covered in grass and sagebrush. Now they moved through a forest of tall pine trees. The interior of the coach felt even colder than before, as if the sun had no reach in this place.

Don't think that way. It's going to be lovely in Chickadee Creek. Remember the photograph of the schoolhouse. You're going to make a wonderful and . . . and safe life for yourself.

Safe.

The word reverberated in her chest. She couldn't help it. Even after all these months and despite the thousands of miles she'd traveled, she didn't feel safe. She was still afraid her father would find her and force her to marry Duncan or another man like him.

"Miss?" The driver's voice came to her above the noise of the creaking coach and the rattle of harness. "Miss, we're coming into Chickadee Creek."

Drawing a breath, she loosened her grip on the strap. When the coach slowed even more, she lowered her hand and tried to straighten her clothing. She didn't want everything to look askew when she disembarked. Chickadee Creek was to be her new home, hopefully for many years to come. She wanted to start off by making a good impression.

OCTOBER 1895

Preston stood on the boardwalk outside the general store. In lieu of the mayor, who was away from Chickadee Creek until November, he'd been called upon to welcome the new teacher to town. It wasn't as if he didn't have other places to be. But there he was, waiting for some old-maid schoolmarm to get off the stagecoach.

I should've refused when I was asked to do it.

He sighed as he checked his pocket watch. The coach was running late. No surprise there. In the months Preston had called Chickadee Creek home, he couldn't remember when it had ever arrived according to the schedule posted on the wall of the mercantile.

Before he could put the watch back into his pocket, the stagecoach rolled into view. Good. He could welcome the teacher, show her the schoolhouse, then drop her at her living quarters. And if he had his way, he would do so in record time.

The coach stopped in front of Preston. The driver stepped onto the wheel, then hopped to the ground. He then came around, opened the door of the coach, and offered his hand to the lady inside.

Preston felt his jaw go slack when a vision in golden brown leaned into view. Her dark hair was topped with a hat the same color as her gown. He was no expert on women's dresses, but he thought it must be the height of fashion. Probably too fashionable for a place like Chickadee Creek, where clothing tended to be more practical than decorative. Definitely too fashionable for the spinster schoolmarm he'd imagined.

The driver reached to take hold of her arm at the elbow. As she stepped to the ground—holding a carpetbag in one hand and a violin case in the other—her gaze met Preston's, and he forgot everything else. He'd noticed already that she was pretty, but he hadn't expected those eyes. Large dark-brown pools surrounded by thick black lashes. Extraordinary.

He swallowed hard.

"Thank you," she said to the driver.

"My pleasure, miss. I'll get your trunk." The man bent his hat brim before heading to the back of the coach.

Preston stepped off the boardwalk. "Miss Anderson?" He wondered if she would give him a different name, if Cora Anderson had missed the stagecoach or changed her mind about coming to this small community. This woman wasn't anything like the schoolmarm he'd pictured in his mind for the past week.

"Yes." She looked at him again, expectancy in her gaze.

"I'm Preston Chandler. Welcome to Chickadee Creek."

"Thank you. It's a pleasure to be here."

The stagecoach driver dropped a large, battered trunk on the ground near Cora. "There you go, miss."

She thanked him again, and he moved away.

Preston reached for the trunk. When he lifted it, he was surprised that it wasn't heavier. Cora Anderson looked as if she would be the type to travel with dozens of gowns and shoes. Again, she was nothing like he'd expected.

"If you'll come with me, I'll show you the schoolhouse and then to your living quarters."

"Thank you," she said once again.

It wasn't far to the schoolhouse, and they walked in silence. Preston noticed that Cora took in her surroundings, looking from one side of the winding street to the other. Perhaps she was memorizing the location of every shop and business. Perhaps she was wishing she could get back onto the stagecoach and return to the comfort of some home far away.

Suddenly she stopped. Preston took two more steps before realizing she wasn't beside him. He stopped, too, and turned to look at her. She smiled, her eyes not on him but on the school-house beyond him.

"Oh my," she breathed.

The school was an ordinary white-clapboard building with a half-dozen windows and a small bell tower with a rope dangling down to the side of the door. As far as Preston could tell, it looked like hundreds of other schoolhouses throughout the country. But the expression on Cora's face said she saw something much more than that, although he wasn't sure what.

"I've got the key," Preston said. "I'll show you inside."

She nodded.

He set the trunk on the ground, and she put her carpetbag and violin case on top of it. For a moment, he considered offering a hand to help her climb the steps. It would be the gentlemanly thing to do. But instinct stopped him. He had the feeling she would rather make her own way.

"I'll get the door." Taking the key from his pocket, he climbed the steps. After unlocking the door, he opened it, then looked behind him.

Cora still stood in the street, her gaze taking in not only the schoolhouse but also the terrain that surrounded it.

Preston cleared his throat.

"I'm sorry." Holding her skirt out of the way, she quickly climbed the steps, stopping in the doorway to look at him. "You must have other things to do than to wait on me, Mr. Chandler. I won't delay you much longer."

"No problem, Miss Anderson." But that wasn't the truth. It *was* a problem. He had work to do. Still, he didn't want to rush away as originally planned.

She stepped inside and walked toward the front of the room.

Her gloved fingers touched the dust-covered teacher's desk. A chalkboard took up the entire wall beyond it, and a large globe rested in a stand in the left corner. A woodstove sat in the corner on the right. Judging by the student desks taking up the better portion of the room, Preston guessed they were prepared for twenty or thirty students.

Cora returned to the door. "I'm ready to be shown to my lodgings." She held out a hand, palm up.

It took him a moment to realize what she wanted. When he did, he gave her the key. As her fingers closed around it, another smile blossomed on her lips, and it seemed to Preston that the cool room warmed by at least ten degrees.

Liam's Journal

Dad called yesterday. He's thinking about selling off some more of the land up here. I hate the idea, although I can't give him much of a reason. I don't need any of it.

I've got 20 acres where my house is. What would I need with the lots he wants to sell in town or the property on the other side of the river? When that old ranch sells, the land will become another one of those upscale communities with houses way beyond the price the people who've lived in the area for years could afford. It's happening everywhere, but I hate to see it happen here. All those people fleeing the big cities. Trouble is they seem to want to change this area into another big city.

It bugs me that Dad's going to sell, but who am I to tell him not to? I've got my acreage and a nice house. Is it because I'm a Chandler that I resist the idea of letting go? Dad never seemed too caught up in how he inherited so much land in the Boise Basin. I guess by the time it came to him, it was less than half as much as it once was. But it's still a lot.

I wonder why he didn't sell it before now.

A while back, I wrote that Jacob wanted me to be more real. I've been thinking about that a lot. What it means to be "real." It's easier to do in the mountains of Idaho than it was in Hollywood. Not that I want to blame the industry or my chosen career for my behavior. I've had a choice how to act. I've had the choice to be more true to myself.

More true to God.

There. That's what I needed to write. More true to God.

I've laid low a lot all these years. Does everybody know I'm a Christian? Not hardly. I've followed Kurt's advice. I've kept the "God talk" to myself. Wouldn't want anybody to dismiss considering me for a movie because of my faith. Yes, I've been a member of a church in LA. A good, Bible-teaching church. But how much beyond that have I gone in living my Christianity? Have I found myself a mentor or become part of a group of men who will hold me accountable? Short answer: no. Why? Because then I might have to grow. Because out of principle, I might have to turn down some of those roles I accepted. Somebody might ask, "Do you think that's what God wants you to do?"

If somebody asked me that in the past, I would have answered with something like, "If God opens a door, who am I not to walk through it?"

But who says all of those doors were opened by God?

Jacob asked me that one night. I ignored him. I wish I hadn't.

Another thing I wished we'd talked about: Chickadee Creek. We've had family here for over 150 years, but I don't know near enough about those roots. The lady at the antique store knows more than I do. Probably more than Dad does. Whenever we came up to the cabin as kids, Dad would mention things here and there. But never much. Funny how it never occurred to me to ask more. Jacob did. Jacob was always more curious about stuff than I was.

I'm more curious now. But to be completely honest (that's what a journal's for, right?), my new curiosity may have more to do with an attractive redhead. I can't seem to stop thinking about her. And it isn't just because she's pretty, although she is that. But I've known plenty of beautiful women. I've <u>dated</u> plenty of beautiful women.

No, there's something else about Chelsea Spencer that makes me think I'd like to get to know her. Then again, would that be smart? I haven't figured out what's next in my life. I don't feel like God's told me if I'm to stay here or go back to LA.

But it wouldn't have to be romantic. A man can still have friends, even while he's working through stuff. Right?

Wish I could bounce all of this off Jacob. Even when we were little kids, he seemed to figure things out faster than me.

Lord Jesus, I miss my brother. I know he's with You and is without pain and sorrow. But I still miss him.

Chapter 8

My girl? Whatever is the matter?"

Chelsea blinked as she looked toward her great-aunt.

"Who was that on the phone, dear?"

"George Frost. The man from the music store."

"Well, it's about time he called." Aunt Rosemary gave Chelsea a hard look, then straightened away from the back of the chair. "Is something wrong with the violin?"

The past three days had gone by at a snail's pace. Chelsea had worried that the violin couldn't be repaired, despite what she'd been told when she left the instrument at the store in Boise. She'd worried about the cost of repairs, if they were possible. She'd been tempted to drive down to the city and take it back, whether or not it could ever be played again.

But Mr. Frost hadn't said anything about repairs on the phone just now.

"No." She shook her head, as if trying to shake away her confusion. "He said . . . Aunt Rosemary, he said it's a valuable instrument. *Very* valuable."

"My goodness gracious."

"Perhaps twenty thousand or more." Chelsea sank onto the chair opposite her great-aunt. "He also said there was a piece of paper inside the lining. It gives the first name of the owner. The violin was a gift for her birthday." She drew a breath, trying to hide the disappointment growing inside of her. "If it's that valuable, it must have been brought to your shop by accident. The person who sold it or gave it must not have known its worth. If we know who the rightful owner is, we'll have to return it."

"If they're still around. Remember, whoever owned it may have left the area. Maybe that's why they brought the violin to the shop. They were getting rid of things they no longer wanted."

"Maybe," Chelsea whispered. For three days she'd believed the violin was hers. For three days, she'd imagined learning to play it. She'd even dared to dream she might become at least somewhat proficient, that she would be able to create beautiful music with it.

"What was the name?" Aunt Rosemary asked.

"The name?"

"You said the violin was a birthday gift. To whom?"

Chelsea shook her head again. "I'm sorry. I was so surprised by what he said about its value, I didn't pay attention to the name." She frowned. "No. Wait. I think he said Cora. Or maybe it was Laura."

"Cora?" Aunt Rosemary covered her mouth with her fingertips. "Cora Anderson Chandler."

"You know her?"

Aunt Rosemary smiled briefly. "No, more's the pity. Cora died the year before I was born. She was Liam Chandler's great-grandmother." She frowned. "No, his great-great-grandmother."

"Chandler. Of course. Then the violin rightfully belongs to Liam." She swallowed the lump in her throat.

"Perhaps. I'd like to think whoever sold it or gave it to the shop knew what it was worth or who it once belonged to and didn't care. But I don't know that we could ever prove that, one way or the other. Even if we could find a receipt. And that would take a miracle." Aunt Rosemary leaned her head back and closed her eyes. "Thirty or forty years ago it could have been. Sometime in the eighties, more than likely, but it's possible it was as far back as the seventies. That chest of drawers wasn't there when I took over the antique store. I bought the dresser at a yard sale. It was too ugly to resell, but it was handy for storage. That must've been about 1974 or 1975. So sometime after that was when we got the violin, although how it got stuck behind that dresser I couldn't say." Her great-aunt looked at Chelsea once again. "It must have come from either Oliver Chandler or his wife, Eunice. Oliver was Liam's grandfather. It just might be that Liam's father would know something about it, but if memory serves, he would've been a teenager at that time. Come to think of it, the old Chandler mansion was still standing back then. The violin may have been something they got rid of before the old house was torn down. It was badly damaged in a storm. A tree fell on it. And the Chandlers decided the house wasn't worth saving. Too bad. It was a grand old place. Almost a museum. Tourists got to walk through it way back when."

Chelsea nodded to show that she listened, but her chest ached a little more with every word. Aunt Rosemary had confirmed what she knew was true. The violin didn't belong to her. She would have to return it.

❧

Liam was chopping wood when he heard a vehicle approaching on the road from Chickadee Creek. He rested the ax head on the block and waited. Moments later he saw the vehicle coming down his driveway. If he wasn't mistaken, that was Rosemary Townsend's car, the one he'd helped her into on Sunday. He set the ax aside and walked toward the front of the house, getting there the same time as the car.

Chelsea Spencer got out a short while later, looking every bit as pretty as he'd remembered her.

"This is a nice surprise," he said, smiling.

She didn't smile in return. "Do you have a few minutes? I need to talk to you about something."

"Sure." He gave her a quizzical look, but she didn't respond. "Come on up to the porch." He led the way, stopping near a couple of deck chairs. He motioned for her to take one. "Would you like something cool to drink?"

"No. Thank you." She sat and clasped her hands in her lap.

"Something's bothering you." He might not be as curious as his brother, but he was observant. He supposed it was one of the skills that made him a decent actor. "What is it?"

"I found something in the antique store that . . . that probably belongs to you."

"To me? Can't imagine what that would be. I haven't lived here that long. Haven't lost anything that I'm aware of."

Chelsea shifted on the chair. "Not to you, precisely. But to your family."

She proceeded to tell him how she'd found a violin in a storage room of the antique store, that her great-aunt said she could have it, and so she took it to be repaired and refurbished, and then she was told the instrument once belonged to his great-great-grandmother, Cora Anderson Chandler.

"Aunt Rosemary thinks it must have come into the antique store around the time the Chandler mansion was torn down."

"Really?" Liam leaned back. "That came down before I was born."

"The man at the music store believes the violin could be worth twenty thousand dollars. Possibly more." She paused to take a deep breath and release it. "It was likely made in the eighteen hundreds, he said. If . . . if he's right, it really should be returned to the Chandler family. It must have been brought to Rosemary & Time by mistake."

The Chandlers had never been a prolific lot. It was easy to trace their family tree back through time because it was a single branch. Liam had no aunts, uncles, or cousins on the Chandler side. Now that Jacob was dead, there was just Liam and his father, Richard Chandler, in the bloodline. While not what one would call filthy rich, Liam's dad was well-off and didn't have a sentimental bone in his body. He was a practical man who had little interest in anything other than business. He wouldn't care about a violin that had belonged to an ancestor, not even one of value.

But Liam felt a spark of interest. Not in the violin itself or what it might be worth. But in the woman who'd found it.

Chelsea lowered her gaze to her hands, but she couldn't hide the sadness that flickered across her face.

"Miss Spencer . . ." He said her name softly. "Chelsea . . ."

She looked up again.

"You may keep the violin."

Her eyes widened in surprise. "But it's rightfully yours and—"

"If it's rightfully mine, then I'm able to donate it to Rosemary & Time. And the owner of Rosemary & Time has the right to give it to you."

The sadness and surprise he'd seen earlier vanished, and for a moment, the joy he saw replace those other emotions stole his breath away. It made him feel like the hero in one of his movies and was worth far more to him than twenty or even thirty thousand dollars.

He leaned forward. "But maybe there's something you can do for me in return."

The change in her expression was abrupt. Suspicion filled her eyes and hardened her jaw.

He knew he'd blundered, although he wasn't sure exactly why his words caused such a severe reaction. He rushed to finish. "I'd like to learn more about the woman who owned the violin. Cora Chandler, right? Mrs. Witherstone at the general store said your great-aunt knows the history of the area and of my family better than anyone else. But she's still recovering from her surgery. So I was hoping maybe you could be of assistance."

Technically, what he'd said wasn't a lie. He *was* curious—if only because spending time looking for answers might allow him to know Chelsea Spencer better.

The wariness in her eyes didn't completely go away, but the stiffness in her shoulders eased a bit. "Have you forgotten I'm new to the town myself? I probably know less about the people and its history than you do."

"I haven't forgotten. But maybe that's good. Fresh pair of eyes and all that." He leaned back again, sensing she'd rather he wasn't too close. "Are you still trying to reorganize the store?"

She nodded.

"Then maybe I could help with that. Mrs. Witherstone says your great-aunt has lots of old newspapers and books and such. You've got to sort through it anyway. Maybe we'll find information about my family while we're at it. Maybe we'll get to know more about the woman who owned the violin and how it came to be in that storage room."

"Maybe," she replied softly.

"I could sort through papers and books and organize at the same time. Under your direction, of course."

Her forehead furrowed in thought. "Aunt Rosemary would be glad for someone to take an interest in everything that's been collected through the years."

"That's me." He smiled again. "I'm taking an interest." More by choice than inclination. But wasn't that splitting hairs?

Silence seemed to stretch out for an eternity before she spoke again.

"All right," she said, her voice barely above a whisper.

He didn't know why, but her acquiescence felt like a great victory.

Chapter 9

As the truck rumbled along the highway, Chelsea glanced over from the passenger seat toward the driver. A baseball cap covered Liam's hair, and dark glasses hid his eyes. Country music played from the stereo speakers in the cab.

How did this happen? What am I doing here?

Before she left Liam's house yesterday, Chelsea had agreed for him to come to the antique store to do research on his family. After all, Rosemary & Time housed a great deal of written material from and about Chickadee Creek and the Boise Basin, from the time of the gold rush all the way up to the present. But somehow, as he walked her to her car, the violin had come up again. She'd told him she meant to drive down to Boise to pick it up from the music store, and before she grasped what was happening, he'd talked her into letting him drive her there.

And so here they were, in this big fancy truck of his, rolling down the highway out of the mountains toward the capital city.

Liam pressed a button on his steering wheel, turning down the volume on the stereo. "I thought after we get the violin, we could stop for something to eat. There's a little restaurant that my brother really liked on that end of town."

Chelsea didn't care for the idea. The less time she spent with Liam Chandler, the better. Not that she had anything against him. He seemed nice, polite, and caring. But Tom had seemed those things, too, in the beginning. She'd learned that charm and good looks often disguised ugly personality traits.

"Hey, Chelsea?"

She looked at him again.

"Have I done or said something to upset you?"

"No. Why?"

"Because you've about plastered yourself to that door. As if you can't get far enough away from me to suit you."

She felt warmth rush to her cheeks. "I'm sorry."

"You don't need to apologize. I just wondered if I'd done something wrong."

"No." She shook her head. "You haven't."

He looked at the road, then glanced at her again. Uncomfortable, she turned her head to look out the window at the passing scenery. After a short while, the volume on the stereo went up again.

When Chelsea was young, she and her siblings had ridden in the back of the ancient pickup truck her father owned. Rain or shine, snow or sleet, blazing heat or frigid temperatures, if the Spencer family went somewhere, the kids were in the open bed of the pickup. Thinking of her sisters and brother, remembering how things had been, she felt guilty sitting in the luxury of this cab.

An older Martina McBride song was playing through the speakers when the volume went down again.

"Chelsea, are you sure I haven't done something wrong?"

She drew a steadying breath and looked at him. "I'm sure."

"Then something else is bothering you. Whatever it is, I'm a good listener. Maybe I can't do anything about it, but I can listen." He glanced at her quickly, then back at the road. "I got good at listening last year. To my brother. That may have been my main job. Listening. Letting him talk. Letting him say whatever he needed to say."

It surprised her, how tempted she was to take him up on the offer. She'd grown guarded lately. No, not true. It wasn't just lately. She'd lived like that since she was a child. She'd learned to weigh her words before saying anything. She'd learned that punishment could come out of nowhere. She'd learned that the slightest comment could bring retribution without explanation.

But Liam is kind. I'm not wrong about that. He let me keep the violin.

Pleasure washed over her at the thought, but the feeling was of short duration. Because on its heels came the reminder that others in the past had manipulated her with gifts and kindness. What made her think Liam Chandler would be different? Besides, the violin and its worth meant nothing to him. He was a rich movie star.

So, what was she doing on this stretch of highway, alone, with this man she barely knew?

She closed her eyes as a chill ran up her spine, that all too familiar panic rising to cut off her breath. "Stop the truck."

"What?"

"Pull over. Stop the truck. Please."

The music playing over the stereo stopped. A moment later, the crunch of tires on gravel sounded before the engine, too, went silent. Chelsea grappled with the door handle. When it opened, she half jumped, half fell out of the cab, stumbling into the underbrush before she fell to her knees.

"Chelsea?"

She didn't look behind her, but in case he meant to approach her, she held up a hand to stop him. "I'll . . . I'll be all right. Just . . . just leave me alone for a while."

"Okay." He sounded unsure, but he did as she asked.

The heels of Chelsea's hands pressed into her thighs as she dragged in air and released it slowly. Colors flashed on the backs of her eyelids. A sound similar to a rushing river filled her ears. She had no sense of time.

Whether short or long, time did pass, and at last the fear began to drain from her.

"God, help me," she whispered.

From behind her came a soft but strong voice. "'For God has not given us a spirit of timidity, but of power and love and discipline.'"

She twisted to look at Liam. He knelt on the ground, watching her with concerned eyes. Not judgment. Only concern.

"I'm sorry," she said.

He shrugged. "No reason to be."

"I hate to appear weak."

"Nobody likes that. But sometimes we are weak. Sometimes we're afraid. Sometimes the circumstances of life feel like too much."

She turned and sat on the ground, drawing her knees up to her chest and clasping them with her arms. "What makes you afraid?"

Pain flickered in his eyes. "Watching my brother die. That made me afraid."

"Your brother." Understanding dawned. "The one you listened to."

"Yeah. His name was Jacob."

"Jacob," she echoed—and wished she knew words that might comfort him as he'd tried to comfort her.

Liam could tell the moment Chelsea turned her thoughts from whatever had brought on her panic and focused on something else. In this case, his brother.

As if to confirm the thought, she said, "Tell me about him. Please."

"He was a special kind of guy." He looked at the mountain rising to his right. "Everybody liked Jacob."

"How did he . . . What . . ."

"Cancer. It was advanced when they found it. Unusual in one that young, one doctor said." He released a humorless laugh. "Jacob said he always wanted to be unusual. Just not in that way."

"You two were close." It was more comment than question.

He looked at her again. Whatever had caused the panic to rise in her appeared to be gone. "Yeah. Real close."

It was her turn to look away, staring at the trees and the rugged terrain surrounding them. "I've always loved the mountains. I feel lost when I'm too far away from them."

"Mmm." He watched her, trying to judge her mood, trying to be sure she was all right.

"Tell me more about your brother."

He hesitated, then did as she asked. "There was a little over a year between us. I'm the older one. Our mom doted on Jacob, as far back as I can remember. I don't know why. He wasn't a sickly kid. Serious. Gentle. But not sickly. Just a good, all-around guy." He plucked a long blade of dry grass and twirled it between his fingers. "It was hard on him when I left for LA. I tried to get him to go with me, but he didn't want any part of that scene. And he was right, of course. He wouldn't have liked it there. But I wish—" He broke off, not sure what he wished.

That he'd stayed in Idaho and never chased the acting dream.

That he'd paid more attention to what was going on in his family, between his parents.

That he'd been there to see the physical changes in Jacob and maybe taken his brother to see a doctor sooner. Soon enough to save him.

"We can't revise the past," Chelsea said, almost too soft for him to hear.

"No. We can't. We can only try to make today all it should be and try to be a better person tomorrow."

A small smile tipped the corners of her mouth. "Have you always been this smart, Mr. Chandler?"

He laughed, surprising himself. Surprising her, too, if her widened eyes meant anything.

Without warning, she stood, brushing dirt and small twigs off the seat of her pants. "We'd better get going. I've delayed us long enough."

Liam didn't know why, but he wished they didn't have to be on their way. He wouldn't have minded staying there and talking awhile longer. He would like a turn to ask her some questions, to get to know her better. For one thing, he would like to know what had brought on that panic attack. It had been real and vicious. No doubt about that. So what was behind it? Not so much what triggered it. That could have been anything. But what was behind it?

He got up and headed for the truck. When he got in, he was glad to see Chelsea wasn't clinging to the passenger door the way she had before. She seemed more relaxed than when their journey began. Liam started the truck and pulled onto the two-lane highway. He considered turning on the stereo again, then thought better of it. Maybe they would talk some more without any background music. It was worth a try.

"Tell me something," he began. "I know you're excited about the violin, and I'd wager good money that it doesn't have anything to do with its age or value or who used to own it. So why so excited? Do you play?"

There was a lengthy pause before she answered, "No, I don't play. But I've always wanted to. Since I was a girl. I thought I was going to get to learn, but my . . . But it wasn't possible. After I left home, I didn't have money for luxuries like a violin or the lessons I would need to learn to play. So I thought . . . I just forgot about it. Put it behind me."

"And then you found a violin in your great-aunt's antique store."

"Yes."

"To me, that sounds like a gift from God."

Another pause, then, "Yes, it does." The words were flecked with wonder.

Liam felt as if he'd done something meaningful. He supposed he had, in a small way. He'd let her keep the violin. But that hadn't been hard to do. Only a little common sense was needed to know that, no matter who took the violin to the antique store and however many years before, the Chandlers no longer had a legitimate claim to it. In fact, he thought Chelsea deserved it, knowing she'd tried to do the right thing despite wanting the instrument so much.

He'd thought before that Chelsea would have liked Jacob. Now he believed his brother would have liked her equally as much. He'd had a good heart. So did she.

Liam's smile grew as the truck rolled on toward Boise.

OCTOBER 1895

Cora walked beside Preston Chandler, nerves tumbling in her stomach. It wasn't an unfamiliar feeling. She'd lived with the sensation for many months now.

"That house over there," he said, indicating the direction with his head since his hands were holding her trunk. "That's where you're staying."

As they approached the house—made of clapboard, like the schoolhouse she'd seen only minutes before—a woman stepped onto the front porch, wiping her hands on a dark apron.

"That's Mrs. Mason," Preston added. "Sarah Mason. Nice woman."

Cora hoped so since they would share a house for at least the next year, if all went well.

"Here she is, Mrs. Mason. Safe and sound." He set the trunk on the porch. "Cora Anderson, Sarah Mason. Sarah Mason, Cora Anderson." He touched his hat brim. "I'll let the two of you get acquainted." His gaze met Cora's. "A pleasure to meet you, miss." With that, he strode away.

Cora relaxed a little now that he was gone. Since leaving New York, she'd remained cautious around men. Any man she met could be the one her father had hired to find her. Aaron Anderson was not the sort to give up easily. It wouldn't matter that months had passed since his daughter broke her engagement and defied him by leaving home. In fact, the passage of time would make him even more determined to find her. He would spend any amount necessary to bring her to heel. But surely he wouldn't be able to find her in this secluded town. Surely she would be safe in Chickadee Creek.

"Mr. Chandler's a man of few words," Sarah said, intruding on Cora's thoughts.

She turned to face her new landlady.

"Come inside. Let's get you settled. It's no easy journey up from the valley. All that jostling about in the coach takes a lot out of you." Sarah picked up Cora's trunk as if it weighed nothing and led the way inside.

The front living area was small but cozy. There were two rocking chairs near a fireplace, a table with benches on two sides and one straight-backed chair on an end, a sideboard, a cookstove, an icebox, and a sink with a pump. There were two doors beyond the living area, leading, Cora could only presume, to a couple of bedrooms. Everything was sparse but clean.

"The room on the right will be yours." Sarah went to the door and opened it with a bump of her shoulder. She set down the trunk inside the doorway, then stepped to one side so Cora could enter as well.

The room held a narrow bed covered with a patchwork quilt,

a chiffonier, and a small stand with a pitcher and bowl in its center. A rag rug covered much of the floor. Instead of a wardrobe for her dresses, there were hooks on the wall.

Cora smiled. "This is nice."

"Why don't you come out to the table and have a cup of tea? You can unpack your trunk after you've rested a spell."

"Thank you. I would love a cup of tea, if it isn't too much trouble."

"No trouble. And if you need the necessary, use the side door off the kitchen. You can see it soon as you step outside."

Cora gave her head a slight shake. "I'm all right."

"Very well." Sarah left the bedroom.

From the doorway, Cora watched the other woman as she filled a kettle with water and set it on the stove. Sarah then took two china cups from the sideboard and set them on the counter. Glancing up, she motioned for Cora to join her at the table. She did so.

"All right, then." Sarah sat opposite her. "Let's do as Mr. Chandler said. Let's get acquainted. Why don't you begin by telling me where you're from? Plain as the nose on your pretty face that you're not from around these parts."

"No." Cora looked down at her hands folded in her lap. "I'm not."

"I'm guessing by the way you talk, when you've managed to say anything at all, that you come from back East somewhere." Sarah's eyes narrowed. "New York, maybe."

Alarm coiled inside Cora. "You can tell that?"

"Mercy, child. I've lived in these parts for almost thirty years. In that time, we've had men and women come through Chickadee Creek from near about everywhere in this country.

Other countries too. I learned I've got an ear for accents, I do, so there aren't many who fool me when it comes to their roots."

Cora sat straighter. "I have no wish to fool you, Mrs. Mason."

"Oh, I'm right sorry. I never meant to say you did." Sarah took a breath and released it. "Maybe it would be better if I told you about me and what you'll find here in Chickadee Creek."

Cora relaxed. "Please."

"Well, like I said, I've lived in these mountains near on thirty years. Came here with my husband, Jack. He started out looking for gold, like most everybody else, then decided he'd do better hauling freight for other miners." She glanced around the living area. "It was a smart decision, becoming a freighter. He built a good business, and we made a nice life for us in this town."

Cora nodded.

The water in the kettle came to a boil, and Sarah rose from her chair and went to prepare the tea. Soon enough, the two cups sat on the table, along with a small pitcher of milk and a sugar bowl.

As if there'd been no break in the conversation, Sarah resumed talking as she added sugar to her tea and stirred it with a spoon. "Chickadee Creek's a good place to live. In addition to the school that Mr. Chandler showed you already, we've got a church, a post office, a mercantile, and a feed store. Even got a ladies' dress shop. County seat is up north, but the mountains between us don't make it easy if there's official business to be done, so we got a little courthouse and a sheriff's office, too, with our own deputy and judge, when the need for them arises. It doesn't arise often. Judge Goodnight, he runs the lumber mill outside of town, and Rafe Sooner, the deputy, spends most of his time locking up stray dogs or trying to catch kids who make mischief."

Sipping her tea, Cora wondered about Preston Chandler. What did he do in this town? Why had he been the one to meet her coach?

"As for me, I work as the housekeeper for Mr. Chandler, the man who brought you here."

Cora lifted her gaze. Had Sarah Mason read her thoughts? Had Cora's curiosity shown on her face?

"He's kind of new to Chickadee Creek too. Inherited his house, land, and mining interests from a cousin. Likable fellow, though I can't say I know a whole lot more about him. Not even sure where he came from before he got here. He isn't a man who talks much." Sarah grinned. "Unlike me, who's been doing all of the talking." She beckoned with one hand. "So now it's your turn. Tell me how you became a teacher."

Thankfully, Cora wasn't required to lie in order to answer. "After I left the East—and you're right, I did live in New York— after I left, I traveled to Colorado. A friend helped me get my teaching certificate, and her niece helped me obtain this position."

"A pretty thing like you should have men lining up to want to take care of you. Marriage, I mean. Surprised that hasn't happened already."

"I'm not interested in having a man take care of me." Her voice sounded terse in her own ears. "I was engaged to be married. Once. Some time ago. I chose not to marry him after all."

"Ah."

"He didn't break my heart, if that's what you're wondering." As the words came out of her mouth, Cora thought again of her father. If any man had broken her heart, it was Aaron Anderson. Her father was the one who hadn't cared what Cora wanted, who'd refused to listen to her, who'd expected to be obeyed no matter what. He'd been the one willing to sell his only daughter without a care for her present or future happiness.

Cora gave her head a shake, chasing away the thought. "I didn't mean to imply that I didn't want to become a teacher. I did. I knew it was meant for me the first moment I stepped into a schoolroom."

"Where did you teach before here?"

"I had a temporary position in Boulder, Colorado, but the original teacher returned after a short while, so I applied for this position. And I'm excited to begin teaching the children of Chickadee Creek."

"Well, that's good, because the children in these parts are looking forward to having a teacher again. The last one didn't make it through the winter. Besides, he was a mean sort. Nobody cared for him, parents or students. Whole town was glad to see his back as he left town."

Cora could only hope the townsfolk wouldn't think the same about her a year from now.

Liam's Journal

Jacob used to say that I liked to study people. He was right. Even as a kid I liked to observe, see what people did, listen to what they said. I liked to find out what made them tick. I still do. Jacob said it taught me empathy, which made it easier for me to play lots of different parts.

"Wouldn't you like to play somebody who keeps his shirt on?" Jacob asked me one time.

I was insulted. It made me angry. I didn't understand what he meant then. I do now. He was challenging me about the direction my career was taking me. Not that he hated my films. He found them exciting and funny. They were good entertainment. But he said there was more to me as an actor and that I ought to find the films that would make me go deeper. Films that would make viewers feel and think, not just laugh or have me flexing my chest muscles.

I miss him saying stuff like that to me. (Although I wanted to slug him at the time.)

I may have been the brother who studied people, but he was the one who understood them on a gut level or a heart level. Way more than I do. Sure, I catch on, but he was always there before me. Understanding. Forgiving. Encouraging.

I don't mean to make a saint out of him, even in these private pages. He wasn't a saint (except in the way my pastor starts each

Sunday by saying, "Morning, saints"). Jacob had his flaws, like any-body. But fewer than me, that's for sure.

I wonder what the movie is that Grayson Wentworth is about to make. The one he talked to Kurt about. Was it something Jacob would've liked me to do?

Chapter 10

A small bell chimed as Liam opened the door to Rosemary & Time on Saturday morning.

"Good morning, Liam."

He looked to his right to see Rosemary Townsend seated in the wingback chair she kept near the window.

"Chelsea told me you'd be prompt, and so you are."

He glanced around. "She isn't here?"

"Not yet. She had an errand to run."

Disappointment sluiced through him. He'd looked forward to seeing her again.

"But she'll be back before long," Rosemary finished.

"Right."

The older woman pushed up from the chair. Using her cane, she walked toward the back of the shop. "Come with me."

"Right," he repeated.

"Chelsea and I got some things out last night before we went to bed." Rosemary motioned for him to come closer.

On the counter near a window lay several stacks of old newspapers, another stack of magazines, and a final one of books.

Rosemary placed a hand on the first stack. "Newspapers don't last a long time, as you probably know. They get yellow and go brittle. These only go back to the seventies, and you'll need to be careful with them so they don't fall to pieces on you. But there was a regular column in here about the early years of Chickadee Creek, and of course, Chandlers had a lot to do with the early years in these parts. So I figure you'll find a good bit of information about your family. And what we don't have here, you'll at least know enough so you can do a search on the internet or go down to the library in the valley. They'll have older copies of the newspaper on microfiche or in some other electronic files."

"I didn't know Chickadee Creek had a newspaper."

"We don't. Not anymore. The *Chickadee Press* went out of business in eighty-five. But it was around for a long time before that. In fact, my grandfather was the owner and editor for a spell." Her gaze roamed over the room. "This was the newspaper office at one time. Way, way back. During the Depression and World War II."

"I never had a clue."

With a sigh, Rosemary returned to the front of the store. "After my grandfather gave up on the newspaper, he used this building to store old things. 'Junk,' he called it, and it mostly was." She sank onto the chair with another big sigh. "I suppose that's mostly what's in here today. Years and years of other people's junk."

Liam smiled at the affection in her voice. She might say it was mostly junk, but she didn't believe it. He could tell that much from the way her gaze roamed the room.

As if hearing his thoughts, she said, "All this represents

other lives." She pointed to a jewelry display. "That string of pearls there. Can you see it? It was a gift from a husband to his new bride. I was a little girl when they got married, but I remember the wedding ceremony clear as day. Took place out on the meadow the other side of the creek. Behind the Chandler mansion."

Liam stepped to the case to look at the necklace, partly to please the older woman, partly out of curiosity.

"The groom was your grandfather Oliver Chandler. The bride, your grandmother Eunice."

Liam glanced at Rosemary. "How did the pearls end up here?"

"Oh, that's a long story." She shook her head.

"I like long stories." He drew up a chair from the opposite wall. "Most movies take about two hours to tell one."

"They're just my memories. Probably not as reliable as what you'll find in those newspapers and books." She motioned with her head toward the stacks she'd shown him earlier.

"I'll risk it."

She responded with a smile. "I was nine years old. I remember because that was the same summer I got a brand-new bike from my grandparents for my birthday. Most of the time, I got hand-me-downs from John, my brother. But not that year. That year, I got a new bike with streamers flowing out of the handlebars."

Liam thought he caught a glimpse of the happy little girl reflected in the sparkle in her eyes.

"Anyway, we were all dressed up in our Sunday best for that wedding. After all, the Chandlers were the first family of our little town. Oliver's father was dead by then, and his mother was living in Boise. But Oliver and Eunice wanted to get married here and planned to live in the Chandler mansion after their honeymoon. He had some scheme to get the mining going again. Young and full of grand ideas, he was, and not that long out of college. He'd studied to be an engineer." She turned a questioning glance in Liam's direction. "Do you remember him?"

"Vaguely. I was about four years old when he passed."

"Mmm." She nodded, then was silent for a lengthy spell, seemingly lost in thought. Finally, she drew a deep breath and continued. "The Chandlers weren't nearly as wealthy as they once were. The Depression was as hard on them as everybody. But they were better off than most. Still owned a good share of the land in these parts. The wedding was quite an affair. All the folks from Chickadee Creek were invited, and lots of people came up from Boise too. I suppose I remember the reception afterward more than anything about the ceremony. Except for the kiss. I remember that kiss." She smiled and clapped her hands together once.

Liam grinned in return.

"At the reception, Oliver gave Eunice that string of pearls. He fastened them around her neck and told her how much he loved her while all the guests watched. It was the most romantic thing I'd seen up to that moment."

"You were nine."

"I was nine. And before you ask, yes, I've seen other romantic things since then. Experienced a bit of romance myself, for that matter."

They laughed in unison.

But her smile faded after a while. "I suppose that's why it was so sad when Eunice brought those pearls to me fifteen years later." She blew out a huff of air. "Your grandfather's gold-mining schemes didn't go well. He lost a lot of money, and they finally moved to Boise for Oliver to find other work. Eunice came back to Chickadee Creek one day to collect a few more belongings from the old mansion, and she stopped in here to sell me the pearls. I told her I couldn't give her anywhere close to what they were worth. Truth is I didn't know what they were worth. She didn't care. She simply said she didn't want them any longer." Rosemary shook her head slowly. "I don't know if she was that desperate for money or if the love those pearls represented was gone. It could have been either . . . or both."

Liam thought of his parents rather than his grandparents. They weren't desperate for money. Or at least he didn't think that was the cause of the rift between them. Had love just died, the same way it appeared to have died between his grandparents?

Rosemary cleared her throat. "I never could bring myself to sell those pearls. I've had offers through the years, but I always asked more than anybody was willing to pay. I don't know why. Sentimental, I guess. At first, I thought Eunice might come back for them. Later . . ." She shrugged. "So there they stay. A show-piece in a decrepit old antique store."

Liam glanced toward the jewelry case but remained silent.

"Would you like them? I never could sell to anybody else, but maybe they'd mean something to you, being part of your family and all."

"What is it with you and Chelsea?" He shook his head, trying to sound insulted. "Trying to force old Chandler stuff on me."

"We've done no such—" She stopped when she saw him grinning at her. "Oh, you are a rascal, aren't you?" Rosemary pat-ted his knee. "But at least we know how the pearls got here. That violin still puzzles me. So I hope the two of you will be able to solve that mystery as you sort through all those papers and books and things."

That sounded like it was time for him to get to work. He stood.

"Liam?"

"Yes, ma'am."

"I will never forget your kindness to Chelsea in letting her keep the violin. I'll never forget it."

Anne McNalley looked to be in her late fifties or early sixties. Her brown hair, worn shoulder length, was streaked with gray. Although her smile was brief when she welcomed Chelsea into her home, her eyes seemed kind, and her voice had a calming quality.

"So you've never taken lessons," Anne said when Chelsea finished giving a limited amount of information about herself.

They were seated in a room on the south side of the house. Sunlight streamed through tall trees to bathe the room in a golden light.

"A few when I was twelve," Chelsea answered. "At school. But basically, no. No real lessons. Not much beyond how I should hold the violin, and I've forgotten that, I'm sure."

"But you're serious about learning now?"

Chelsea nodded. "Yes. Very."

"You are older than most of my beginning students. You probably have a job and other responsibilities. Will you commit to daily practice and to not missing your weekly lessons?"

"Yes."

"May I see your instrument?" The teacher extended her arms.

Chelsea passed the case to her and watched as she opened it. The expression on the instructor's face changed to one of surprise, then disbelief.

"Good heavens," Anne McNalley breathed at last. "This is beautiful. And you never learned to play it?" She looked up.

"It was given to me recently."

"Given?"

"A gift from my great-aunt." In her mind, she pictured Liam driving his truck back from the music store the previous day. "And from a friend of ours."

After a moment, Anne asked, "May I?" even as she lifted the violin from the case.

When the teacher drew the bow across the strings, the pure sound made tears rise in Chelsea's eyes. She'd wanted to do that very thing ever since she found the violin, but she hadn't had the courage. She hadn't wanted to spoil anything by creating a noise that would make her cringe, like fingers on a chalkboard.

Anne smiled as her gaze returned to Chelsea. "When would you like to begin your lessons?"

"As soon as you have an opening." She reached for her purse. "I can pay you for the first lesson in advance, if you'd like."

Anne waved a hand. "That's not necessary. You can pay me when we begin." She put the violin into the case, then reached for an appointment book that rested on a nearby piano, flipped it open, and ran a finger down a few columns. "I don't teach often in the summer. Most students want the time off, and my family prefers it when I do the same. Shall we say Tuesdays at ten in the morning?"

Chelsea's heart raced with the excitement. "Tuesdays at ten would be perfect." She would have said the same for any day of the week except Sunday. She would have agreed to any time as well, and Aunt Rosemary would agree to whatever worked best. She'd said as much before Chelsea left the house.

"Wonderful." Anne rose, effectively ending the meeting.

As Chelsea walked to her car a short while later, it was difficult not to break into a happy dance. There was a lightness in her steps that made her feel as if she were floating on air. The violin had been a gift from her great-aunt and from Liam, but this feeling was a gift from God.

She turned her face toward the sun and said, "Thank You!"

Preston

NOVEMBER 1895

The first snowstorm of the season arrived in Chickadee Creek in early November. Preston stood outside the office of the Chandler Mining Company and watched large flakes float lazily toward the ground.

"It's gonna blow soon," Ethan Sooner said from the protection of the doorway.

Preston looked over his shoulder. "How can you tell?"

"Dunno." The man shrugged. "Can feel it, I reckon."

"You can feel it?"

"Makes my bones ache when a bad storm's comin'."

Ethan Sooner—father of the local sheriff's deputy—was the first man Preston had hired after his arrival in Idaho the previous spring. He'd been assured that no one knew more about mining in this county than Ethan Sooner, and the man had proven his reputation true. Not that they were actually in business as of yet. Gold nuggets were gone from Chickadee Creek. All that remained in these streams and mountains was fine gold. Very fine gold. And Preston planned to bring the first dredger to the area to go after it. Dredging had been employed three years earlier at the mouth of the Raft River. With any luck, the dredger Preston had ordered would be delivered in the spring, and the new and improved Chandler Mining Company would be up and running again by early summer.

At the moment, summer seemed far away because snow was no longer falling lazily toward the earth. Large, languid flakes had become tiny and numerous, and as Ethan predicted, the wind was on the rise, driving the snow before it. It stung as it hit Preston's face and neck. He turned and went inside.

A fire burned in the potbellied stove, warming the roomy office. Over-warming it, as far as Preston was concerned. The heat made his nose and throat feel dry and scratchy. He swallowed some coffee, hoping it would ease the discomfort.

"I forgot to tell you something," Ethan said, drawing Preston's attention. "The missus wants you to come to the house for Thanksgiving dinner. And I may as well tell you now: she won't take no for an answer. She's got her heart set on it."

Preston hadn't thought about observing the holiday. Sarah Mason had asked if he would like the cook to prepare anything special, and he'd told her he would make do with whatever was in the icebox and pantry. He didn't need anyone working on Thanksgiving.

"Ethan, I'll be fine at—"

"I'm tellin' you, she won't take no. You may as well agree to come eat with us so she doesn't have to come drag you from your house."

Preston grinned. "All right. I'll plan to be there. What can I bring?"

"Not a thing but yourself. Nora wouldn't have it any other way. We'll see you at the church service at ten. Then you'll come home to eat with us."

If there was anything Preston had learned since coming to Chickadee Creek, it was that it was foolish to try to resist the hospitality of the locals. He was surprised he'd tried, even for a moment. "Sounds good."

Ethan reached for his coat, hanging on a hook near the door. "If it's all right with you, boss, I'm going to head home before this storm gets much worse."

"Go on. I won't be far behind you."

"Mind that you don't dawdle. You don't want to get stuck here."

Preston looked out the window. The world had turned completely white. "No. I don't."

Ethan nodded, opened the door, and stepped outside. Cold air rushed into the room, pushing heat into the far corners. As soon as the door closed behind Ethan, the whistling sound of the wind softened, leaving behind silence broken by the crackle of the fire.

Preston had been on his own since he was fourteen. His mother died when he was a kid. His father took to drink after that, and when he was liquored up, he was mean. One day, Preston had decided he'd had enough and left the small town on the banks of a river in the Midwest.

Over the years, he grew used to being the only one in a room or in a house, the only one riding a horse through a vast, lonely stretch of earth. He was comfortable with silence. He never minded hard work, and he'd managed to support himself without breaking the law—although he was tempted a time or two, when the hunger got to him. For much of his life he'd owned little more than the clothes on his back. Sometimes he had a horse and saddle. He knew how to get by on little. In some ways, it was more difficult to know what to do with plenty. He was still getting used to that, all these months later.

He rose from his desk and walked to a window. He hadn't been caught in the worst of storms in the Sierras or the Rockies, but he'd seen enough to know Ethan was right. He'd better leave the mining office before the snow got too deep. Besides, he didn't like it when his thoughts went to the past. With any luck, the wind would blow them away as he made his way to the house.

It was slow going. He had to lean into the wind, tucking his face down into the collar of his coat like a turtle into its shell. By the time he opened the door to the Chandler house, he felt battered and half frozen.

"Mr. Chandler! Look at you."

At the sound of Sarah's voice, he glanced up. He hadn't expected her to be there.

His housekeeper bustled over to help him out of his coat. "You need to remember a scarf and gloves next time. Anybody with a lick of sense could've told you this morning that a storm was coming."

While there were many in town who gave an extra measure of respect to Preston simply because of his last name and his inherited wealth, Sarah Mason wasn't one of them. She often spoke to him as if he were a troublesome child instead of a grown man. Like now. As if he wasn't smart enough to know what to wear in cold weather. From somebody else, it might irritate him. Not from Sarah. He liked the woman. Her plainspoken ways suited him, and they'd gotten along well from the start of her employment.

He gave her a wry smile. "Perhaps you ought to think of bundling up and getting home yourself."

"Not before I've seen to your supper. Cook left it warming in the oven before I sent her home."

"I can fend for myself when I need to."

"I know that, Mr. Chandler, but I also know what my job is. And that's to see you have a well-run household and meals on the table when it's time."

Preston knew it was useless to argue with the Widow Mason. He would eat his supper, as she insisted. But he would also escort her home, whether she liked it or not.

Cora

NOVEMBER 1895

On Thanksgiving Day, Cora and Sarah walked along the road toward the Sooner home, Cora carrying two pies and Sarah bringing a basket of rolls fresh from the oven. It was nearly noon, but the temperature had yet to rise above freezing. The bitter chill quickened their steps, and they wasted no energy on words as they leaned into the wind and hurried to their destination.

Sarah's knock on the door was answered by Ethan Sooner.

"Come in. Come in, before you blow away."

Nora Sooner looked over her shoulder while continuing to

stir something on the stove. "Give Ethan your coats and go sit near the fire. We're so glad you could join us."

In the weeks since Cora began teaching in Chickadee Creek, she'd visited many of her students' homes. But the Sooners had no school-age children, so she hadn't had a chance to get to know them beyond brief hellos after church on Sundays. Still, she wasn't surprised that she'd been included in their invitation for Thanksgiving dinner. She'd found her new hometown to be filled with gracious, friendly people.

Ethan took the pies and basket of rolls and carried them to the kitchen. By the time he returned, both of the women had shed their coats. He held out his arms to take them, then motioned with his head toward the fireplace. "Make yourselves at home."

Sarah put a hand in the small of Cora's back and urged her forward. "You take the rocking chair." She pointed with her free hand.

Cora complied, then watched as her friend sat on a straight-backed chair nearby. It seemed to rock more than the rocker, and Cora immediately understood why Sarah had steered her away from it.

Emotions tightened her chest. She'd experienced so many kindnesses since leaving New York. Without the benevolence of strangers—particularly Mabel Johnson and Sarah Mason, but others too—Cora wouldn't have survived long in her reckless dash for freedom. She probably wouldn't have made it as far as Denver, let alone to Idaho. She wouldn't be employed as a schoolteacher. Her own schooling had left her well educated, but it hadn't given her much in the way of common sense. She'd had no understanding of how the world worked beyond the parlors and ballrooms of high society. Not really.

The door opened again, admitting Rafe Sooner and his pregnant wife, Lauretta.

"Oh, for pity's sake." Nora bustled over to the new arrivals. "Son, you two look half-froze to death. I told you you shoulda found a place closer to us." Holding the sides of Rafe's head between her hands, she kissed him on both cheeks, then repeated the gesture with her daughter-in-law. "Get yourselves over by the fire and thaw out."

Cora rose and moved away from the rocking chair. "Please," she said when Lauretta looked her way. "Sit here. You'll be warm in no time."

Lauretta smiled as she waddled toward the vacated chair, one hand resting on her enlarged belly, the other on the small of her back. "Thank you," she breathed as she sank onto the rocker. "I do get tired when I stand for long."

Another blast of cold air drew Cora's gaze to the door. This time it was Preston Chandler who Ethan invited into the house. She'd expected the members of the Sooner family, but Mr. Chandler was a surprise. She didn't know why. She supposed because she'd seen so little of him since the day of her arrival.

"You know everybody," Ethan said to Preston, motioning with his hand to indicate the people in the room.

"Yes." Preston's gaze met with Cora's. "Miss Anderson." There was a moment when it seemed he wouldn't look away, but then he did. "Mrs. Sooner. Mrs. Mason. Nice to see you."

"Here," Ethan interrupted. "Give me your coat, and then go sit yourself down at the table. Care for some coffee?"

Cora took a few steps back, uncertain why she felt the need to retreat. Maybe it was the way Preston Chandler seemed to look through her. No, not through her. Inside of her. As if he could read her secrets. A disturbing thought.

In her former life, when she'd been nothing more than the decoration on a man's arm, she'd been used to the stares of others. Women trying to decide if she was the prettiest female in the room or if she had the nicest gown or the most expensive jewels. Men trying to decide if her beauty and wealth were enough to tempt them into a marriage contract with a woman whose lineage wasn't quite upper crust.

But the way Preston Chandler looked at her wasn't like that. It wasn't superficial. It seemed to go deeper than that. He seemed to look for the person within.

Something fluttered inside Cora. This man *saw* her. And knowing he saw the *real* Cora Anderson was both disturbing and . . . and delightful. The knowledge seemed to pull at her, to want to draw her closer to him.

She held her breath for a moment, and sanity returned. This strange attraction she felt wasn't good for either of them. The real Cora Anderson didn't want to be seen, didn't want to be known.

She took another step back and hoped he wouldn't look her way again.

Liam's Journal

I was thinking last night about generational sins. I know the Bible talks about them, but I don't fully understand what they are or how they work in a Christian's life today. Did they end with the New Covenant? Some Christians seem to think so. Did the death and resurrection of Jesus put a stop to them, at least for those who trust Jesus for their salvation? Or is the evil in this world proof that generational sin goes on to the third and fourth generations even today?

Rosemary Townsend says my grandparents' marriage was in trouble back before I was born. I never got to know them, so I don't know what they were like. I was two when she died and four when he died. I have a fuzzy picture of him in my head, but that might be from seeing photos more than an actual memory. But could their troubles as a couple have impacted my dad? Did seeing his parents' marriage become unhealthy influence him to walk out on Mom all these years later?

Then again, his parents didn't separate (that I know of) or divorce, so it doesn't seem like the same thing as what's happening to my parents. Maybe he didn't even know that Grandpa and Grandma went through a bad patch. Maybe whatever caused Grandma Eunice to sell her pearls was soon forgotten, a momentary tiff.

I always thought Mom and Dad had a solid marriage. I thought they set an example for others. You don't see many successful marriages in Hollywood, that's for sure. Do a lot of couples go into marriage thinking they can get out of it if it doesn't work? Do they already have an escape plan in their minds? Or do most actually think it will last a lifetime?

If I ever decide to get married, I want to marry a woman who's as committed to me as I am to her. And committed to the Lord. To being faithful. To being devoted. I'll want her to respect me, and I'll want to love her as Christ loves the church, enough that I would die for her. Sounds like a lot, but that's how the Bible says it's supposed to be between a husband and wife. So that's the way I'll want it to be, if and when the time comes.

Chapter 11

After returning from church that Sunday, Liam grabbed an apple to eat, then took Chipper outside for a bit of exercise. Between throws of the Frisbee, he managed to finish off the apple. He carried the core to the trash bin and dropped it inside just as Chipper barked a warning.

Turning around, Liam saw the approach of his dad's car. That was a surprise. His dad hadn't mentioned anything about coming up when they'd talked the previous week.

"Still got the dog, I see," Dad said when he got out of the car a short while later.

"Chipper? Yeah. Why wouldn't I?"

His dad raised an eyebrow. "Don't know why I said that. I guess I thought you got him for Jacob, and now that Jacob's gone . . ." He let his words trail off.

"Come on up to the porch. I'll get us something cool to drink."

"Got any beer?"

It was one thing when Kurt Knight had asked him a similar question when he visited a week ago. But this request from his dad rubbed Liam the wrong way. Made him even more irritated than when Dad wondered about Chipper still being around. Because his dad should know the answers.

"I take it that's a no."

Liam looked behind him. "It's a no."

"Water'll be fine, then."

"Be right back."

Chipper followed Liam inside. The dog knew there wouldn't be any affectionate ear scratching if he stayed outside with Richard Chandler.

Liam grabbed a couple of plastic tumblers from a cupboard, filled them halfway with ice, then added cold water from the refrigerator door. When he was done, he paused a moment to take a breath, hoping to regain the peace he'd felt at church less than an hour before. *Lord, help.*

Outside again, he set both glasses on the small table between the chairs, then sat in the empty one. Chipper lay down near his right foot, releasing a sigh that reflected Liam's feelings.

"What brought you up here, Dad?"

"I haven't seen you in a while."

"No, you haven't." He heard bitterness in his voice, and it surprised him. He hadn't thought he cared that his dad had withdrawn as much from him as from his mom. Liam had called his dad at least a couple of times a month since coming to stay in Chickadee Creek. It never happened the other way around.

"And while I'm here," his dad continued, "I wanted to look at some of the property I plan to sell."

Business had brought him to Chickadee Creek. Of course. Even on a Sunday, for Richard Chandler everything was about business—making deals, succeeding, getting ahead.

Strange. Liam hadn't noticed that about his dad when he and Jacob were growing up. Maybe it hadn't been as bad back then. Maybe his dad hadn't been as absent. A hard worker but not a workaholic. However, Liam had definitely noticed the absences throughout Jacob's illness.

"I thought you might want to go with me," his dad said. "Give me your opinion."

"You want my opinion?"

"Said I did, didn't I?"

Liam reached for his water glass, hoping to hide the frown furrowing his forehead. He hated this adversarial feeling. He loved his dad. He wanted them to be close again. When he thought of his dad, he wanted to remember the good times, the fishing trips, the holidays and summer vacations at the old cabin. Maybe he was the one who needed to make that happen. "Sure. I'll go with you."

"Good. Good." His dad stood. "Let's do it."

Liam stood too. "We can take my truck. That way Chipper can ride along in the back."

His dad grunted.

Leading the way down the steps from the deck, Liam called for the dog to follow. A few moments later, he dropped the tailgate, and Chipper soared into the bed of the truck, taking his place up near the cab. For longer or faster trips, the dog rode shotgun or in the back seat. But for local trips, he seemed to love the freedom of the truck bed.

Liam pulled open the driver-side door. "You ready?"

"I'm ready." His dad walked around to the opposite door and got in.

"Where to first?" Liam started the engine.

"Chandler Road. Site of the old house."
"Okay."

Aunt Rosemary fell asleep in her easy chair not long after she and Chelsea finished eating lunch. Chelsea read for a while, then decided to take a walk.

All of Chickadee Creek seemed to be following the example of her great-aunt. No one else was about on this Sunday afternoon. Unlike in the cities, the few businesses in this small town still closed on Sundays, with the exception of the cafe. No cars came down the road. No people sat on decks or porches along this stretch of road. The only sounds she heard were the gurgling creek and birds flittering between trees.

Chelsea didn't walk fast. Instead, she allowed herself to enjoy the play of light and shadow as they fell across the road before her and to breathe in the fresh, pine-scented air. A few Bible verses replayed in her thoughts. Meditation, she'd recently learned, meant devouring the Word. It meant taking in the Scriptures and letting them become a part of her. That's what she hoped would happen with those favorite verses whispering in her memory, that they would become a part of the fabric of her inner being.

"'The name of the LORD is a strong tower,'" she said aloud. "'The righteous runs into it and is safe.'"

Proverbs 18:10 was a verse Aunt Rosemary had given her to memorize after she learned of Chelsea's panic attacks. Saying it now, remembering it word for word, made her smile. She felt stronger and more centered with the verse as a weapon against fear.

At the place where the two main roads crossed, Chelsea turned off of Alexander and headed north on Chandler. On the bridge, she stopped to stare down at the crystal-clear stream as it flowed beneath her. The summer when she was eight, she'd thrown painted sticks into the stream, then rushed to the other side of the bridge to see which one would appear first. Would it be the red one or the blue one or the yellow one? It made her wish she had some colored sticks with her now.

"Maybe another time." She continued on.

But only a few steps later, she noticed Liam's truck on the site of the old Chandler mansion. An instant later she saw Liam himself. He stood with another man near the steps and foundation, all that remained of the large house. When Liam saw her, he raised an arm to wave, then motioned her forward.

"Hey, Chelsea," he said as she drew closer. "Didn't get a chance to talk to you at church this morning."

"I know. Aunt Rosemary had something in the oven for our lunch and didn't want to linger."

"She seems to be feeling better than last week. Her limp is less noticeable."

"Yes. I think so too. But she still gets worn out rather quickly."

He took a step toward her. "She and I had a great talk yesterday. I was sorry you didn't get back before I had to leave." He turned halfway and looked toward the man behind him. "I'd like you to meet my dad, Richard Chandler. Dad, this is Chelsea Spencer."

"It's nice to meet you, sir," she responded with a smile in Richard's direction.

He nodded but didn't return the smile.

The family resemblance between the two men was strong.

Richard Chandler could have been a movie star himself, she thought, although not in the same kind of roles. Even from where she stood, she could tell he wasn't as physically fit as Liam. No adventure films with dangerous stunts for him. And something about him told her it wasn't as easy to discover a smile on his face as it was on Liam's.

"Dad's thinking about selling this property," Liam said into the lengthening silence.

"Oh, really? How sad."

Richard frowned. "Why sad?"

"Well," she answered quickly, "it's belonged to your family for about a hundred and fifty years. This house was the center of everything in the area for decades. That's a lot of history."

"It's just land." Richard turned away and walked toward the foundation.

Chelsea caught an angry expression as it flashed across Liam's face. But it was gone so quickly she wondered if she'd seen it at all.

Liam motioned with his head. "Have a look with us?"

"I don't want to intrude."

He lowered his voice. "You'd be doing me a favor. Dad's in a mood. Don't know why."

"Okay. If you're sure."

He waited for her to step forward, then turned, and they walked side by side.

As a child visiting her great-aunt, she hadn't explored the old foundation or the rest of the grounds that surrounded it. Her father had taught her never to trespass on someone else's property. But since her arrival in Chickadee Creek this summer, she'd seen many photos of the Chandler mansion in its former glory, making her more curious. Seeing the size of the crumbling foundation up close, it was easy to understand how grand the house had been. It must have dwarfed every other building in the town for the hundred years it stood in this spot.

"Cora Chandler had an amazing rose garden in the back." Liam pointed. "Your Aunt Rosemary showed me an article about it in one of her books about the area. There was a pond and fountain right back there. Come on. I'll show you what's left of it."

Chelsea glanced in the direction of Liam's father. He'd kept his back toward them and seemed to be staring off toward the north. But she sensed his irritation and was certain he wanted her gone.

"You know what." She faced Liam. "I'd better get home to Aunt Rosemary. But maybe you could show it to me another time."

He smiled. "I'd like that."

A warning bell chimed inside her. She'd allowed herself to relax in Liam's company, little by little. She'd allowed herself to like him, despite everything she'd experienced in the past. So much so that *she* was the one asking to spend time with him. Would she come to regret this budding friendship?

Maybe she regretted it already.

Liam's Journal

I did something crazy. I'm going to buy the land where the Chandler house and gardens stood. About seven acres in all. I don't even understand why I made the agreement with Dad. Not only am I buying the land, I agreed to pay him his full asking price. I think I could have talked him down, but I didn't even try.

Things were strained between us from the moment he arrived in Chickadee Creek. I didn't know he was coming. He just showed up. I thought maybe he came to talk. I thought maybe I could ask him what was happening between him and Mom, what went wrong in their marriage, how things could get better. I thought maybe we could talk about Jacob. I miss my brother, and when nobody talks about him, it feels like I lose a little more of him each day.

But Dad never let the conversation veer in either of those directions. For the most part, there was just tense silence between us.

We ran into Chelsea Spencer while we were looking over the grounds. I introduced her to Dad, but he wasn't friendly. I don't know why that was. I told her Dad was going to sell the land, and she said it was a sad thing to do. Dad didn't agree and wondered why she called it sad. She told him it was sad because it belonged to the Chandlers for a hundred and fifty years. Dad answered that it was just land.

That was the moment I decided to buy it. It made me mad. Mad that Dad cares so little about his own family. Family from the past. The family he's got left. Which isn't much now. It made me want to know more about the Chandler history. For real this time. I told Chelsea I was curious, but it was only sort of true. But if it could help make sense of my dad, why he is the way he is, it'd be worth it.

God, how do I honor my father and at the same time try to do what's right? You're going to have to show me the way.

Chapter 12

When Liam made up his mind to do something, he wasn't one for delay.

On Tuesday, he drove down to Boise to take care of the initial paperwork necessary for buying the Chandler mansion property. He and his dad met at the office of the real estate agent handling the sale. When they finished, they parted ways. His dad was in a hurry to get back to his office, and Liam wasn't inclined to delay him.

He watched his dad's car until it disappeared at the next intersection. Then he got into his truck, thinking he meant to make his way out of the city and back to the mountains. Instead, he found himself driving to the cemetery. He hadn't been to Jacob's grave site since the funeral. It had been winter then, with snow covering the ground and a frigid wind swirling around the mourners. Today was hot, the sky cloudless, with no breeze stirring the air.

On the opposite end of the cemetery, a groundskeeper mowed the grass, the sound muted by the distance between them. Liam looked around, uncertain about the location of his brother's grave. Things looked different now with the trees and bushes in full leaf. He set off in the general direction, wondering if he would fail to find it, but then his gaze fell upon the headstone bearing Jacob's name and the dates of his birth and death. His breath caught for an instant, and he felt the grip of grief tighten around his heart.

Bro, I sure do miss you.

He stood still, as if waiting for a reply from Jacob. He knew he wouldn't get one, but he waited all the same.

Finally, he said, "I'm buying the old Chandler property from Dad. The acres where the big house was. Before our time, but I've been reading up on it and other stuff about our family. Wish I could talk to you about it."

It still surprised Liam, his newfound interest in his family's history. Perhaps his mom's family would be of interest as well, but it was his dad's side that intrigued him. In fact, he wondered why he hadn't been interested long before meeting Chelsea and learning about Cora Chandler and her violin or about the pearls his grandfather gave his grandmother on their wedding day. Strange how all of that knowledge gave him a sense of belonging, something he hadn't felt for a long time.

"But you understood how I felt. Didn't you, Jacob? You looked at me and knew that I felt . . . different . . . like an outsider. Even when I didn't realize I felt that way."

Perhaps that's what drove me into the acting profession. Perhaps it was the need to be noticed by someone. Anyone.

He released a mirthless laugh.

If that was the case, if he'd felt so different and like an

outsider, where did the idea of his happy childhood and perfect family come from?

"It came from you, didn't it?" He swallowed the lump of emotion that threatened to choke him. "You made me believe in the ideal, even when underneath I sensed the truth."

With a sigh, he turned away from the grave site and walked to his truck. Once again he meant to drive back to Chickadee Creek, and once again he turned in another direction, this time toward his mom's home. He didn't know if she would be there. He hadn't called or texted to let her know he would be in Boise. He went anyway.

Seeing an unfamiliar car in his mom's driveway, he felt relief. A visitor meant he wouldn't be expected to stay long. The sense of relief was followed by a familiar sting of guilt. He shouldn't want to escape her company as quickly as possible. Wasn't that behaving like his dad? A behavior he resented. Not how he wanted to be.

As he'd done countless times before, he strode up the front walk while using a phone app to unlock the electronic keypad before he got there. As he rapped twice, he opened the door.

"Mom, it's me," he called as his gaze shifted toward the living room.

He wasn't quite sure what happened between his quick knock and the moment he saw the man rise from the sofa. He registered the flustered look on his mom's face, followed by a rush of color into her cheeks.

"This is unexpected," she said as she stood, her hands smoothing the fabric of her tan capris.

He realized then what he must have interrupted, and it sent a shock wave through him.

"Liam, I believe you met David Harris at Jacob's funeral."

His gaze turned to the man, instant dislike making his blood run cold, then hot.

"Hello, Liam." David's voice sounded low, almost apologetic in tone.

"Mr. Harris." Liam turned his gaze on his mom again. "I was in Boise to sign some papers. I'm buying the Chandler property."

His mom's brows rose in question.

"Where the mansion stood in Chickadee Creek. I'm buying it from Dad."

"Good heavens. Whyever would you do that?"

"He's selling off quite a bit of land up there. I assume he's in need of more cash. I decided I wanted to keep some of the property for myself."

"Susan," David said in a near whisper, "I think I should go."

Liam couldn't have agreed more.

"No," his mom answered quickly. "That isn't necessary."

David Harris gave her a firm look. "I think it is." He took one step back. "It was good to see you again, Liam." He left the house, seeming to take the oxygen with him.

"You were rude." His mom sank onto the sofa again.

"Who is he?"

"A friend of mine."

Liam narrowed his eyes at her. "What *kind* of friend?"

"Now you're insulting me."

"Am I?" He sat on the nearest chair. "I'm not an idiot, Mom. I've got eyes in my head and can see what's in front of me."

She shook her head slowly. "David and I have known each other for over thirty years."

"So why haven't I seen him before?"

"Because he moved away from Boise when . . . when you were a baby. He only moved back to Idaho a few years ago."

Liam suspected she was telling the truth but not the whole truth. He pressed harder. "Is he a friend of Dad's too?"

Silence stretched between them.

"No," she answered at last, her gaze unflinching. "He isn't."

Her words were like a punch in his midsection, and they propelled him to his feet. "He's the reason Dad moved out."

She stared at him, her expression a mixture of anger and guilt.

An affair. His mom was having an affair. No wonder his dad had moved out. No wonder his dad had said Liam needed to ask his mom what was going on.

He drew in a slow, deep breath and released it. "How long?"

"How long what?"

"You know what. How long have you been having an affair?"

She didn't answer.

A worse thought occurred to him. "Were you seeing him while Jacob was sick?"

"It's complicated."

"People say that all the time. Maybe your reasons are complicated, but my question isn't. Were you sleeping with that man"—he pointed toward the door—"while my brother was dying?"

She pressed her lips into a thin line, and he knew he wouldn't get an answer from her today. Without another word, he turned and strode out of the house.

❧

Chelsea was driving toward home on Alexander Road when she saw Liam's truck ahead of her make a right onto Chandler Road. For some crazy reason—perhaps she wanted to share with him about her first violin lesson—she decided to do the same. By the time she could see beyond the bridge, he'd turned into the horseshoe-shaped driveway on the mansion site.

When she stopped her car behind his truck, Liam already stood near the steps, fingers tucked into the back pockets of his jeans, his head bowed. Was he praying?

Suddenly uncertain, she drew her hand back from the door handle. But he must have heard her arrival, for he turned and looked in her direction. She couldn't tell from his expression if he was glad to see her there or not.

Not knowing what else to do, she drew a deep breath and got out of the car. "Am I intruding?"

He shook his head and moved toward her.

"I saw your truck and . . . and I wanted to thank you again for allowing me to keep the violin. I finished my first lesson about fifteen minutes ago."

His smile was brief, and the look in his eyes, now that he was closer, was sad. "How was it?"

"If you don't mind the sound of a cat howling in the middle of the night, then you wouldn't mind the sounds I managed to make. My teacher is patient. Sainted, even. Or maybe she's hard of hearing."

This time his smile was more genuine and lingered a few

moments longer. "Are you going to love playing it as much as you thought you would?"

"Yes. I feel joyful just holding the violin." The admission embarrassed her, and she glanced downward.

"I'm glad, Chelsea. Seeing your joy brings me joy too."

She looked up again.

"I was in need of that at the moment."

"You were?"

He nodded.

"I . . . I'm sorry. For whatever's wrong. For whatever's made you unhappy."

She thought she understood, at least in small part. There were times in her life when a smile from a perfect stranger gave her the hope she needed. Like a ray of sunshine breaking through a cloud on a rainy day. She watched as Liam drew a deep breath and squared his shoulders. Determination replaced the sadness she'd witnessed.

"While you're here," he said, "let me show you around. I didn't get to do that on Sunday."

"Are you sure? I don't want to intrude."

"Not intruding. Come to think of it, you don't know that I decided to buy it. Signed the paperwork today. Won't take long for the transaction to go through. Nothing to be inspected, unless you count the old shed at the back of the property."

"You're buying the land from your father?"

"Before he could sell it off to somebody else. Yeah." A frown creased his brow.

The look made her sorry she'd asked that particular question. "So, what do you intend to do with it?"

"I'm not sure." He motioned for her to walk with him, and

they set off along one side of the crumbling foundation. "Maybe I'll build another house where the original one stood. Maybe a replica. I even thought it might make a good resort of some kind. A destination resort. Maybe for weddings and anniversary celebrations and reunions. That might be something."

"That would be something, all right."

He glanced her way, the hint of a smile returning. "Are you ridiculing me? Or is that a challenge?"

"Neither." She returned his smile. "I'm not sure what anybody would do with a house of that size in this small town, but a resort might work."

"Of course, if I built a replica, I could get married and have a dozen kids to fill up all the rooms."

She sent him a look of disbelief. She remembered all too well the challenges of supporting a family on a limited income in a remote community. And her parents only had four children, not twelve. "How would you provide for them? Or do you plan to abandon them while you run off to Hollywood?" She heard the critical edge in her voice and half expected him to react in anger—as her father would have, as her former boyfriend would have.

But he didn't. "I was kidding. About the dozen kids. Not about building on this site. Not about the possibility of a resort. The grounds are big enough. With the right landscaping, it could work."

"But what about making movies? Do you intend to give that up to run a destination resort?"

"I don't know yet." He shrugged. "I'm waiting for God to make that clear to me."

As quickly as it came, her annoyance vanished. Perhaps it was because Liam had declared his reliance on God for direction in his life. Or perhaps she realized she'd overreacted. She opened her mouth to apologize, but he didn't give her a chance.

"If *you* owned the property, what would you build on it?" he asked.

"Me?" She let her gaze sweep over the grounds. "I can't even imagine."

"Think about it. I'd value your opinion."

She looked at him, and pleasure spread through her. Had anyone ever valued her opinion before? What a rare and precious thing.

MAY 1896

Spring came late that year to the mountains of Idaho—or so everyone told Cora. It was nearly the end of May before the last traces of snow disappeared in Chickadee Creek.

The afternoon air was crisp but not cold on that Monday afternoon as Cora followed the rushing creek higher into the mountains, away from the town. She was accompanied by Rambler, the stray dog that had adopted her soon after the start of the new year. The dog had entered the school with some of the children one morning and had somehow become her constant companion. He was a rather ugly canine with wiry hair that hid his eyes. A piece of one ear had been torn away at some point, presumably in a fight with another dog or a large forest animal. Despite his appearance, though, Rambler wormed his way into Cora's heart. Sarah's, too, although the older woman grumbled about "the beast" on a regular basis.

The chatter of a chipmunk caused Rambler to dash into the forest underbrush. Cora stopped walking so she could watch his antics. It took him a while to locate the critter, sitting on a low branch of a tree. It scolded the dog, who continued to leap and bark and make a general ruckus, as Sarah would call it.

After a while, Cora called to him. "Let's go, Rambler. Come on."

She began walking again. In her right hand, she clutched the handle of her violin case. In the year since her flight from New York, she hadn't once played her beloved instrument. She'd scarcely even looked at the violin for fear doing so might cause her resolve to waver. By now the instrument must be out of tune. Perhaps it would need repair. She couldn't be sure. But today she meant to find out.

At first her decision not to play had to do with her father. He must know she'd taken her violin with her. Even he knew how much she loved to play. Whoever he'd hired to search for her— and she was certain, even now, there must be someone seeking her location—would be on the lookout for a woman who played the violin and played it well.

But a year had passed, and her father was unlikely to look for her in a place like Chickadee Creek. He wouldn't be able to imagine her washing and ironing her own clothes or standing in a one-room schoolhouse, teaching twenty students ranging in ages from six to fourteen. It would never occur to him that she would walk through a forest accompanied by a scraggly-looking dog. Anyone searching for her would be sent to larger cities. Places where there were balls and theaters and operas. Cities where modern conveniences abounded. Surely it was safe for her to go off by herself and play her violin, to let the music embrace her heart and allow her spirit to soar.

Smiling, she drew in a deep breath through her nose. As she exhaled, she spread her arms wide and shouted, "I'm free!" As her words echoed through the forest, she began to laugh and turn in a slow circle.

MAY 1896

Preston leaned forward, his forearm resting on the pommel of the saddle. He grinned as he watched Cora Anderson turn in a slow circle, laughing, her head thrown back. Even from where he rested on the ridge high above her, he felt her joy.

"I'm free," she'd shouted moments before.

Free from what? he wondered.

Chickadee Creek was a small town, and in the months since Cora's arrival, Preston had heard only good things about her. Students and parents seemed to like her. His housekeeper, Sarah Mason, praised her on a regular basis. Still, Preston had little firsthand knowledge of the young woman. Except for Sundays, he spent nearly every daylight hour in the mine offices or surveying the various Chandler lands. That had left him little time to get to know the pretty schoolteacher. And the demands upon his time had increased with the arrival of the dredger.

In fact, he'd been returning from the dredger to the mine offices when he saw Cora walking on the trail below him. Something compelled him to rein in and watch her pass. Only she'd stopped, shouted, and twirled, all of it completely unexpected. When he saw her at church on Sundays, she was reserved and quiet. Nothing like the joyous woman he saw on the trail below.

The change intrigued him.

Cora stopped turning in that slow circle, then stepped to a fallen tree a short distance off the trail. A dog followed her there, and Preston remembered Sarah telling him about the stray Cora had adopted this past winter. But the dog he saw wasn't the sort of canine Preston had imagined with her. It was as ugly as she was beautiful.

Cora sat on the log and opened the violin case she carried. The same one, he assumed, that she'd clutched when disembarking from the stagecoach the previous fall. A short while later, she took the instrument from the case. She held it, stared at it, as if not quite sure what to do with it. But that was a mistaken impression. Moments later, she played a single note. The sound rose and spread through the forest. She played the same note again, touched something on the instrument, then repeated the actions a number of times. Only when she moved on to another note did he understand what she was doing: tuning the violin.

He couldn't have said why he continued to sit there, waiting and watching, listening to a single note repeated again and again. But he received his answer when the tuning was complete and she began to play. At first, it seemed a simple enough melody, but after a time it grew more powerful. So powerful and moving that he forgot to breathe. It was as if the forest became a cathedral. Never in his life had he heard anything like it. Truly, the instrument wept, and he wanted to weep with it.

Preston was a stranger to the emotions rising within him, and he felt the need to escape the music before he lost control. He tightened the reins to back his horse away from the edge of the ridge. At that same moment, however, the music stopped. In an instant Cora's head lifted, and her gaze met with his. Even with the distance between them, he read fear on her face.

What should he do now? Ride away. Or go to her. He preferred the first option. He chose the second.

The way down to the trail was steep, but his horse had traversed it before. Somehow he managed to pay attention to both the descent and the woman who was his destination. By the time he reached her, the violin was put away and she clutched the case against her chest as if it were a shield.

"Miss Anderson." He tipped the brim of his hat before stepping down from the saddle.

She took a step back.

"Sorry I frightened you. I can see you weren't expecting an audience."

"No." She shook her head. "No, I wasn't."

"I'm surprised Mrs. Mason hasn't told me you can play like that. It was the most moving thing I've ever heard."

"Sarah hasn't heard me play," she answered softly, her gaze dropping to the ground between them.

"That's a shame. A gift like that ought to be shared."

She looked up again. A little of the fear had left her lovely eyes, replaced by a sliver of pleasure.

"I've heard my share of fiddling at barn dances and such," he continued. "But nothing like the song you played. I imagine those are reserved for concert halls." He arched an eyebrow. "Would I be right about that?"

"Do you mean, did I ever play in a concert hall? No. Appearances by women musicians are rare in such places. There are exceptions, of course, but those are most often in Europe rather than in America."

He remembered his first impression of Cora Anderson as she'd stepped from the stagecoach. He'd thought she couldn't possibly be a schoolteacher, let alone that she would want to live in this little town. Everything about her seemed to cry privilege, education, and the upper class. She was polished and refined, and he'd expected her to be spoiled and egotistical, even selfish.

"Why did you come to Idaho?" he asked impulsively.

She stiffened. "I beg your pardon."

"Sorry. I didn't mean for it to sound like that. I just . . . It's so obvious that . . . that—" He broke off.

"That I don't belong here?"

He shrugged. "I suppose."

"Being raised in a certain place or in a certain way does not mean a person belongs there, Mr. Chandler." She stood a little taller, her shoulders squared, her chin lifted. "I came to this town to make a new life for myself. It has become my home. Is there some reason you don't think I should be here?"

Preston swept the hat from his head and raked the fingers of his free hand through his hair. "No, miss. That's the last thing I want you to think." As he spoke the words, he realized how true they were. He knew her only slightly, and yet he knew he would feel the loss if she left Chickadee Creek. "Please, forgive me if I spoke out of turn." He drew a deep breath. "And I want you to know, I'd give just about anything to hear you play that song again."

Heat rose in her cheeks, but it was accompanied by a smile.

Preston should have realized then and there that he was a goner.

Chapter 13

*T*aking a breather from sorting and organizing, Chelsea sat in the window seat at the back of the second story of the antique shop. Her cell service didn't work most places in Chickadee Creek, but thanks to Wi-Fi she could still receive and send internet calls and text messages. She smiled when she saw she had a new text from Evelyn. But the smile didn't last long.

> Tom went to see Mom. So angry when she wouldn't tell him where you are. He didn't believe she didn't know.

Chelsea hadn't seen Tom Goodson in almost two months. Why wouldn't he give up? She'd made it clear when they last spoke that she wasn't interested in getting back together, that she was done with him, that anything they'd once shared was over for good.

A shudder passed through her when she remembered the night he'd sat in his car outside of her apartment. In the light from the parking lot, she'd seen him staring up at her windows. Something malevolent hung in the air that night, and she knew she had to get away soon. Aunt Rosemary's invitation to stay with her in Chickadee Creek arrived two days later.

A miracle, of sorts.

A miracle . . .

"I'm still waiting for God to make that clear to me."

Remembering Liam's words from a week before, she frowned. Since God had been able to bring her to safety in Chickadee Creek, without any effort on her part, she knew He could handle her other worries, that He would either open a door or give her wisdom to know what she was to do.

With her thumbs, she typed:

Are you safe? Is Mom safe?

The reply came:

Yes. Mom's friend sent him away with a warning. He won't come back.

Chelsea wondered if her sister was being entirely honest. Their father had been unpredictable in his rages. One moment he'd laughed with his wife and played with his children. The next he'd struck out in anger, harming whoever was in his path. There'd been no way to predict when or how or why it would happen or who would bear the brunt of it.

Tom's behavior had been much the same, only she and Tom were almost four months into their relationship before she experienced his first explosion. In hindsight, she realized there'd been warning signs, but she hadn't recognized them. Or perhaps she hadn't wanted to recognize them. She'd been caught up in a romantic haze and had allowed herself to be swept along, even when doubts began to surface.

Lord Jesus, I brought this on myself and on my family by not listening to that little voice telling me Tom wasn't who I thought. Please keep Evelyn and Mom safe from him. I don't know that he would threaten or hurt them. It's me he wants to hurt. It's me he's angry with. But I'm unsure what he'll do when he can't find me. He's erratic and volatile, and he knows where they live. Keep them safe, please.

Eyes still closed, she drew in a deep breath and released it. After a few seconds more, she realized she was waiting for panic to rise up, for fear to overtake her. It didn't happen this time. Not the uncontrollable panic. She was concerned for herself and for her family, and she wondered what Tom might do next. But she was calm at the same time. She was able to think clearly and rationally. This must be what the Bible meant when it promised God would keep her in perfect peace if she kept her thoughts focused on Him.

The chime above the shop door sounded. Chelsea opened her eyes to see Liam enter the store. He glanced toward Aunt Rosemary's favorite chair. Finding it empty, his gaze swept the lower level, then rose toward the second. He smiled when he found her.

Her heart stuttered as their gazes met. A moment before, she'd prayed about the danger she believed Tom posed, and now she reacted with pleasure because Liam walked into the shop. It was wrong. All wrong. And yet—

"Morning," he called.

"Good morning." She rose from the window seat and slipped her phone into her back pocket as she stepped to the railing. "How goes the research?"

"Good, I think. I drove down to Boise yesterday to get a look at the original plans for the mansion. They have a set of them at the museum. Not the original drawings, but copies of them. Some historical preservation expert showed them to me. I was afraid to breathe the whole time we were in that small room. He really didn't want to show them to me."

"That bad?" She moved toward the stairs.

"He didn't like me before I met him. I'm a Chandler, and we—as in my family—allowed the old mansion to fall into disuse, and then we tore it down after it was damaged in the storm. Those Chandlers who are left—meaning me and my dad—should be taken out and shot at dawn."

"You'll be missed." She tried to keep a straight face.

He grinned. "Thanks a lot."

How easy things were between them. It surprised her how much she liked Liam. It surprised her how she wasn't leery of his charm and good looks, as she'd been when they first met. In her quieter, solitary moments, she could admit it wasn't wise for her to feel this comfortable in his presence. Comfort meant her guard was down. A lowered guard meant she could be in danger. And yet she couldn't seem to care when he smiled up at her the way he was now.

Lord, make me wise.

"Hey, how was your violin lesson yesterday?"

She shook her head as she walked down the stairs. "Not quite as screechy as before. But I'm a long way from playing real music."

"I'll bet you're not as bad as you make it sound."

"I wouldn't test that theory with Aunt Rosemary. She's a very honest woman. She'll tell you what my practicing sounds like."

He chuckled before asking, "Speaking of which, where is she?"

"Aunt Rosemary said she had some bill paying to catch up on, so she sent me over to the shop on my own."

"Ah." He looked around. "She told me to come by. She has some more books she wanted me to look at."

"Oh, that's right. They're over here." Chelsea led the way toward a back corner of the store. "I poked through them this morning. There's one that was written in the early part of the twentieth century. Aunt Rosemary said it should be of particular interest to you. It's by a minister's wife who knew both Preston and Cora Chandler when they were new to Chickadee Creek. That's what the author said in the foreword. It's mostly another history of the area, but there looks to be quite a bit about your family too. And there's a photograph of your great-great-grandmother holding a violin." She hesitated before adding, "I'm sure it's *the* violin."

"*Your* violin?"

Something relaxed inside when he confirmed, once again, that the violin was hers. "Yes."

"That should be interesting." He picked up the indicated book and opened the cover.

"The photo with the violin is on page 270."

He nodded as he flipped the pages.

Unable to resist, Chelsea sidled closer to his side so she could look at the book along with him. When he arrived at the page, she reached out and placed her index finger next to the photograph. "I think I can see some family resemblance. Same dark hair. Same dark eyes."

He glanced at her with a bemused expression. "It's a black-and-white photo," he replied dryly. "Everything looks dark."

"I know." She laughed. "But the resemblance is still there. Cora Chandler could have been an actress. She's beautiful." *And so are you*, she finished silently.

Liam felt the warmth of Chelsea's body through the cotton fabric of his shirt. The hair on his arms stood on end, as if he were near an electrical charge. His mouth went dry, and his brain felt fuzzy. It would have been easy and natural to turn and take her into his arms. The strength of the desire to do so caught him unawares.

Did she feel it too? Perhaps, for she took a quick step away from him. Then, as if that wasn't enough space, she moved to the opposite side of the table.

Cora Chandler. He needed to think about his great-great-grandmother and not Chelsea Spencer. Learning more about his family, about Cora and her violin, about the Chandler mansion. Those were the reasons why he was at the antique shop.

Besides, a romantic involvement wasn't a good idea, no matter how attractive the woman in question was. His life was too uncertain. He wasn't sure if he would stay in Idaho or return to California. He didn't know if he would keep acting or start over in a totally different career. He was trying to get his faith life back on track. He didn't need another distraction. Sure, he could admit he was drawn to Chelsea. She was nice. She was pretty. As a bonus, she had that beautiful ginger hair. Why wouldn't he like her? But pursuing those feelings could derail him on more than one front. And it might not be good for Chelsea either.

Just look what happened to Mom. She got derailed too.

He winced at the thought, unwilling to remember that his mom had a lover. She'd always seemed strong in her faith. It would have been easier to believe his father, the workaholic, would have an affair. All those hours in the office, away from his family. That would have made sense to Liam, even if he wouldn't have liked it. But not his mom. She—

"What's wrong, Liam?"

He met Chelsea's gaze. "Nothing."

She tilted her head slightly, her eyes saying she didn't believe him.

"Okay, you're right. Something's wrong." He gave her an apologetic smile, along with a slight shake of his head. "But I'm not ready to talk about it yet."

"Fair enough." She nodded. "But if I can help, even by just listening, I'm game."

He cleared his throat, lifting the book in his hand. "I'd like to take this with me. How much for it?"

"Oh, Aunt Rosemary meant for you to have it. No charge."

"Not a very sound business model. Giving away what's in the shop."

"She would say you gave us—*me*—a lot more than that book is worth."

"Okay. But you can tell her this is the last time. We're square from here on out. I won't budge about that."

Chelsea's smile lit up her face. "I'll tell her, but don't go holding your breath. She can be way more stubborn than you ever thought of being."

"Really?" He grinned. "Sounds like a challenge to me."

"If you like." She gave a little toss of her head.

How had she done that? How had she managed to chase his dark thoughts into a corner? Not that it mattered how. It only mattered that it happened.

Liam's Journal

Mom is having an affair.

I write it, but I don't want to believe it. Haven't wanted to believe it from the moment I realized what was going on.

His name is David Harris. When I saw him at Mom's house, he looked familiar. He was at Jacob's funeral, so that must be where I saw him before. Takes guts to show up like that. Why would he do it? Some kind of sick way of supporting Mom? I don't get it.

I wonder if Dad knew it was going on even before that. From some of the stuff Jacob said, I'm guessing he did.

Should I tell Dad I know? He said I should ask Mom what went wrong between them. Now I know why. But would he want to know that I finally know too?

At least his mood makes more sense to me. Not all of it but some.

God, how does a son react appropriately about something like this? How do I honor my mother when she's having an affair? And while still married to my dad.

Funny. The prayer in my last entry was similar but about my dad.

I know people divorce at the drop of a hat these days. One actor

I know has been married three times already, and he's my age. But I never thought my parents would divorce. They seemed solid, most of the time. Or maybe I wasn't looking for the signs.

Show me how I need to respond, Lord. I sure don't know on my own.

Liam's Journal

I dreamed about Jacob last night. The old Jacob before cancer. The strong and healthy one. I'm not sure where we were. The house felt familiar, but it wasn't the old cabin, and it wasn't the house where we grew up. But we both seemed at home there. We were joking and laughing. TV was on. There were snacks on the coffee table. Jacob's favorites. Junk food. Nothing healthy.

And then all of a sudden he looked at me, real serious like, and said, "Thanks for lovin' me, bro. Despite everything."

Right then I woke up. I was disoriented at first. The dream seemed so real, and what he'd said kept echoing in my head. It didn't make sense to me. Jacob and I were close. Always. I don't remember any time I didn't love my kid brother, because from my first memories, he was right there beside me. Everybody loved Jacob. What was that "despite everything" business? Why would my mind even come up with a dream like that?

Funny thing is we used to talk about how Jacob was Mom's favorite. There was never any doubt about that. If anybody felt unloved sometimes, it was me. And maybe I said or inferred that I was glad Jacob loved me. But I wouldn't have said "despite everything." What everything?

And I know Jacob never said anything like that to me. Not ever. I would remember.

So why did it seem real? Like it was something important. Like it was something I needed to hear or know or think about?

If I was writing this dream for a film, it would be a turning point in the plot. But I'm not a writer. My brain doesn't work that way. Sometimes I'll get an idea for a script for a movie I'm in. I'll think I would do a scene a different way if it was up to me. And sometimes the director and writer agree with me.

But I don't see how this is a turning point.

Chapter 14

Wentworth pursues Chandler for lead in next film.

*L*iam stared at the tweet, unsure if he wanted to follow the link to the article or not. But he couldn't resist the impulse for long. He clicked it and quickly scanned the post.

> An unconfirmed source at the studio reported that Grayson Wentworth is not giving up on his first choice for the lead role in his next film . . . Liam Chandler hasn't been seen in Hollywood for more than a year due to a reported illness and subsequent death in the family . . . When questioned, Chandler's agent, Kurt Knight, had no comment . . . Where is Liam Chandler?

Liam closed his laptop. Was it true or just words needed to fill up space? Was Grayson Wentworth determined to have him star in his next movie? What was the role? He hadn't asked when Kurt mentioned it last month. Maybe that was proof he didn't want to go back to acting. Maybe his lack of curiosity showed that he no longer belonged in the Hollywood scene.

Jacob's voice whispered in his memory, *"Don't you want to go deeper?"*

"Yeah," he answered aloud. He would like a role that wasn't about escaping from aliens or prehistoric beasts, roles where he wasn't running for his life or making a move on a female costar. Maybe a role he could play with his shirt on, as Jacob suggested. Maybe he would like to be in a film that moved a viewer to tears. Or at least to feel something more than an adrenaline rush.

He frowned as he reached for the phone. Kurt took his call within moments.

"You heard about what's online?" his agent asked without preamble.

"I read a piece." Liam gave Kurt the name of the source.

"The news is picking up speed. Been forwarded a lot on Twitter and Facebook. Many people in the business wondering where you are and why you don't have another film in production. And that's good for your career. Trust me. It's all positive chatter."

"Is it true? What the writer said. Wentworth still wants me?"

"It's true."

Liam got up and walked to the living-room window. "I didn't ask before. What's the part?"

"The starring one. Top billing."

"That's not what I meant, and you know it. What *kind* of movie?"

"It's a drama."

"Set where?"

"On Earth." Kurt laughed at his own joke before adding, "Oklahoma during the Great Depression."

"The Great Depression," Liam echoed. He'd long been

drawn to the history of the thirties, particularly the cause and effect of the Dust Bowl.

Kurt continued. "The script's based on a bestselling book that came out a few years back. Focuses on a family who's caught up in the Dust Bowl. But instead of heading for California, like so many did, they stuck it out."

Liam's pulse skittered. Did his agent know his interest in the subject?

"Don't you want to go deeper?"

This was it. This was what Jacob meant when he'd asked that question. A role like this could be Liam's chance to go deeper. He felt it in his gut. He didn't have to read the script to know, not with Grayson Wentworth at the helm.

God, is this what I'm supposed to do? Is this what I've been waiting for?

Despite his quickened pulse, he felt calm embracing his excitement. "Kurt, tell him I'm interested. See if you can set up a time for us to talk."

"Really? You sure?"

"I'm sure." Even as he spoke the words, he felt his certainty increase.

"You want him to come to you?"

"Are you kidding?"

"No. No, I think he'd be willing to fly up to Idaho, if that's what it takes."

"You know, if he's willing, that is what I'd like. Maybe for him to see me in my own environment, in my own home."

His agent was silent for a moment. "Home, huh?"

"Yeah. Looks like I'm ready to work again, but when I'm not filming, this is where I want to be."

"I'll see what I can set up and get back to you."

"Great. Talk to you soon."

"Will do."

"Wait. Kurt, can you remember the name of the book the film is based on? I'd like to read it."

"Can't think of it right off. I'll have my assistant find out and text it to you."

"Perfect."

The two men exchanged a few more words, then ended the call. Liam remained at the window, staring out at the forest while trying to wrap his mind around the decision he'd made. It seemed to have happened in seconds. Or had it been weeks and months in coming?

Chipper came to sit by his master, placing his head beneath Liam's hand. He took the hint and ruffled the dog's ears.

"And here I was thinking I might be done with acting." Liam looked down at the dog. "Looks like I might be headed back to California, boy. What do you think about traveling a bit?"

Chipper licked his hand.

There was no denying his dog loved to go places in the truck. But what would Chipper think of being locked in a crate in the belly of a plane? How much would he hate being stuck in a strange place while Liam was at the lot, filming? Of course, they might work on location. Would they allow Liam to bring his dog wherever that was?

Liam sat on the sofa and resumed petting the dog's head.

"We might have to make other arrangements."

He couldn't ask his dad. The man was no fan of pets and pretty much lived at the office anyway. And he wouldn't ask his mom. This was no time to be asking her for favors. Not when just thinking about her made him angry.

I could ask Chelsea.

He didn't even wonder what her answer would be. She would agree to look after Chipper. He pictured her, smiling, nodding in agreement, then turning her attention immediately to the dog, bending over Chipper, patting his back, talking to him.

The urge to call her was strong. Crazy, since he didn't have the role yet, despite what Kurt said. He didn't even have a meeting set up. Besides, deals fell apart all the time. Wentworth might want him now and change his mind tomorrow after meeting a guy who was even better for the part.

Then again, Liam didn't need to be going out of town before he called Chelsea. Did he?

Aunt Rosemary had made a lot of progress since her return to Chickadee Creek. She'd improved so much that Chelsea felt superfluous. Her great-aunt took a brief nap each afternoon, but otherwise her energy level seemed greater than her own. When Aunt Rosemary was in the antique shop, she stayed busy, for the most part. Chelsea would tell her to sit and rest, but the rest never lasted long. Perhaps because customers had finally begun to enter the shop after a long absence. Mostly it was townsfolk coming by to see what changes Rosemary had made, but summer tourists had also discovered Rosemary & Time.

"I let this place go to pot long before my fall," Aunt Rosemary said after a customer left the store, the soft chime of the bell still echoing. "Years before. I should have asked you to help me long ago. You've done wonders with it, downstairs and up. People can find things to buy, even if they didn't know they wanted to take something home. It all looked like junk before you came. Now it looks like valuable antiques."

"Not everything looks valuable." Chelsea slid a book onto the waiting shelf. "And not everything looked like junk before. When I came to stay with you as a girl, I remember the shop as wonderful and . . . and cozy."

"You were a little girl. We see things differently when we're young."

"Maybe."

The telephone rang and her great-aunt answered it. "Rosemary & Time. How may I help you?"

Chelsea riffled the pages of another thick book, this one about the Napoleonic Wars. Pausing to look at a drawing of a battlefield, she thought of Liam and wondered if this history book would interest him or if he only cared to learn more about his family's history in Idaho.

"Chelsea," Aunt Rosemary called, intruding on her thoughts. "It's Liam Chandler."

Her heart did an odd little dance in her chest as she closed the book and put it on the shelf. "Did he say what he wants?"

Her great-aunt shook her head.

Chelsea walked to the counter and took the phone from Aunt Rosemary's outstretched hand. "Hi, Liam."

"Hope I'm not interrupting anything important."

She laughed softly. "It isn't rocket science, what I do around here. I can handle an interruption."

"Right." He chuckled too. "I get your point."

Chelsea turned to lean her backside against the counter, but mostly she didn't want Aunt Rosemary to read her expression. She didn't want it known by anyone how she'd begun to think and feel about Liam Chandler. Because what girl from a backwater town in Idaho let herself fall for a movie star, even one in seclusion? The man she thought he was might be an act. She'd been fooled before, and not by someone trained to pretend to be someone else.

"The reason I called," he said, "is that I'm planning to barbecue tomorrow evening. I know it's last minute, but I wondered if you'd care to join me."

"Just me?"

He was silent a moment, then said, "No. Rosemary, too, if she's able to come."

She wasn't sure if she was gladdened or disappointed by his reply. "She's able."

"I'll have both chicken and beef, plus corn on the cob and salad. I'm not a gourmet chef, but I'm not bad on the grill."

"Can we bring anything?"

"If you've got a particular soft drink you prefer, you might bring that. I've got a couple of flavors of sparkling water, and I can make tea or coffee."

"Time?"

"How about six thirty?"

"Okay. We'll be there. Thanks." With the call ended, she turned to face Aunt Rosemary again. "We've been invited to a barbecue at Liam's tomorrow night."

"How nice. But are you sure he wants me there?"

"Yes, I'm sure. It's what he said."

Aunt Rosemary released a sigh. "I've meant to have him over for Sunday dinner, and now he's beaten me to the punch. Where were my manners?"

"It wasn't a race."

"Maybe not, but my mother would roll over in her grave all the same."

Cora

SEPTEMBER 1896

The smell of autumn filled the air on that September morning as Cora walked toward the mercantile. The crisp scent reminded her it wouldn't be long before another school year began.

She was ready, even if her students weren't. She much preferred days filled with lessons. She loved watching the children as they bent over their slates. It was exciting when a young student suddenly understood two plus two equaled four or discovered a jumble of letters made a word. It was magical when one of them got swept away by a story or when someone realized there was a big, wide world beyond the mountains of Idaho.

Silently she thanked God for His wonderful provision, for allowing her to meet Mabel Johnson on that train. She couldn't have imagined that the chatty woman who took the seat opposite her would become the catalyst for her employment as a teacher. She hadn't known it was something she wanted. At first she'd thought teaching was simply a way to support herself. Respectable employment options for women were few. Marriage was expected and thought to be the path every woman wanted.

Even in Chickadee Creek, people seemed determined to marry off the schoolmistress. Cora had eaten more than one Sunday dinner with a family where another guest happened to be a local bachelor. Although why they would want to find her a husband, she didn't understand. Marriage usually meant a woman stopped teaching. And since the parents seemed to approve of her, why would they want to have to find another teacher to take her place?

One bachelor who hadn't eaten opposite her—not since last Thanksgiving, a dinner without matchmaking at its center—was Preston Chandler. In truth, she'd scarcely seen him outside of church since the beginning of summer, the day he'd observed her playing her violin. Rumor had it that he almost lived at the mining office—when he wasn't on the dredger. Yet she thought about him often. She wasn't sure why.

Worrying her lower lip between her teeth, she opened the door to the mercantile.

"Mornin', Miss Anderson," Alexander Harris called to her from behind the counter.

"Good morning, Mr. Harris."

"Anything I can help you find?"

"No, thank you. I know where everything is." For some reason, the words made her smile. She loved that she knew where to find things in this store. It meant she belonged.

Alexander gave her a quick nod before turning back to Mr. Hemplemeyer, the owner of a sheep ranch to the west of Chickadee Creek. The three youngest of his six sons had been students of Cora's in the previous term. Thinking of them, all three shooting up beyond their trousers last spring, made her smile. Only two would return to the school when classes resumed. The older boy, Bruno, would join his other brothers and father on the ranch.

As she filled the basket on her arm with items for the kitchen, she thought back to when she'd been the same age as Bruno.

There'd been no expectations of her whatsoever beyond that she make life as pleasant as possible for her father, his friends, and any suitors who might be interested in her hand in marriage. Nor had her father shown any love or affection toward her. Mr. Hemplemeyer, on the other hand, loved his family and wasn't afraid to show it. He wanted the best for his sons, and she found herself envying the Hemplemeyer boys. How different her life might have been if she'd been loved like that.

She blinked away the unexpected emotions. It had been many months since she'd allowed herself to feel that particular pain. She was happy with her life as it was today. She had wonderful friends such as Sarah Mason and Nora Sooner. She loved her work as a teacher. She lacked nothing of importance. She had a comfortable place to live, plenty of food to eat, and good clothes to wear. She didn't miss the large house or the fancy balls or the exotic delicacies served at meals or the fine gowns and jewels that used to fill her wardrobe. But apparently she missed what she'd never had: the true affection of her parents.

"Miss Anderson?"

She knew that voice. Drawing a quick breath, she turned toward Preston Chandler. How strange that she'd thought about him on her way to the mercantile, thought how she almost never saw him outside of church, and now there he was, standing close, speaking softly.

"You looked distressed," he said. "Are you feeling well?"

"Oh. Yes." She felt heat rise in her cheeks. "I'm well. Thank you."

The smallest of smiles tugged at the corners of his mouth.

His question had flustered her. His smile irritated her. She lifted her chin and answered, "I was remembering my family." The words were true, but the meaning behind them was less so.

"You must miss them."

She longed to agree. She couldn't.

Softly, he said, "You're free?" He paused, then nodded. "I see. You're free of them." This time it wasn't a question.

It came back to her, that day in May when he'd descended from the ridge on horseback. She'd thought he'd only heard her play the violin. She hadn't known he'd been up on that ridge even longer, long enough to hear her declaration of liberty.

Preston cleared his throat. "You're safe here, Miss Anderson."

Something danced in her chest as she looked into his eyes. She found kindness there, kindness without judgment. Nor was he laughing at her or teasing her as she'd feared he might.

He took a short step back. "I must return to the mining office. But I . . . I wondered if we might have supper one evening at Nellie's Restaurant."

She felt her eyes widen with surprise.

"Say this Friday night. I could come for you at five thirty."

She nodded, meaning that she understood.

But he took the gesture as an agreement. "Great." He touched the brim of his hat. "I'll see you then." He turned and strode away.

SEPTEMBER 1896

Nellie's was the only eating establishment in Chickadee Creek. At one time there'd been a restaurant in the hotel, but the hotel was destroyed in a fire in 1889 and never rebuilt. By that time, there wasn't the same need for a hotel as in the early years. Visitors to Chickadee Creek had the option of a couple of boardinghouses, and that seemed to be enough. Preston had stayed in one of the boardinghouses when he first arrived in town, and he ate quite a few meals at Nellie's at the time. After Sarah Mason hired a cook, soon after her own employment, there'd been no need to return to Nellie's. He hoped he'd made the right choice to bring Cora there on that Friday night. Not that there were any other options.

Preston opened the door and stepped out of the way, allowing Cora to enter before him. She gave him a hesitant smile as she moved inside.

It was crazy, he thought, how many months he'd allowed to pass before he tried to make tonight happen. An evening with Cora had been on his mind ever since that day he heard her play the violin up on that forest trail. Why hadn't he acted sooner?

The answer was obvious, especially when he was seated across from her at this table. Her sophistication couldn't be disguised by a simple white blouse and dark-blue skirt.

Preston had lived a rough-and-tumble existence in his earlier years. More often than not, he'd lived hand to mouth. He had less schooling than some of the children in her classes. Yes, he was the richest man in Chickadee Creek, but he'd inherited the money through no virtue or effort of his own.

Cora Anderson, on the other hand, came from privilege. It was evident in the cultured way she talked—both the tone of her voice and her vocabulary. In her elegant posture when standing and the way she seemed to glide when she walked. In the amazing way she played her violin. He would even swear it was found in her delicate smile. At the same time, she never looked down her nose at him or anyone else in Chickadee Creek. She fit into this community as if born to it.

She's too good for the likes of me, but that won't stop me from trying.

"Do you dine here often?" Cora asked into the lengthening silence.

"No." His voice cracked on the single word. He cleared his throat. "No. One of the first things Sarah did when I made her my housekeeper was to hire a cook. Although I haven't been at home much over the summer. I'm working most days at the dredger, and it's easier to stay up there at night. We—the men and I—have made a good camp. I've lived in worse, that's for certain."

"I know they're all thankful for the employment."

"And I'm glad to have them. I've got good men working for me."

The waitress came to take their orders, and Preston was thankful for the interruption. He didn't want to talk about the dredger or the amount of gold they'd found. Especially since it wasn't as much as he'd expected.

After the waitress left, Preston leaned forward. "Miss Anderson, I didn't bring you here to talk about mining. I'd much rather talk about you."

"About me? I'm afraid that isn't a very interesting topic." Her color heightened, and she lowered her gaze to the checkered tablecloth.

"I'm sure you're wrong about that."

She didn't answer, didn't look up again. Still, he saw her discomfort in the set of her shoulders and the way her fingertips played with the white cloth napkin on the table. Making her uncomfortable hadn't been his intent. He wanted to know her better. But he didn't want that to come at a cost to her.

He leaned back, hoping the extra space would soothe her. "Then tell me about that violin of yours."

At this, her gaze lifted.

"Tell me how old you were when you learned to play."

She took a breath. "I was twelve when I took my first lesson. I learned the piano before that, but then I attended a concert and heard the violin played as I'd never heard it before." A look of joy brightened her eyes. "From that moment, I talked of almost nothing else. I pestered my parents unmercifully." As quickly as it had come, the look of joy vanished.

Preston wondered what had driven Cora from her home, why she'd needed to escape. What had made her feel a captive? He leaned forward again. "What was the song I heard you playing that day in the forest?"

She thought for a moment, then answered, "A piece from Tchaikovsky. His violin concerto. It's one of my favorites."

"I think I knew it was a favorite from listening as you played."

The blush returned to her cheeks. "Thank you, Mr. Chandler. You're most kind."

"I'd like to hear you play it again sometime. If you'd let me."

She gave her head the slightest shake.

"Others in town would like it too. Before you refuse, please consider it. Maybe talk to Sarah Mason before you make up your mind. I've found she gives sound advice."

Her eyes narrowed as she looked at him. "Mr. Chandler, I suspect you are a good businessman."

"Why's that?"

She laughed softly. "You are a shrewd negotiator."

Chapter 15

*D*elicious odors wafted from the grill on the back deck of the house when Chipper announced the arrival of Liam's guests. After wiping his hands on a towel, he headed around to the driveway in time to watch both women get out of the car. But he had eyes only for the driver.

Chelsea's hair was captured in a messy bun, revealing the slender length of her neck. She wore peach-colored shorts, a matching summer top, and flip-flops on her feet. *Adorable* was the word that sprang to mind. When their gazes met, she sent him a quick smile before she hurried around the car to join her great-aunt, the two of them then following the stone walkway that led to the back.

Liam met them halfway and took hold of Rosemary's other arm. As soon as he did so, Chelsea fell back behind them.

"I don't need much help these days," Rosemary said.

He nodded but didn't release his grip. "Don't want you tripping over one of those uneven stones. Better safe than sorry. You've already had a fall. Don't want a repeat."

"True enough." She patted his hand. "Thanks."

Liam and Rosemary made their way onto the deck, Chelsea in their wake. Once Rosemary was comfortably seated, Liam asked what they wanted to drink, then went to fulfill their requests. He was back in short order.

"Thanks for accepting my invitation." He gave the older woman her beverage. "I know it was last minute, but I'm getting tired of my own company."

There was something in the way Rosemary looked at him that said she wasn't convinced about his reasoning. And since what he'd said wasn't entirely true, he couldn't be surprised she saw through his excuse.

Liam cleared his throat. "The food will be ready in about ten minutes."

"Why don't you give Chelsea a tour of your house?" the older woman said. "I'm sure she'd love to see it, and then she can tell me, and I can satisfy all of my curious friends who are dying to know what it looks like inside."

Liam glanced at Chelsea. "Maybe it'd be better if we wait until after we eat. I'd hate to burn our dinner because we got distracted while I showed you around inside."

"Good idea," she answered with another of her brief smiles.

In truth, Liam was already distracted. He'd been distracted for the past twenty-four-plus hours. Ever since he'd thought about asking Chelsea to take care of Chipper if he had to travel. He hadn't slept worth beans last night. He hadn't heard much of the sermon that morning at church. And even now, despite what he said, he was in danger of forgetting to check the food before it turned to charcoal.

Giving himself a mental shake, he stepped to the grill and opened it.

"Need help?" Chelsea appeared at his side with a large platter in one hand and tongs in the other. Both had been on the nearby table moments before.

"Thanks." He took the items from her.

Fortunately for all, the meat and vegetables were cooked to perfection. It didn't take long for the food to settle in the center of the table, including the salad fixings from the refrigerator. And after a word of thanks, they began to eat.

Chelsea remembered Liam telling her that he'd built his house thinking it would be for hunting trips or brief getaway retreats between films. By design, it reminded her of a mountain lodge with its spacious floor plan, high ceilings, and open beams. She could also see that no expense had been spared, from the top-of-the-line appliances in the kitchen to the rustic decorations throughout the house.

"I have to ask," Chelsea said as she stood in the center of the master bedroom. "Did you hire a decorator, or do you think like this?"

He laughed at the question. After he brought his amusement under control, he answered, "Hired a decorator. If it was up to me, I'd have a TV and a leather recliner downstairs, my bed and nightstand in here, and not much else. There probably wouldn't even be anything hanging on the walls." He let his gaze roam the room as if to remind himself what *was* hanging on the walls.

It was a good time for Chelsea to do some reminding of her own. She needed to remember their differences—and there were plenty of them. She preferred to stay hidden in the shadows, while he was famous, although the good people of Chickadee Creek pretended otherwise, respecting his desire for privacy. He was wealthy, while she'd never had much in the way of money. She'd never been a homeowner, while he owned homes in California and Idaho. In fact, she felt lucky to own a car.

On the desk in front of a large window, she saw a Bible and an open, spiral-bound book with lined pages filled with writing in blue ink. Something told her the latter was Liam's personal journal. If so, those two items on his desk represented something they did have in common. Faith and a determination to remember what God had done in their lives. Perhaps their differences weren't too great to overcome.

"Nice view, isn't it?" Liam asked.

She glanced at him, glad that he'd thought her only interested in the scenery beyond the window. "Beautiful. I've always felt at home in the forest."

"Me too." He moved to the window, looking out. "Don't get me wrong. I love the ocean, and I can't complain about the weather in California. But this? This is home for me." He looked down. A moment later, he closed the journal and set the Bible on top of it.

Had he guessed what had drawn her attention? She hoped not. "Maybe we should go back. Aunt Rosemary must think we got lost by now." She headed for the door.

"Before we do . . ."

His words stopped her, drew her around again.

"I wanted to ask a favor."

"Of course. If I can."

"There's a chance I might start a new film in the near future. Not sure when. My agent's setting up a meeting with the director."

The news made her breath catch. Not that she was surprised. Only that she disliked his going. Dreaded it. Despite everything.

"Anyway, if it all works out"—his gaze dropped to the dog now seated at his side—"I'm not sure what to do about Chipper."

"You don't want to take him with you?" Had she misread him? Would he abandon his dog when he returned to California? Was he that kind of man?

"Sure, I'd like to take him. But I'm not sure he'd enjoy being shut up in a crate while we fly back and forth. I'd rather he'd be able to stay with people who care about him when I'm away."

When I'm away. His words echoed in her heart, easing some of the tension. He didn't mean to abandon Chipper. She hadn't misread him.

"What I was hoping is that you might agree to keep him when I'm gone. You're good with him, and he likes you. It's a lot to ask. If I get the part, I might be gone for weeks at a time before I could fly home for a quick break. I don't know anything about where the filming will be done or how long a shoot they expect it to be. It could be on location in the South, which would make it even harder to fly home on a regular basis."

She lifted a hand to let him know he didn't have to convince her. "I'll be glad to keep Chipper when you're away."

"Maybe you'd better check with Rosemary first." He took a step toward her. "Chipper kind of takes over a house."

"I'll check, but I already know what her answer will be."

As if understanding what had transpired, the dog got up and trotted to Chelsea's side, bumping her leg with his muzzle, then sat, pressing tight against her.

"You know," Liam said dryly, "I've got a feeling I'm not going to be missed. At least not much."

Looking down, Chelsea stroked Chipper's head. "Time will tell. Huh, boy?"

But she knew, even if the dog didn't miss Liam, she would.

For the first time in a long while, I'm liking the thought of making another film. Nothing is for certain, but the chances are good. And just as this comes up, I find myself thinking more and more about Chelsea Spencer than anything else.

How crazy is that?

If Jacob were here, he'd have a good laugh at my expense. He wanted me to make movies with more depth, and it looks like that's what this film will be. But he also wanted me to find somebody to love. I don't know if that's what I'm feeling for Chelsea. Something close to it, I think. Or the start of it.

Why'd they both have to come up at the same time? I'm thinking one might cost me the other if I'm not careful. And I'm not sure what I'd hate most to lose.

Liam's Journal

Talked to Dad. Told him I knew about Mom. He said there was more to it that he thought I should know.

More than Mom having an affair? If there's more than that, I don't think I want to know. Seems like plenty already.

We're told the truth will set us free. I've wondered if, the way most people use it, that verse from the Bible is taken out of context. Does the truth <u>always</u> set us free? I need to do a study on that. Figure it out. Because it seems to me some truths imprison people. Maybe that's their own fault. Maybe it's a mistaken truth.

Right now, the truth about Mom that I already know feels like it's weighing me down, not setting me free. How will the next round of truth leave me feeling?

Chapter 16

There were directors whom actors worked with, knowing the films would be great but the experience would be somewhat less so. Grayson Wentworth wasn't one of those directors. All reports were that his films were great *and* he was terrific to work with. Meeting him in person the following Friday, Liam could see why the reports were all positive.

In his fifties with a laid-back demeanor, Grayson had a kind of easy charm. He answered Liam's questions about the script without any sign of holding back or wanting to keep information to himself. He made it clear that, yes, he did want Liam in the starring role. He mentioned details from several of Liam's past films, praising him in some areas and telling him how he would have done other things differently if he'd directed the scenes. But even in that, he didn't seem to be criticizing the actual director. It was merely an exchange of creative ideas.

After a couple of hours on Liam's front deck—Chipper moving between actor, agent, and director for attention—Grayson got up, stretched, and asked if Liam would show him around Chickadee Creek.

"Not a whole lot to see. You probably noticed that on your way through town."

"Must be something worth seeing if this is where you plan to live year-round."

Chelsea's image popped into Liam's head, but he forced himself to think of other reasons for his choice. "My family roots go back in these mountains for more than a hundred and fifty years. I didn't give much thought to it when I first built this house. I like the mountains, and when I was a kid, this was where we came a lot. But I've gained an interest in the Chandler family history since staying here. Been doing some research on the internet, reading books and old newspapers. I've had help from some of the locals too." Again he thought of Chelsea, this time picturing her inside the old antique store.

"Intriguing," Grayson said, interest in his eyes.

"The woman who owns the general store in town thinks I should write a book about Chickadee Creek."

"Who knows? Maybe you will." Grayson's eyebrows lifted. "Or a movie script. Was one of your ancestors an outlaw? Could be a good story there."

Liam chuckled as he shook his head. "Nothing as colorful as that. At least not that I've come across."

"Well, let's have a look at Chickadee Creek. One never knows where a story awaits."

Kurt stood, his phone in hand. "You two go on without me. I've got some messages I need to reply to and a couple of phone calls to make."

"Okay. I'll leave Chipper with you, then."

Kurt motioned agreement with his hand before turning toward the front door, already typing something on his phone.

Before heading into town, Liam drove his pickup along a narrow road to the location of the old dredger. The dredger itself was long gone, but evidence of its one-time presence remained along the banks of the stream.

"From what I can tell," Liam told Grayson as they stood beside the truck a short while later, "dredging made a mess of the surrounding terrain. You can't see it as much anymore. It's mostly overgrown. But there are still signs." He pointed to some large piles of rocks and gravel. "Owen Chandler, the first Chandler to come to the Boise Basin, made his fortune while there were plenty of gold nuggets in these streams. Easy pickin's, as they say. Preston Chandler was my great-great-grandfather. He inherited the land and money from his cousin Owen. He wasn't anywhere near as successful with dredge mining, but he diversified and did well through investments as well as in sheep ranching and logging."

Grayson walked around the level parking area, looking at the remains of an old building, a battered container up against a rock wall, and the mountain rising sharply to their right. "People move around in the modern world. Families don't stay in one place. They lose their roots. It's something that your family stayed in Chickadee Creek for a century and a half."

Liam motioned with his head, and the two men got into the pickup before Liam corrected Grayson's assumption. "We've owned land in Chickadee Creek all these years, but I'm the first Chandler to live up here since my grandparents moved to Boise about fifty years ago. My mom and dad had a vacation cabin up here, but the old Chandler mansion was torn down in the late seventies."

"A mansion, huh?"

"I've got copies of the floor plan back at my house. It was definitely big." As he turned the truck in the direction of town, he added, "I'll take you to the site now. I recently bought the property from my dad. I've even thought about building a resort on it."

"A resort?"

Liam shrugged. He couldn't share details, even if he wanted to. The idea was too new to him.

Grayson chuckled. "You really don't mean to return to LA to live, do you?"

"Not full time. I may keep a place to stay, for when I'm filming on a lot. At least for now. I guess I'll see how it goes."

"If this film turns out the way I think it will, Liam, your career is about to change dramatically. You'll be in more demand than ever." Another pause, then, "Are you ready for it?"

Liam didn't answer at once. He mulled the question around in his mind. *Am I ready for it, Lord?* He was convinced one reason God had brought him to Chickadee Creek was so he could get his life back on track, so he could learn to put first things first. For many months, he hadn't been sure he would ever go back to acting, but God had nudged him about Grayson Wentworth's film. He'd felt the Lord open that door and gently push him to go through it.

"Yes," he answered at last, "I think I'm ready for whatever comes. But for now, I'll focus on this one film and not what the future'll bring."

"Kurt said you were levelheaded."

He laughed softly. "Sometimes."

"Aunt Rosemary? Look at this." Heart racing, Chelsea stared at the sheet music in her hand. The paper was yellowed with age, a little wrinkled, and torn on the edges in a couple of places. But the print itself was still easy to read.

"What is it, Chelsea?"

She stood and walked to her great-aunt, seated in her chair near the shop window.

Aunt Rosemary waved a fan in front of her face. "It's so hot today," she said as Chelsea drew closer. "We should close the shop and go home. No one is going to want to purchase anything today. Tourists have all gone to seek relief in the water somewhere, and our neighbors have more sense than to come shopping on a day like this."

Chelsea knelt beside her great-aunt.

"What do you have there?"

"It's some old sheet music. Published in 1936. It's called *Freedom's Sonata*. But look who wrote it." She placed her finger beneath the name near the title.

"I don't believe it. Cora Chandler." Aunt Rosemary looked up to meet Chelsea's gaze. "I had no idea she composed anything. I'm not musical myself. Can't look at the notes written on a piece of paper and hear it in my head like some folks can. Can you?"

"Maybe a little, but not really. Not something this complex."

"I'd like to hear it. Who do you suppose we should call?"

Chelsea frowned in thought. "Karen Bishop gives piano lessons."

"Yes, I'm sure Karen could play it if we asked. No. Wait!" Aunt Rosemary's face glowed with delight. "Cora played the violin. We should get Anne McNalley to play it for us on your violin. On *Cora's* violin." She clapped her hands once. "I'll go with you to your lesson next week."

Chelsea felt her own excitement increase. "That's a great idea. Although maybe Anne would like to practice the piece before she plays it for us."

"Could be. But she's very talented. I'll bet she can play it well enough we'd get the gist of it."

Chelsea sank back on her haunches and rested the sheet music on her thighs. She wasn't sure she wanted to "get the gist" of the melody. She would rather hear it the way Cora intended, the way she must have heard it in her own head when she composed it.

"*Freedom's Sonata*," she read softly before looking up again. "Why do you suppose she called it that?"

"Have no idea. But it's intriguing, isn't it? Maybe it'd be worth going back through some of the history books to try to figure out." Her great-aunt leaned to the side, looking down toward the sheet music in Chelsea's lap. "Although I'm much more curious about that composition. Why haven't I heard anything about it before? Was that the only song she wrote and published? Do others know about this, or has it been forgotten over time?" She shook her head as she clucked her tongue. "Heaven knows what else might be in this old shop. A valuable violin. Now that sheet music. Gracious. I've got no business running an antique store. I don't even know what I've got to sell."

Rising to her knees again, Chelsea kissed the older woman's cheek. "I'm glad you have the shop, Aunt Rosemary. It's like a daily treasure hunt." She got to her feet. "Maybe I should call Liam. He'd be interested in seeing this."

"I'm sure he would."

She didn't turn around to look at her great-aunt, but something told her neither one of them was fooled by her reason to want to call Liam. He hadn't been far from her thoughts since the barbecue on Sunday. She thought of him when she awakened each morning. She thought of him when she crawled into bed each night. She thought of him as she sorted through old books and emptied more boxes at the shop.

Today was the day the Hollywood director was coming to Chickadee Creek. Liam had told her so when he and Chipper stopped by the shop on Tuesday. "I'll pray about the meeting," she'd promised him. She'd kept the promise, although her heart wasn't entirely in those prayers, knowing she could be praying for something that would take Liam away from her for good.

DECEMBER 1896

Everybody in Chickadee Creek seemed to expect an engagement between Preston Chandler and Cora Anderson to be announced soon. The two of them had been seen out walking together when the weather was nice, dining together at Nellie's on most Friday or Saturday nights, and sitting together at church for the past eight Sundays.

But unlike her friends and neighbors, Cora didn't know what she expected. With Preston's earnest demeanor and easy disposition, he'd slowly but surely wormed his way past her defenses, past her insecurities, past her determination to remain unentangled. He wasn't anything like her father or the men who'd called upon her in New York. While he had wealth, he didn't shy away from hard work. Although he'd never gone far in school, he educated himself through reading and taking his questions to men with answers. She enjoyed the time she spent in his company, and she believed he felt the same about her. But neither of them had spoken about anything more than friendship between them. Certainly he'd never used the word *love*. Nor had he mentioned a desire to marry.

And wasn't that the way she wanted it?

"You're lost in thought," Sarah said as the two women sat near the fire in their comfy home.

Cora looked at her friend. "Did you know Mr. Chandler asked me to play for his party guests next week?"

"No, I didn't. Did you agree?"

"I haven't decided. I . . . It's been a long time since I've played for others. I'm not sure I want to."

"Why is that, Cora? I've never understood your reluctance. It's obvious you love the violin."

Besides Preston, Sarah was the only person in Chickadee Creek who'd heard Cora play, and that—the same as with Preston—had been by accident.

"You have an amazing gift," Sarah added, her gaze dropping to the yarn in her lap.

Cora frowned. Sarah was more than her landlady, even more than her friend. She was a mentor, an encourager, someone to be held in esteem. Cora knew she could talk to the woman about anything, and yet she remained tight-lipped about her past, about her family, about her reasons for fleeing her father's home. Could she truly be Sarah's friend if she didn't share that secret part of herself?

"You don't have to tell me, Cora."

She drew in a breath. "No, I should tell you. There isn't any reason I shouldn't. It's only . . . It's difficult to talk about. I've kept it inside for so long."

Sarah nodded, not looking up from her knitting.

"I haven't wanted to play my violin where anyone might hear me because . . . because . . . Well, I think I became superstitious about it. As if not playing has protected me, kept me safe."

This admission drew Sarah's gaze.

Speaking slowly at first, Cora told the story of her family, of her mother's detachment, of what her father expected of her, of the man she was supposed to marry with no care for her own feelings about it. She shared about her sudden decision to escape, about her fearful journey by train, always wondering if the next stop would be where a hireling or business associate of Aaron Anderson would take hold of her arm and drag her back to New York, to a way of life she detested. Once started, the words poured out of her. She held nothing back, not stopping until she came to the day of her arrival in Chickadee Creek. Then she fell silent.

For a long while, the only sounds in the room were the crackling of the fire, the soft creak of Sarah's rocking chair, and the click of knitting needles.

But at last, Sarah stilled and looked at Cora. "May I ask you something?"

"Of course," she answered, although she couldn't think what else she might reveal.

"Do you believe the good Lord guides your steps?"

"Yes." She spoke with a confidence she hadn't felt two years ago.

"Then it seems to me you have a choice. You must choose

between superstition and faith. You can't have both. You can choose one or the other."

Cora frowned. Superstition or faith. One or the other. The choice was hers.

The choice is mine. She felt a quickening in her heart, a new understanding of how God wanted her to live. In faith, not in fear.

She would make the right choice.

DECEMBER 1896

Preston often felt as if he rattled around in the enormous Chandler house. Rarely did he have visitors in his home. He saw Sarah Mason most days on his return from the mining office, and he often saw the cook long enough to thank her for his supper. He'd never laid eyes on the maid, but since the house was kept clean, he knew she came in to do her work, overseen by Sarah.

But on this Christmas Eve, the house almost burst at its seams. Guests sat or stood in the hall, the reception room, the parlor, and the dining room. He'd even seen a few men gathered in the library. He wouldn't be surprised if more guests had made it up the stairs to check out the bedchambers and bathing room on the second floor.

Not that he cared where anyone went. His attention was focused on Cora Anderson.

For months now, he'd felt himself falling in love with her, little by little. He'd tried to resist the feelings, for a number of sound reasons. For one, the dredging hadn't gone as well as he'd hoped. Buying the dredger and having it shipped to Chickadee Creek had been a huge expense, and thus far it hadn't paid for itself. He wasn't sure it would ever pay for itself. What if he kept losing money? Could he ask a woman like Cora to take a risk?

Of course, if he'd wanted to resist falling in love with her, he wouldn't have sought her out on so many different occasions. Losing his heart was his own fault.

Cora moved to the side of the large fireplace, holding the violin with one hand and the bow with the other. She wore a gown of gold. He imagined she'd worn it to much more glittering affairs than this local Christmas party, and he suspected that, two years ago, it would have been accented by precious jewels around her delicate throat and wrists. But she seemed to sparkle without diamonds or emeralds or topaz.

When Preston had asked her to play tonight, he hadn't thought she would agree. He imagined he had Sarah to thank for it.

Cora lifted the instrument, bracing the end of it with her chin. Because of the nature of the evening and the layout of the house, Preston had told her to simply begin to play, without any kind of announcement. "Let the music draw their attention," he'd said. "I guarantee it will."

And so it did. She started with "Joy to the World" before moving into "O Come, All Ye Faithful." By the time she was finished with the second song, the house had fallen silent. Guests had filled the parlor, and those who couldn't get into the room crowded closer to the doorways.

Cora glanced Preston's way, perhaps wondering if she should continue. He smiled and nodded.

She lifted the bow again, closed her eyes, and played the first notes of "Silent Night." The music was totally pure, completely beautiful.

And Preston knew he would never be the same after that night.

DECEMBER 1896

Two days after Christmas, Cora stared at the headline on the second page of the *Chickadee Press*, reading it for the third time, trying to make it say something else or to disappear entirely:

LOCAL WOMAN ASTOUNDS
GUESTS ON CHRISTMAS EVE

She closed her eyes.

Please, God. Please, no.

She drew a slow, deep breath, opened her eyes again, and read the brief article beneath the headline.

Cora Anderson, the schoolteacher in Chickadee Creek, played her violin for the guests of Preston Chandler at his Christmas gathering earlier this week. Everyone present that evening was amazed by the quality of the performance, no one more so than this reporter.

Miss Anderson came to our fair town in the autumn of last year, and she has become a valued member of our community. But no one seems to have known that she is accomplished not simply in teaching children reading, writing, and arithmetic but also is a virtuoso of the first order on the violin.

Cora sucked in another breath and read the two paragraphs again. When she was done, she set the newspaper aside and closed her eyes once more.

It's a small newspaper. It only matters to the residents of this community. No one else will see it. Father will never know about it. His spies won't look here.

All these months, for more than a year and a half, she'd been careful to remain hidden, inconspicuous. And then she'd risked everything because she wanted to play her violin for others. No. No, it was more than that. She'd done it to please Preston. She'd done it because he asked her to play.

Would her father find her because she'd lost her heart to Preston Chandler?

Chapter 17

C helsea waited until the next morning to call Liam about the sheet music. She got his answering machine but didn't leave a message. For all she knew he was still with his agent and the director.

Feeling restless, she went for a walk, wanting to beat the heat. At first her thoughts were jumbled, her emotions warring with her better judgment. Finally, deep in the forest, she settled onto a log and tried to sort through her feelings about Liam Chandler.

How could she dread the departure of a man who'd never asked her out on a date, never held her hand, never kissed her? Was there any reason to think he was interested in her beyond a casual acquaintance and perhaps as someone who shared an interest in the history of Chickadee Creek? Not really. And yet . . . And yet there was something between the two of them, something that had grown over the weeks since they'd met. She felt it, and she couldn't help but hope he felt it too.

A chipmunk scolded her from the limbs of a nearby tree, and smiling, she looked in its direction.

One summer, Chelsea and her sister Evelyn had managed to trap a couple of chipmunks. Ben and Jerry, they'd named them, after the ice-cream magnates. They kept them in an old cage discovered weeks earlier in the trash bin behind a car repair shop in Hadley Station. There was no telling what had lived in the cage before the two little girls found it.

They didn't have to ask to know their father wouldn't approve of them trying to make pets of a couple of chipmunks, so they hid the cage inside a large forsythia bush at the back of their yard. For several weeks, they snuck nuts and fruit to the forest rodents at different times of day, and they kept the small water dish filled. But one morning, they discovered an empty and mangled cage—perhaps destroyed by a bear, perhaps by their father. The chipmunks were nowhere in sight.

Tearfully, Evelyn had asked, "Do you think they got away?"

Chelsea had nodded, but she hadn't been all that sure.

Now she looked at the scolding chipmunk and asked, "You wouldn't happen to be Ben or Jerry, would you?"

The little guy sat up on his hind legs, front legs folded, and stared right back, refusing to give a reply.

She rose from the log. "Thanks for the distraction anyway."

He chirped at her.

"You must be Ben, the chatty one."

He scampered up the tree, disappearing in an instant.

Strange how much better she felt. Nothing in her thinking had changed. She hadn't hit upon any answers. Nonetheless, her spirits felt lighter as she continued on.

Half an hour later, she was on Chandler Road, headed into Chickadee Creek, when she saw Liam's truck parked at the old mansion site. Her pulse skittered as her eyes searched the grounds for Liam himself. There was no sign of him. She wondered where he could be.

At that moment, Chipper burst from the trees at the far end of the property and raced in her direction. She stopped walking to await his arrival. Laughter bubbled up inside of her at the dog's exuberant greeting, as if they were long-lost friends.

"Chelsea!"

She straightened to see Liam standing beside a large, old shed that leaned to one side.

He motioned for her to join him. "Come have a look."

She couldn't imagine what was worth seeing, but her heart delighted in being asked. She walked in his direction, Chipper running on ahead of her.

"You'll never guess what I found," Liam said as she drew closer. "There's a concrete fruit cellar at the back of this shed."

The discovery didn't seem worth the excitement he exhibited.

"There are wooden crates filled with stuff down there."

"Stuff?"

"I don't know what all. Books. Dishes. Junk. Could all be ruined by this time, but stored in a cool, dry cellar, maybe it's okay. Come have a look."

She eyed the leaning shed. "Doesn't look safe to me."

"It's been like this for as long as I can remember, and it hasn't come down yet. Not even in the worst windstorms. It should be okay." He held out an arm toward her. "Come on. Have a look."

She would much prefer to wait until the crates were brought out into the daylight, but she found it hard to resist Liam when he looked at her that way. Mesmerizing.

His hand closed around hers. She hadn't realized she'd extended her arm until that happened.

He drew her inside the dilapidated shed. Dust hung in the air, as if no breeze had reached the interior in years. Untrue, for light came through where slats were broken off or missing altogether. Straw still covered parts of the earthen floor. A wheelbarrow, lacking its wheel, sat tipped against a sawhorse. A hemp rope hung from a beam, the ends frayed. Two halters, the leather worn, clung to nails in the wall.

"The cellar's back there." Liam pointed toward a dark corner. "I'm surprised kids didn't break in and haul the boxes off long ago. Or at least break them open to see what was inside."

"Probably nobody expected to find anything in here except a worthless wheelbarrow. You don't see the cellar from the doorway."

He drew her closer to the steps. The concrete seemed out of place in the shed, and the open door at the bottom showed nothing but pitch black beyond.

"There are a few photos in one of those books I got from you that give a glimpse of this shed when the estate was in its heyday. Off to that side was a large vegetable garden and some fruit trees too. But from the house and the formal gardens, the shed was entirely hidden from view by the flowers and vines. A genius design."

"Genius," she echoed, despite feeling the need to get back outside in the fresh air and daylight.

Liam switched on a flashlight. "There's at least a dozen crates." He went down one step. "They must have been there since at least the seventies. Maybe longer." He looked back, as if expecting her to follow him.

Recognizing the fear rising within, Chelsea shook her head.

"You don't want to see the crates?"

"Not down there." The words came out a whisper, her throat too tight for more.

Her pulse raced in her ears. Her lungs seemed incapable of drawing a deep breath. She spun on her heel and hurried outside, not stopping until she reached an open space flooded with sunshine. There, she tipped back her head so she could feel the warmth of the sun on her face. She drew a deep breath in through her nose and blew it out her mouth. One, then another, then another, until the world began to right itself.

Liam stuffed his fingertips into the back pockets of his jeans. He wanted to go to Chelsea, take her in his arms, and protect her from the terror he'd caught sight of a moment before she bolted. But instinct told him to stay back, to wait it out.

He remembered that day by the highway, when she'd said she didn't like to be weak. The panic that had overtaken her then had disappeared almost as fast as it came. Which, he supposed, was why he hadn't thought of it again. Until now. Until he saw her, standing in the sunlight, fighting for control.

Perhaps sensing him watching her, she turned.

"Are you all right?" he asked.

She nodded.

He took a couple of steps toward her. "Sorry for back there. I had no idea—"

"Small, dark places frighten me."

"You're claustrophobic."

She nodded again, her shoulders rising and falling on another deep breath. Then, in a voice almost too soft to hear, she said, "It was my father's favorite punishment for me."

Liam frowned, the words making no sense to him.

"When I disobeyed, he locked me in a closet. Sometimes for hours."

Cold fingers seemed to squeeze his heart as he imagined a little girl, curled in a corner in the dark, waiting for release.

Chelsea looked up at the sky again. "I'm okay most of the time. I don't have panic attacks very often. Not anymore."

It took Liam a moment to realize how very little he knew about her life before she'd come to Chickadee Creek. He knew her father was dead. He knew she had younger siblings but wasn't sure how many. A sister was closest to her age. He knew she'd grown up in the panhandle of Idaho and had moved to Spokane as a young adult. He knew she loved her Aunt Rosemary and that she also loved God. And now he knew why she feared small, dark places. But he knew little else. Why was that? Especially since he liked her so much. Had his Hollywood years made him completely self-absorbed? Did he only want to talk about himself, and he liked her because she was willing to listen to him? The questions made his gut knot. If that was true, there wasn't much about him to like.

As if she knew his thoughts, Chelsea said, "I never talk about it."

"The claustrophobia?"

"My family. My past. All of it. I avoid it."

Her words made him feel a little better about himself. But only a little.

The hint of a smile touched the corners of her mouth. "I learned a lot of self-talk over the years. Ways to remind myself that I would be okay, that I had plenty of air, that I wouldn't suffocate. And now I'm learning to lean into God and let His Word bring me out of the fear." She paused, her gaze unwavering.

"'For God has not given us a spirit of timidity, but of power and love and discipline.' Do you remember quoting that to me?"

"Yes. I remember."

"It helped, you know. In the last few weeks, I've made it a point to memorize more verses from the Bible. It beats self-talk because there's real power in it. It's living and active. Right?"

The urge to hold her close swept over him again. Instead he answered, "Right."

"I almost forgot." The expression on her face changed to one of excitement. "I have something to share with you. I found something of Cora's yesterday."

"Another violin?"

"No." Her smile blossomed. "Some sheet music. Music that Cora wrote. You must come over to the shop and see it for yourself."

He could fall in love with Chelsea Spencer, he thought as he moved toward her. It would be as easy as falling off a log.

— *Liam's Journal* —

It looks like I'll be doing the Wentworth film. Details still to be worked out, but I've read enough of the script to know I want this part. I want it bad. Jacob would love it. Wish I could tell him about it. Wish we could sit together in the basement family room and hash over all the possibilities for the role.

Filming will be on location. Oklahoma or Texas. Which means I'll be gone from Idaho for weeks at a time. Maybe as many as eight. That's Grayson's guess.

I need to talk to Mom before I go. She's left a couple of messages that I've ignored. I can't go on doing that. It's tempting to leave it that way until I'm back from location, months from now. I'd rather not tell her I'll be going away. But I can't do that either.

I remembered something Jacob said to me, not long before he died. He said there's doing what's easy and there's doing what's right. I need to choose what's right.

Liam's Journal

The script is even more amazing than I thought at first. I finished reading the draft Grayson left with me. He said there are changes to be made, but even if there wasn't a single line altered, I'd be impressed.

And the part I'm to play—the husband and dad, fighting for his land, fighting for his family . . . I only hope I'll do it justice.

Jacob would love this. If this sort of thing matters in heaven, I hope God will tell my brother about it.

Chapter 18

C helsea's pulse sped up again, but it wasn't fear that caused it this time. It was the way Liam looked at her as he drew closer. Her breath caught in her throat. Did she want to run to him or away from him?

He must have seen her uncertainty. He stopped, then said, "Let's walk to the shop. To see the sheet music. I'll come back for my truck later."

"All right."

She half expected him to reach for her hand. He didn't.

"So tell me about this new find of yours." They fell into step, walking across the mansion grounds to the road. "You said Cora Chandler wrote it. Do you mean it's something written in her hand?"

"No. It's published. The copyright date says 1936, and the piece is called *Freedom's Sonata*."

"Have you played it on your violin?"

"Me? No." She laughed. "An off-key 'Twinkle, Twinkle, Little Star' is more my speed at this point. But I called my instructor, and she's going to play it for me and Aunt Rosemary at my next lesson."

"Did she recognize the title?"

"No. And she was surprised it wasn't part of local lore, at the very least."

They paused on the bridge and, in unison, leaned forearms on the rail and looked down at the creek running beneath them. Chipper stuck his head through the boards and barked once, as if to let them know he paid attention.

"Funny, isn't it?" she asked after a while. "The way we try to hide so much about ourselves from the people around us, but we hope we can uncover the truth about people who lived a hundred years ago."

There was a lengthy silence before Liam asked, "What do you try to hide from others, Chelsea?"

The tenderness she heard in his voice made her eyes water.

"Never mind. You don't have to answer me. I shouldn't've asked."

She blinked, then looked over at him. "No. I'd like to answer. But not right now." She straightened from the railing. "Right now, I want to show you Cora's song."

"All right." He smiled. "Let's go."

As they turned toward Alexander Road, she caught a glimpse of a pale-green sedan as it passed out of view. Her heart hiccupped. It was a common reaction to pale-green cars, but not one she'd experienced since coming to Chickadee Creek.

Liam's voice intruded on her thoughts. "Did you check the internet to see if Cora published any other songs?"

"What?" She looked at him. "No. No, I didn't. I should have done that first thing. Now that we know she published something, maybe we'll discover more. We'll do that now."

She quickened her steps. When they reached Alexander

Road, she glanced left before turning to her right. There were no cars in sight, in either direction, green or otherwise.

She drew in a quick breath. What a crazy day! She'd fretted over Liam's leaving town. She'd talked to a chipmunk. She'd let panic overtake her because of a dark fruit cellar. And now she was seeing cars where there weren't any.

When they entered the antique store minutes later, Aunt Rosemary was ringing up a sale on the ancient cash register. Her great-aunt glanced their way, then turned her attention back to the couple—tourists, by the look of them—on the opposite side of the counter. "I hope you'll enjoy your purchase," she said to the woman.

"I know I will. I've been looking for the perfect pie safe for more than a year, but everything I've found has been far too expensive."

"A little love and a bit of polish, and it'll be beautiful again." Aunt Rosemary showed the couple a bright smile.

They turned and left the shop, the pie safe carried between them, the bell ringing as the door closed again.

"You sold the pie safe?" Chelsea asked.

Aunt Rosemary nodded. "Three hundred and fifty dollars. I may just close up shop and relax for the rest of the day." Her gaze took in Liam. "What about you two?"

"Liam's come to see Cora's sheet music." Chelsea started toward the back of the shop.

"Of course he has." Aunt Rosemary laughed softly.

Chelsea was tempted to glance back to see what was funny but decided against it. She suspected her great-aunt might have winked at Liam as he passed by.

Oh, please, no. Not that.

She took a key from behind an unabridged dictionary with a tattered paper cover and unlocked a cabinet that held items not for sale or too valuable to be left out in the open. From a manila folder, she withdrew the four-page sheet music and held it out to Liam, who was by this time standing at her side.

He took it from her, his gaze moving over the artwork on the front. "Looks like one of the forest trails around here."

"I thought the same thing." She pointed. "When I was walking this morning, I sat on a log like that one. Who knows? Maybe the same one."

Liam looked at her, amusement in his eyes. "You know better than that."

"Yes, I know better than that. They decay over time. Weather and termites and all. But it's fun to imagine it *could* be the same log on the same trail."

Liam's expression changed, the amusement gone in an instant. Slowly, he leaned closer. Chelsea's breath caught when she realized what he was about to do. The touch of his lips upon hers was light, almost imperceptible . . . and yet gloriously real. Her heart fluttered as fast as a hummingbird's wings. She couldn't tell if seconds or minutes passed before he drew his head back from hers.

A smile returned to the corners of his mouth. "Were we talking about logs?"

"Or maybe sheet music," she answered in a whisper, her brain struggling to work again.

Silly, really, to feel that way. It wasn't as if she'd never been kissed before. And more than kissed, before she gave her heart to the Lord. Remembering her former way of life, she drew away from Liam.

He gave her a puzzled look.

She took a quick breath, then pointed at the sheet music in his hand, wanting to distract him. "You haven't even looked beyond the cover."

"No." His gaze didn't waver from hers. "I haven't."

She turned her head slightly, glancing toward the counter. Aunt Rosemary had her back toward them, and Chelsea suspected the woman wouldn't have turned around even if a bomb exploded.

"Okay," Liam said. "I'll look." He opened the sheet music. "Lots of notes on a page. I can see why you're excited. No wonder it was published."

She heard both teasing and encouragement in his voice. And it worked. But it also reminded her that she'd promised to open up to him, to share with him the hidden things in her life. That wouldn't be easy, no matter how much she liked him.

It took all of Liam's resolve not to pull Chelsea into his arms and kiss her again. He wanted to prevent her from drawing farther away from him. He wasn't sorry he'd kissed her, and she hadn't resisted him, so he didn't think she objected. But something changed soon after the kiss ended. He didn't know what or why.

Pretending a real interest in the music, he said, "Let's check for more information on the internet."

"Yes. Let's."

When they walked by the counter, Rosemary kept her eyes locked on an open book. Liam suspected her goal was to avoid looking up at either of them. Somehow he knew she was rooting for him to win over her great-niece's heart, and he loved her for it. Someday, if things went well between him and Chelsea, he would tell Rosemary Townsend how he felt at this moment.

The desktop computer was old and ran like a tortoise. It made Liam itch for his top-of-the-line laptop back at his house. But the computer finally managed to connect to the internet, and they were able to browse for more information regarding Cora Anderson Chandler. They didn't find a great deal. Mostly references to books they'd already seen. And they found nothing about her composing music for the violin.

Chelsea released a sigh as she leaned back in the desk chair. "I hoped we'd find something of more interest."

"Not everything makes it onto the internet, I guess."

"Maybe you should write something. She's your great-great-grandmother. You should combine everything you've learned and write a book."

He grinned at the suggestion, especially since it was the very thing he'd told Grace Witherstone he didn't plan to do. "Maybe I will. And maybe you can help me do it. I never claimed to be a writer."

"Neither did I."

"Hey, you two," Rosemary called to them. "I'm hungry. Why don't you go get us some hamburgers and fries from the Hillside Cafe? You can be there and back before you know it."

Chelsea swiveled the chair toward her great-aunt. "We don't need to do that. I can fix something at the house. I was thinking green salads and grilled cheese sandwiches. Liam, would you like to join us?"

He didn't have a chance to answer.

"But what I *want* is a hamburger and fries," Rosemary insisted, a little louder this time. "And one of their yummy chocolate milkshakes." As she finished, her gaze shifted to Liam, and once again he felt the older woman encouraging him. "You can leave Chipper with me."

He stood. "Hamburgers, fries, and a shake. Coming up." He looked at Chelsea. "Ready?"

"Do I have a choice?"

He stilled. "Seriously, yes. You do have a choice." He wasn't sure why he felt the need to tell her that, but he did. "You always have a choice, Chelsea."

Appreciation filled her eyes. *Thank you*, she mouthed as she rose from the chair.

"We'll take my truck. Want to wait here for me to get it?"

"No. I'll walk with you."

"Bye!" Aunt Rosemary called after them.

"I'm sorry you got roped into this," Chelsea said after a short silence.

"There wasn't any roping involved. I'm hungry too."

"For burgers we have to drive miles to get?"

He gave her a quick smile. "It was the milkshake that caught my interest."

"I'll admit, ice cream sounds good on a hot day."

The silence that accompanied the remainder of the walk to his truck was a comfortable one. More like they'd enjoyed before he kissed her. Liam was glad of that, although he still didn't regret the kiss. In fact, he hoped to do it again in the not too distant future.

Chickadee Creek remained quiet. A lazy kind of Saturday. He supposed the temperature was too high for most residents to want to wander far from their homes or businesses. As hot as it was in the mountains, it must be sweltering down in Boise.

When they reached the truck, Liam opened the passenger door for Chelsea, then hurried around to the driver's side and got in. The cab was stifling, and he wasted no time in starting the engine so he could crank up the air conditioner. It didn't take long for the cab to cool off enough that they could close the doors and start on their way.

They met no oncoming traffic as they followed Alexander Road out to the highway, but they did see a couple of young kids playing in the creek, their parents seated on a blanket nearby. The dad waved, and Liam waved back, despite not knowing who it was. It made him feel like he belonged.

At the highway, he made a left and, at fifty miles an hour, arrived at the Hillside Cafe in about ten minutes. Half a dozen cars were in the parking lot, and the outside dining area that overlooked Mores Creek was filled with customers.

"Looks like Aunt Rosemary wasn't the only one with this idea." Laughter filled Chelsea's voice.

"My thoughts exactly." He pulled the truck into a parking spot and turned off the engine.

Chelsea reached for the door handle, then stopped and looked over at him. "What's happening between us, Liam?"

His heart *kerthump*ed.

"Are you leaving Chickadee Creek? You haven't told me what happened with the director yesterday."

"I was going to. I meant to." Liam restarted the engine before the cab got too hot. "I got distracted by the crates in the cellar. Stupid, I guess, since I don't have a clue what's in them. And then we started talking about the sheet music."

She continued as if she hadn't heard him. "Are you going to make the movie?" Her voice dropped a little. "Are you going away?"

"Yes, it looks like I've got the part, although there are still negotiations to be done. And yes, I'll have to go away during filming." He leaned a little to his right, forcing her to meet his gaze. "But I won't be gone for long. I won't be gone forever."

She watched him with a look that said she wanted to have hope, that she wanted to believe him but was afraid. After what she'd told him about her dad, he could understand why, at least partly. She'd been betrayed by someone she should have been able to trust. Her father had failed her. Liam didn't want to do the same.

Slowly, he lifted his left hand to cup the side of her face, keeping his touch light. "Chelsea, this is my home now. I'm coming back. I promise." He smiled to lighten the moment. "After all, you'll have my dog."

She attempted a laugh but failed.

What could he do besides kiss her again?

For a time, the hamburgers, fries, and milkshakes were forgotten.

MARCH 1897

"Miss Anderson."

Emitting a small gasp, Cora turned from the stove, a chunk of wood still in her hand.

Preston closed the door behind him, deepening the shadows

within the schoolroom despite all of the uncovered windows attempting to let in light. "Sorry. I didn't mean to startle you."

"It's all right." She felt flustered. Of late, she always felt flustered around him. She didn't know why. Or didn't *want* to know why.

He took a step forward, at the same time sweeping his hat from his head. The gesture left his dark hair mussed. "There is something of some importance I would like to say to you."

"Yes?" The word sounded paper thin in her ears.

He covered the remaining distance that separated them and took the wood from her hand. After shoving it into the stove, he closed the door, then turned to face her once again. "Perhaps you know what I want to say."

She shook her head. The truth or a lie? She wasn't certain.

"Your friendship means a great deal to me, Cora."

And yours to me, she thought above the rapid beating of her heart.

"And I was wondering . . ." He let his words trail into silence.

She couldn't breathe. She felt her eyes widen. The world seemed to tip beneath her, and she wondered if she would lose her balance.

He smoothed his hair with one hand. "You've told me you left the East because you chose not to marry."

Had she told him that? She'd forgotten. She'd forgotten everything except the way his dark eyes looked at her now and that intriguing lock of hair falling across her forehead above his right eye.

"But I wondered if I might change your mind about that."

Could he change her mind? She was free now. Free to make her own choices. Free to come and go as she pleased. Despite that piece about her in the newspaper in December, no one had come looking for her. No one had found her. She remained free to live her life as she wanted. Whyever would she want to give up her hard-won freedom?

"Because, Miss Anderson, I find that I would very much like to be married to you. It seems you have taken my heart captive, and I cannot imagine a future without you at my side."

In all of the months of their acquaintance, he'd acted the gentleman when with her. But he'd never sounded as stiff and formal as he did now. He was nervous, she realized. As nervous as she was. The discovery allowed her to breathe again, and a smile crept into the corners of her mouth.

Preston cleared his throat. "Did I sound like a fool just then?"

She shook her head, her smile growing.

"Ethan tried to tell me what to say."

That explained a lot.

"Cora." Preston placed his fingertips on her shoulders. "I love you. I adore you. It's as simple as that. Will you marry me?"

Her breath caught again. But this time it wasn't his words that caused it. It was the answer rising in her own heart, a word insisting upon being spoken. "Yes," she whispered.

He drew her into his arms. "Are you sure?"

"Yes."

"I don't know what sort of husband I'll be. I'm not cultured. I'm not educated. But I'll never mistreat you. I'll never let you be in want. I'll always treasure you."

"I know that, Preston."

He stilled. "Cora. May I kiss you?"

"Yes. Please."

He held her chin in the fingers of one hand, tilting her head just enough to give him access to her mouth. When his lips pressed against hers, she felt the world tip on its axis once again, and this time she let herself fall.

Chapter 19

The next day, Chelsea glanced at Liam as he drove north along the highway. "I know a spot," was all he'd told her about their destination. A picnic basket and a cooler rested behind them in the rear seat of the truck, along with Chipper, who had his head poked out a partially open window. Lauren Daigle sang softly through the speakers. It was a favorite song of Chelsea's, one she listened to often.

"Great sermon this morning," Liam said above the music. "I like what Reverend Oswald had to say about old normals being like a tractor beam we need to pull free of."

"'Don't rush back to the old normal.'" As she quoted the pastor's words, she recalled the patterns in her own life, the times she'd returned to the familiar, even when it was bad for her and others, rather than going forward to something new, something that promised to be better. "It's good advice."

It had seemed to Chelsea, when seated in the pew between Aunt Rosemary and Liam, that Vincent Oswald prepared his sermon for her alone, because this was the day she meant to tell Liam her history. She wanted him to know her. Truly know her.

She wanted him to understand who she was and the mistakes she'd made. If she was going to love him—and she thought she was—and if he was going to love her—as she hoped he might—then she couldn't keep secrets from him.

Liam continued, "But not everything old should be jettisoned for the new. When I first went to LA, I didn't hold tight to good things like reading my Bible or being faithful in worship. I didn't act like a Christian in more obvious ways, so it's no surprise that many don't know I'm a believer. Makes me ashamed now. Anyway, I plan to hold those good and important things in a closed hand from now on."

Chelsea hadn't been a follower of Jesus for long. Everything still felt new to her. But she thought she understood what he meant.

"Before he died, Jacob reminded me that nothing we go through is wasted in God's economy. Our hurts. Our mistakes. Even our own stupidity." He released a soft chuckle. "*My* own stupidity. The Lord uses it for my good when I trust Him with it."

"Romans," she said, although she couldn't remember the chapter and verse.

"Eight twenty-eight," he supplied, at the same time pressing on the brake to slow the vehicle.

Chelsea looked out the window as Liam turned the truck onto a one-lane dirt road. It was not much more than a deer track, and the rough going put an end to their conversation. Chelsea reached up to hold the grip, bracing herself to keep from bouncing around like a rag doll.

After about a quarter of a mile or so, the road burst out of the trees. The ground dropped off sharply on the right. More of a cliff than a mountainside. Far below ran a ribbon of water, glittering in the sunlight. On the left, the ground rose just as abruptly. Could even mountain goats climb it?

"Where are you taking me?" she asked above the noise in the cab.

"It'll be worth it. I promise."

Before she could think of a reply, the front right wheel dropped into another rut. Her shoulder struck the door. She gasped as she was jerked the opposite way, although the seatbelt kept her from going too far. She prayed that they would reach their destination soon.

But Liam was right. It *was* worth it.

When the road spilled into a wide-open space after a long, slow descent, the sight took her breath away. The fork of the river she'd looked down upon from a great height at the start of this trek cut through the center of a lush meadow. The long grass, swaying in a breeze, was a mixture of green and pale gold in color. Liam turned the truck off the road and drove to a place in the shade of tall pines.

Cutting the engine, he said, "We made it."

She smiled in answer, then opened the door and dropped to the ground, glad to no longer be bouncing along the road. The melody of the river—wide, shallow, and crystal clear in this place—drew her irresistibly toward its bank. Perhaps it was silly, but she thought the air smelled cleaner than at home. And with the breeze and at this higher altitude, it was definitely cooler than in Chickadee Creek.

"Where are we?" She turned around. "However did you know about this place?"

Liam shrugged. "When Jacob and I were teens, we'd get bored hanging around the cabin, so we'd take off and explore lots of different roads and trails. Most everything around here is national forestland, so it's open to the public year-round. The road we came down is favored by horseback riders in the summer and cross-country skiers in the winter."

"It would be a whole lot less bumpy on horseback than in a truck. Even one as nice as yours."

"Can't argue with that." He leaned down to pet Chipper's head. "I'm hungry. Shall we eat?"

"Yes."

"How about I get things ready while you throw the Frisbee for Chipper? He could use some exercise." He reached into the back seat of the truck and pulled out a fluorescent-orange disk.

Chipper hopped and twirled in anticipation. But instead of letting the Frisbee fly for the dog, Liam tossed it vertically to Chelsea. She caught it, turned, and sent it soaring. As fast as she was, Chipper was faster. He caught it before it hit the ground, then brought it back to her.

"Good dog. Good boy." She ruffled his ears with one hand while taking the disk from his mouth with the other.

About ten minutes later, Liam called, "Chow's on."

Frisbee in mouth, Chipper ran toward Liam as if he knew what the words meant.

But it was Chelsea who held his gaze. He loved the added color in her cheeks, the bright sparkle in her eyes, the long line of her neck. He took all of it in as she approached the blanket he'd spread on the ground. It made him want to kiss her.

But who was he kidding? Everything made him want to kiss

her. Seeing her walk into church that morning had made him want to kiss her. Riding in the truck on the way up here had made him want to kiss her. Watching her throw the Frisbee for Chipper had made him want to kiss her. He'd lain awake for hours last night, remembering the taste of her lips upon his. He longed to taste them again.

"What?" she asked, her eyes narrowing. "Do I have something on my face?" She brushed her fingers across her cheeks, then her chin.

"No." He laughed softly. "I was thinking how pretty you look."

She stilled. "You think I'm pretty?"

"Of course. Because you are."

"But you—" She stopped, then shook her head.

He couldn't know for sure, but he suspected she was comparing herself to various female costars from his films or to the women he'd appeared with in the pages of *People* or *US* or their online counterparts. Comparing and deciding she came up short. She couldn't be more wrong.

He took a step toward her. "I'll never forget when I saw you crossing the road that first day. You carried an old battered pail and a ladder that looked way too big for you. You had on a green top and jean shorts and white sneakers. And your beautiful hair was slicked back in a ponytail. Like it is now."

"You remember all that?"

"I remember all that." He took another step closer.

She tilted her head slightly to one side. "All I remember is your black truck and how it was covered with a thick layer of dust. I didn't recognize you. I'm not sure I looked at you for more than a second."

He laughed. "You aren't very good for my ego."

"Does your ego *need* a boost?"

He sobered. "Humility is a more desired trait."

"I like that you aren't self-absorbed, Mr. Chandler."

"Ditto, Miss Spencer." He motioned toward the blanket behind him. "We'd better eat before Chipper decides to help us out."

He held out his hand toward her, and she took it. It felt as natural as breathing to Liam.

"I went for simple," he told her as they settled on the ground.

"Simple is good."

From the cooler, he took Pyrex containers of cubed watermelon and cantaloupe, fresh strawberries and raspberries, sliced cucumbers and baby carrots, a bottle of ranch dressing, several types of cheese, and several kinds of crackers. There were cans of pink lemonade and bottles of water to wash it all down.

For a while, they were content to concentrate on the food spread before them, but eventually Chelsea broke the silence. "Remember yesterday when you asked me what I try to hide from others?"

"I shouldn't have. It was—"

She shook her head. "No, it's true. I've always kept my feelings hidden. Since I was a little girl. I learned it was better to be invisible whenever possible."

Her words made his heart hurt. "Because of your dad?"

"Yes." The word came out on a breath.

She told him some stories from her childhood. A few were fun, especially ones about her younger siblings. Others were bittersweet. But over everything hung the truth of how hard she'd tried to please the man who emotionally and, all too often, physically abused her. Sometimes with a belt with a large metal buckle. More often in a dark, locked closet.

"After my dad died," she continued, "I got away from Hadley Station. I moved to Spokane and tried to make a new life for myself. My mom and brother and sisters did the same eventually. We had varying degrees of success, I would say." She turned to look at the river and the surrounding mountains.

Liam wanted to hold her, comfort her, but a sixth sense warned him to keep his distance, to let her choose her own way and her own timing.

"And then I met a guy . . . Tom."

She spoke so softly, Liam wasn't sure he'd heard the name right. But that didn't matter. Whoever it was, whatever his name, Liam's heart hardened against him. A long silence followed before she looked his way again. Tears glittered in her eyes, the same way the sunlight glittered off the water flowing past them.

"Tom Goodson. He didn't live up to his last name." She attempted a small laugh. It didn't work. "He was charming in the beginning. He was always charming in front of others. My dad was charming in front of others too. Only his family knew what he was really like. I keep thinking that, because of my dad, I should have seen through Tom from the start, but I didn't."

Instinct told Liam to brace himself for what she would say next.

"The first time he hit me, he split my lip." She touched a spot on her mouth. "I should have left then, but I didn't."

"Chelsea . . ."

She held up a hand, like a traffic cop in a classic film. It silenced him.

"I learned really young that it's possible to go and hide deep inside yourself, to close yourself off from the truth of what's happening." Her eyes pleaded for him to understand. "The brain really is amazing, the way it can put experiences and emotions into compartments so you don't have to look at what is too painful until you're ready. That's how it was for me." She looked toward the river again. "The danger is you might not make it back from that hiding place."

How did you make it back? he wanted to ask. More than that, he still wanted to take her in his arms.

In films, he'd always played one of the heroic characters. He hadn't had a lead role yet, but he'd been on the right side. One of the good guys. Now he wanted to be a good guy for Chelsea. He wanted to rescue her, play the white knight riding in to carry away the damsel in distress.

As if knowing his thoughts, she faced him again. Determination had replaced the broken expression he'd glimpsed earlier. "It was a random comment by a girl I worked with that woke me up, brought me out of the fog of pretense. She wasn't even talking about me or my situation, but suddenly, I knew I wasn't going to live like that any longer. I left work early, went to the apartment, packed my things, and left."

"You lived with him?"

She nodded. "I wasn't a believer when I moved in with Tom. Living together gave him more control over my movements, although I didn't realize that at first. And he hated it when I started going to church, hated it more when I started to question if our living situation was right before God."

She touched the side of her face, and Liam knew she was remembering another time when that jerk had hit her.

"Do you think less of me?" she asked in a whisper.

Only then did he realize there were tears trailing down her cheeks.

"No," he answered, his voice deep, his throat choked with emotion. "I don't think less of you. We've all had to ask God to forgive us for our bad choices. I don't think less of you because you're human. I think you're amazing."

She gave him a watery smile. "Amazing?"

"Without question."

And then he did what he'd wanted to do the whole time she poured out her story. He took her in his arms, held her close, and swore to himself that Chelsea Spencer would never have reason to regret telling him her story.

Liam's Journal

I can imagine Jacob's face as I try to explain my feelings for Chelsea. He knew I had my struggles with desire. Physical temptation was a frequent companion of mine when I was living in LA. But it's way more than that with Chelsea. Not that I'm not attracted to her in that way too. I am.

But my feelings go deeper. I want to take care of her. I want to make sure she isn't hurt again, the way she was in the past. I want to hear her laughter. I want to watch her with Chipper. I can't wait to see and hear her play the violin.

Jacob wanted me to find someone, to fall in love. He believed it was one of the things I needed most. I'm starting to think he was right. No, not starting. I believe it. He was right.

I've put it off long enough. I'm going to see Mom.

Listening to Chelsea talk about her childhood opened up my eyes to a lot. I had it good as a kid. Maybe my childhood wasn't ideal, the way I thought it was for a long time (like <u>Leave It To Beaver</u> or one of those other '50s programs on perpetual reruns), but it was good. My parents never mistreated me. Yes, I knew Jacob was Mom's favorite. Maybe it's because he was younger. Maybe it's because he was better and kinder than me. Sure, Dad worked a lot. More than he probably had to. But he was there for us too. And he loved us. Mom loved us.

I don't know any perfect people. I'm sure not perfect. I can't expect Mom or Dad to be perfect. Guess that's where forgiveness and acceptance come in. Jacob had those in spades. I'm glad I had his example. Now to apply them.

Another thing: Jacob had a way with people. It was like he could look at them and know what they most needed from him. A fist bump. A hug. A word of encouragement. Silence.

He was like that as a little kid. He was still like that as he was dying.

Friends would come to see him, friends meaning to give him comfort, and Jacob would end up comforting them, making them feel better even though he was the one who was so sick.

Sounds like a line for a sappy movie, but sometimes I wonder if

Jacob was too good for this world, if that's why God took him home so young.

Jacob would argue with that. He'd remind me again that God knows the number of our days from the moment He forms us in the womb. He'd tell me that he didn't die one second earlier or one second later than the number that was assigned to him from the start.

Wish it felt that way. Wish it felt like the timing was right. But it doesn't. I miss Jacob. I miss my kid brother. I miss the way we were together and the things he taught me.

There's that old cliché that says the good die young. Cliché or not, it was true of Jacob. He was good and he died young.

Chapter 20

Chelsea watched as dawn inched across the ceiling of her room. Happiness curled inside of her, making her want to sing and laugh and shout.

Liam Chandler was falling in love with her.

No, he hadn't spoken the actual words, but the truth had been in the strength of his arms and in the kisses that followed. It had been in the tenderness in his eyes and the gentleness in his voice.

And I'm falling in love with him. O Lord, I really am falling in love with him, despite wanting to be careful. Really and truly in love. It's wonderful, and it's frightening at the same time. But frightening in the best kind of way. Only You could make something like this happen. Beauty from ashes.

It hadn't been easy to tell Liam about her childhood. It had been even harder to tell him about her relationship with Tom. She'd left out the part about her ex-boyfriend's threats and his attempts to catch her alone after she moved out. She'd left out the part about Tom's middle-of-the-night phone calls and the times she'd sat curled in a corner, afraid he would break into her apartment. She'd left out the relief that overwhelmed her when Aunt

Rosemary asked her to come stay in Chickadee Creek. She'd left out those details because none of them mattered now. Nearly four hundred miles separated her from Tom Goodson. He was her past. God willing, Liam was her future.

Grinning, she got out of bed and headed for the shower. Twenty minutes later, her hair still damp, she went down the stairs and made a beeline for the coffee. Her great-aunt was seated at the kitchen table, her Bible open before her.

"Well, listen to you," Aunt Rosemary said.

"'Listen'?" Chelsea turned around. "To what?"

"To whatever you were humming." Aunt Rosemary picked up her coffee cup, then added with a smile, "You must be happy."

"Am I normally grumpy?"

Aunt Rosemary laughed. "No, dear. But this happiness seems different."

It is different, she thought as she retrieved creamer from the fridge. She'd finished pouring some into her coffee mug when her phone cheeped. Chelsea looked at the phone screen. A text from Liam. This early?

As if hearing Chelsea's thought, Aunt Rosemary said, "It's barely six thirty. When I was your age, we respected people's time. We didn't call anyone before ten in the morning, and we certainly never intruded after nine o'clock at night."

Chelsea barely heard her. She opened the text app and read:

Must go see my mom. May I leave Chipper with you for the day?

She texted back her agreement.

Thanks. See you in 30 min.

She put the phone into the back pocket of her shorts. "I'll be back," she told her great-aunt, then dashed up the stairs to do something with her hair and to put on some eye shadow and mascara.

Funny, she wasn't one to fuss much with her appearance. She preferred a natural, laid-back style. But it felt important to look her best for Liam this morning.

"I was thinking how pretty you look."

Remembering his words from the previous day, pleasure sluiced through her. It was followed by a rush of doubt. Why would he choose her over that actress he'd dated last year? What was her name? Didn't matter. Whatever her name, she was a flawless beauty. Chelsea had plenty of flaws. Her nose was a little too long, her chin too pointed. She wasn't curvy either. Her father had said she was built like a boy, straight up and down.

She turned away from the bathroom mirror, not wanting to continue this particular line of thinking. Besides, Liam was in Idaho. Liam liked to spend time with her. Then again, he would soon be making a movie somewhere down south. Who would be his female costar?

"Stop it!" she whispered as she pressed the heels of her hands against her ears. She'd been so happy when she woke up. Why be negative now? As if in answer to her own question, she remembered something her great-aunt had said a few days ago.

"Aunt Rosemary." She descended the stairs. "What was that verse you quoted to me the other day after I told you about the thoughts that go through my head? It was about an enemy and a hungry lion or something."

Aunt Rosemary replied without any hesitation. "From 1 Peter. 'Be of sober spirit, be on the alert. Your adversary, the devil, prowls around like a roaring lion, seeking someone to devour.'" She flipped through the pages of her Bible. "And the next verse says, 'But resist him, firm in your faith, knowing that the same experiences of suffering are being accomplished by your brethren who are in the world.'" She looked up.

Chelsea sank onto a chair at the table. "Are negative thoughts always whispers from the Enemy?"

"Not always. I believe God speaks to us through our doubts. To warn us what our choices might bring about, for instance. But there's a difference in the way God corrects and guides us and the attacks of the Enemy. God wants to make us strong in Him, dependent but safe in Him. His voice encourages us on the right path. The devil wants to tear us down and make us despair, to lose hope."

"How do I learn to tell the difference?"

Aunt Rosemary smiled briefly. "Practice. Experience. Faith." She leaned forward, reaching across the table to touch the back of Chelsea's hand. "Most important of all, trust. Trust Him. When we look to Him, He will guide us."

"In everything? Even in the little things that might not seem important to others?"

"In everything."

Chelsea nodded.

"My dear, when worries or troubled thoughts or whatever it is come into your mind, turn them over to God. Even if you have to turn them over a hundred or a thousand times a day, cast your cares upon Him." She pressed a finger onto the page of her Bible. "That's the verse just above the two I already quoted. 'Casting all your anxiety on Him, because He cares for you.'"

Something settled inside of Chelsea. She would turn those negative thoughts over to God and be glad in Him.

Liam could have taken Chipper with him to Boise. The dog loved to ride in the truck and was well-behaved no matter where they went together. The truth was he'd wanted an excuse to see Chelsea before he went to his mom's house. He needed the boost that a glimpse of her would give him before he tackled what could be an unpleasant experience.

It worked too. Chelsea's smile, the warm way she looked at him as he passed Chipper's leash into her hand, the sweet sound of her voice as she told him not to worry, all worked to bolster his spirits and calm his nerves.

On the drive down out of the mountains, he played one of his favorite albums, sometimes singing along with Chris Tomlin, other times sending up quick prayers for his heart to be tender, for his mom to tell him the truth, and that she would be ready to do the right thing. He prayed for them both to be able to put their differences to rest.

As Liam pulled his truck into the driveway, his mom stepped into view behind the storm door. A slight glare on the glass kept him from reading her expression.

God, help me get through this.

He opened the truck door and stepped to the ground. Drawing a deep breath, he cut across the lawn toward the front of the house. Before he reached the stoop, his mom pushed open the storm door.

"I've got coffee ready," she said before she turned and walked toward the kitchen.

He followed right behind.

"I didn't expect you to want to come this early." She poured coffee into the two waiting mugs.

"Sorry. It felt like early was better."

She handed him his mug, then carried her own and a plate of cinnamon rolls to the small dining-room table.

He sat in the chair opposite her. "I'd like you to tell me about David Harris."

A wry smile flitted across her mouth and was gone. "You don't waste time."

"No. Enough time's been wasted."

She stared into her mug. "It's not an easy story to tell."

"I guess." He heard the edge in his voice and regretted it. Still, he found it impossible to say he was sorry.

"Years ago, David and I worked in the same office. I knew him before your dad and I got married. He was sweet and funny, and he was ready to listen whenever I wanted to talk."

I'll bet.

"David was my friend, but I loved your dad. Richard and I had so much in common, although we had our differences too. Your dad has the kind of personality that swept me away. He was very hard to resist." She glanced up. "You're like him in that regard."

It was Liam's turn to stare into his coffee mug.

"Your dad and I were excited when we learned I was pregnant with you, but that excitement didn't last long. It wasn't an easy pregnancy. I was sick a lot. There was danger and uncertainty. Problems that had the doctor wondering if I would need a C-section. I was frightened a lot of the time, not knowing if I would be okay or if you would be okay."

"I didn't know that." He looked up. "Why didn't I know that?"

"I never thought you needed to know."

He shook his head slowly.

"By my seventh month, your dad and I were fighting constantly. He spent more and more time at the office. I didn't understand then that he was just as scared as I was. But even after you were born and everything was okay, it seemed like he was never at home. I had a husband, but I was a single mom at the same time. I was tired and so, so blue. I suppose I had postpartum depression, although it wasn't diagnosed. It never occurred to me to say anything to the doctor. Then one day—you were about six weeks old—I went to the grocery store, and I saw David in the bakery aisle."

Liam didn't want her to go on. He knew he wouldn't like what he heard next. He sensed it was going to be worse than expected.

"We went for coffee. I talked and he listened. He *heard* me. I hadn't felt heard in many months." Tears filled his mom's eyes. "We started seeing each other after that."

Seeing each other. A euphemism for the start of an affair. An affair that had begun when he was an infant. Not something recent. Something old. His gut clenched.

"I got pregnant again," she continued in a voice so soft he almost didn't hear her. "And your dad . . . Richard knew it wasn't his baby."

Liam stood so fast, his chair tipped over backward and hit the floor. He couldn't seem to draw breath.

Jacob . . . his baby brother . . . their mom's favorite . . . wasn't his dad's son.

"Your dad knew the truth, but he was determined not to get a divorce. I'm not sure why. I suppose he still loved me. Or maybe it was pride and he didn't want to be the first Chandler to get a divorce. Whatever the reasons, we stayed together. David . . . David knew I was pregnant, but when I told him I wasn't getting a divorce, that I was staying with my husband, he moved to Colorado before Jacob was born. Your dad and I built a new life together. Our marriage wasn't the same as in the beginning, but I think we were all happy enough. Don't you?"

How was he supposed to answer that question? What was "happy enough" for a family?

"A few years ago, David moved back to Boise, but I didn't know it. He honored my request that we never be in touch again, that he would allow Jacob to be Richard's son. Our paths never crossed. But then he learned about Jacob's failing health from a mutual friend from the old days. He was told that Jacob was dying. So he called me, and I let him come to the house. How could I not let him see his son before it was too late?" She took in a deep breath and released it. "I made sure you weren't home that day."

Liam raked his hair with the fingers of one hand. "Did Jacob know who David was? Did he . . . Did he know David was his . . . natural father?"

"No." She drew another breath. "No, he didn't."

"When did you . . . When did the affair resume?" The words felt like they scraped his throat raw on their way out.

249

"It didn't, Liam. I'm not and wasn't having an affair with David. We . . . shared nothing except the loss of a son. A son he only met once. That was all."

Did he believe her? He wanted to believe her. Did he?

"The day you saw David here at the house, he'd come to tell me goodbye. He was moving back to Colorado. It was only the third time I'd seen him since I got pregnant over thirty years ago. The first was when he came to meet Jacob. The second was at the funeral."

"He's gone now?"

"Yes."

"Does Dad know?"

"Yes."

He rubbed a hand across his forehead. "Is Dad coming home again?"

"I don't know, Liam. As I told you before, it's complicated. Even though things were fine on the surface, your dad harbored so much resentment for all those years. Even though he was the one who didn't want a divorce, he resented what I did bitterly. And after Jacob died, I think he just stopped wanting to care or to try. He loved your brother, despite everything. Perhaps it's his grief that made him walk out. Perhaps it was seeing David at the funeral. I don't know. He isn't ready to talk about it with me."

On the way to see his mom, Liam had prayed she would tell him the truth and be ready to do the right thing. It appeared the prayer had been answered. He'd also prayed they could put their differences to rest. His heart said that was up to him . . . and the first step was to forgive her.

Can I forgive her?

He stepped to one side and righted the chair. Then he looked at his mom again. Unshed tears glistened in her eyes, along with that same question: could he forgive her?

"I don't know any perfect people." He'd written those words in the journal he kept. He'd admitted on the page that he wasn't perfect and neither were his parents. Still . . .

"I've got to go," he said gruffly.

She nodded her understanding.

"I . . . I'll call."

"All right," she whispered.

He turned and left the house.

Preston

APRIL 1897

Preston stood in front of the dressing mirror. Wanting to look the best he could on his wedding day, he'd ordered a new suit from a tailor in Boise. But now he regretted it. The suit itself was fine, but Preston didn't look like himself in it. He looked like he was trying to be something he wasn't.

He frowned.

Was he wrong to marry Cora? She might live in a rented room and teach in a simple schoolhouse in a small town in the mountains of Idaho. But she was refined and well educated and so much more than he would ever be, no matter how much wealth he acquired. Was it fair to ask her to tie herself to him?

And yet, he couldn't imagine his life without her. He couldn't imagine not hearing her laugh or seeing her smile. He'd grown to love the way she lowered her eyes so he wouldn't see mischief in them. He adored the bright sparkle of ideas that could burst forth at the most unexpected times. He held his breath when she played her violin, the music stirring something in his soul that nothing had touched before.

"Preston."

He turned to face Sarah Mason, who stood in his bedchamber doorway. They had long since given up the formality of last names, except on those rare occasions when he conducted business at the house. The woman was more than his housekeeper. She was his friend, and he was glad she called him Preston at this moment. It made him feel less a fraud.

"How do I look?" He tugged at his vest.

"Very nice. As does your bride."

The blood seemed to drain from his head. It was a little like the time a mule kicked him in the gut. He'd nearly lost consciousness that day. He wasn't about to do so again. Inhaling a deep breath, he moved toward Sarah with a determined stride. She gave him a quick smile before stepping out of his way.

Voices drifted up the main stairway to greet him. Friends and neighbors come to wish the couple well on their wedding day. Many of these same people had come to his Christmas celebration, but he'd thought of them only as guests then. Now he recognized them as friends. This, too, was because of the woman he was about to marry. She'd helped him see a future for himself that was more than making himself richer. She'd helped him see Chickadee Creek as a place to call home. She'd had the courage to run from an unhappy life, and she'd given him the courage to plant roots. Deep roots.

Smiling now, the light-headedness forgotten, he descended the stairs, suddenly in a hurry to begin living his future.

Cora

APRIL 1897

"You are absolutely beautiful," Sarah said as she settled the bridal veil onto Cora's head.

Cora met her friend's gaze in the mirror of the smallest bedchamber in Preston's home. In what would shortly be *her* home, *their* home. "Thank you."

"I think I knew this day would come since the moment Preston brought you from the stagecoach to stay with me. I knew we would be friends, and I knew you two would fall in love."

"How did you know?"

She tapped the side of her nose with her index finger. "Some things a woman just knows."

Cora laughed softly.

"Now, I believe it's time for you to go downstairs. Your groom's already there, waiting for you."

"I'm happy. I never expected to be this happy." She turned from the mirror. "And I thought marriage was the last thing I wanted. I wanted to be free." She pressed her hands to her cheeks. "But I feel more free today than ever before in my life."

"The two of you." Sarah shook her head and clucked. Then she moved to the door and opened it. "Get on with you now. I'll be glad to have my spare room empty again."

Cora saw the tears swimming in her friend's eyes a moment before she was blinded by her own. Dabbing her eyes with her handkerchief, then her nose, she left the bedchamber.

The conversations began to quiet as she came down the stairs. Through the gauzy white of her veil, she saw heads turn and smiles blossom. Her heartbeat seemed to thunder in her ears as joy coiled around her heart.

Just as her shoe was about to alight on the final step, a knock sounded on the front door. Another guest opened it, drawing her gaze. Her foot slipped off the step, and she grabbed for the bannister.

No! Not you. Not now.

Although she didn't see it happen, she felt everyone's attention turn toward the new arrival.

"Cora!" Aaron Anderson, the man she'd hoped never to see again, stepped into the vestibule, whipping off his hat as he did so.

It was like seeing a ghost, and dread stole her breath away. "Father."

"What the devil do you think you're doing?"

The silence in the house felt different now. Tense. Strained. She sensed over a dozen pairs of eyes on her.

"I'm getting married," Cora answered, stating the obvious.

"So I was told. It's good I arrived when I did." He sent a disparaging look at the guests, then returned his gaze to Cora. "Go and change your clothes. We'll put an end to this nonsense."

"How did you find me?"

"Does it matter? I've wasted nearly two years of my time and wasted a great deal of money on investigators."

The article in the newspaper. He didn't have to answer her question. That insignificant little article in an insignificant little newspaper had given her away and brought him to Idaho.

In a near whisper, she said, "You didn't have to do either."

"By heavens. I won't be defied. We will leave for Boise City at once."

"Father, I—"

"At once. Do you hear me? You will come with me now."

For one horrible moment, Cora thought she had no choice but to obey him. Then movement from the parlor entrance caused her to turn her head. Preston stood there, looking handsome in his new suit. More important, she saw his goodness and his strength. She saw his love. Certainty welled in her chest, a confidence in the life she'd chosen.

She looked at her father again. "No, Father. I will not go with you. But you're welcome to join our other guests."

"Your guests?" His tone was derogatory.

"Our friends," she added, taking the last step.

Her father glowered.

Pity welled within her, and the realization surprised her even more than his sudden appearance. For all his money and power, he was a miserable man. He would never have enough. For every goal he reached, all he saw was what he hadn't achieved yet. He only noticed the men who had more.

Without another word, she turned toward Preston.

APRIL 1897

In the weeks following Preston's proposal, Cora had shared with him the details of her life before she'd come to Chickadee Creek. Seeing the pain in the eyes of the woman he loved, he'd disliked Aaron Anderson, sight unseen.

Having that very same man barge into his home on his wedding day and demand that Cora leave with him made Preston's blood boil. He wanted to drive the older man from the vestibule, off the porch, and into the street. But he didn't act. Perhaps it was seeing the certainty on Cora's face or hearing the strength and determination in her voice. Perhaps it was the confident way she turned from her father and moved toward Preston. It made his heart soar. He held out a hand for her, and when she reached him, she took it.

"She'll have no inheritance," her father shouted. "You marry her without my permission or approval."

Hurt flashed in Cora's eyes. As if her father had declared aloud that he didn't love her and didn't care what happened to her.

But if so, why had he come all this way to take her home? Preston didn't understand any of it. What he did know was that he'd like to smash his fist into her father's face.

With resolve, he curbed the desire for vengeance as he tucked Cora's hand into the crook of his arm. Then, forcing a calm into his voice that he didn't feel, he met her father's gaze. "Mr. Anderson, your daughter is of age. She can marry without your permission." He looked at Cora again. "Nor do we have need of an inheritance. For I am very much in love with her, and I need no inducement to take her as my bride."

Aaron Anderson sputtered a few words under his breath.

Let him sputter, Preston thought as he drew Cora toward the parlor. *Nothing could keep me from marrying her. Nothing.*

Chapter 21

The drive from Boise to Chickadee Creek seemed at least twice as long as the one headed the other direction. Liam had to force himself to concentrate on the road rather than give in to the wild swings of his thoughts and emotions.

He was relieved when Rosemary Townsend's house came into view. He slowed and turned into her drive but sat unmoving for a while after cutting the engine. He hadn't even reached for the door handle when Chipper bounded out of the house and off the porch.

"Hey, fella." Liam got out of the truck, squatted, and loved on the dog, feeling some of the tension ease in his shoulders.

"We didn't expect you back this soon."

Liam looked up at the porch where Chelsea stood, leaning her hands on the railing. She smiled for a moment, then frowned. Obviously, he wasn't a great actor if she'd seen through his mood that easily.

"I didn't expect to be back this soon either." He stood. "Thanks for watching Chipper for me."

"Why don't you come in for a cup of coffee?"

"I wouldn't want—"

"Please."

All that awaited him at home were his own dark thoughts and some leftover lasagna. "Okay." He ruffled Chipper's ears. "Back inside, boy."

The dog seemed happy to obey. He ran onto the porch, greeting Chelsea with the same enthusiasm he'd shown his master. Liam was tempted to do the same thing. Run up onto the porch to be with her. Let her chase away the confusion swirling inside with a comforting hand. And why not? Yesterday, she'd shared some of her own hard truths. If he cared for her, didn't he owe her the same honesty?

He jammed his fingertips into the back pockets of his jeans. "Instead of coffee, would you mind a walk? I could use the exercise."

"No. I don't mind." Her smile returned as she pushed her hair back from her face. "Let me get some shoes on, and I'll be right out."

Chipper returned to Liam once again, and the two of them walked down the drive to the edge of Alexander Road. A light-green car drove slowly by, headed east. Liam couldn't see the driver from where he stood, but he lifted a hand in an abbreviated wave, in case it was someone he knew from church or someone he'd met in town. He watched as the car turned south on Chandler Road, disappearing from view.

"I'm ready."

Liam turned in time to see Chelsea come down the porch steps, her hair now in a familiar ponytail, her feet encased in lemon-yellow sneakers. She looked adorable. How could his mood help but improve at the sight of her?

As soon as she reached him, they set off in the direction of the old mansion site. But they didn't pause on the bridge or make note of the property Liam now owned. Chelsea seemed content to wait for him to speak first. He didn't do so until they'd left Chickadee Creek behind and were following a trail deeper into the forest. Pine needles crunched beneath their feet. Chipper took off after some woodland creature. The *tap-tap-tap* of a woodpecker carried to them through the trees.

"I went to see my mom today because I thought she was having an affair." From the corner of his eye, he saw Chelsea look at him. "Turns out I was both right and wrong."

Chipper ran back to them, tongue lolling from one side of his mouth. The dog circled them twice, then took off into the trees once again.

"She told me she had an affair over thirty years ago. And it turns out my brother Jacob was the son of her lover, not my dad."

Chelsea sucked in a breath of air, soft but still audible.

"Jacob was her favorite son. Now I sort of understand why. It wasn't because he was better than me—although he was. He definitely was. But I think she favored him because she knew my dad wouldn't."

"He knew? Your dad knew."

"Yeah. She says he did. I haven't talked to him yet. Dad loved Jacob. I'm sure of that. I don't think he favored either one of us. We were his kids. But maybe . . . Well, maybe I just couldn't tell. He was gone a lot, working. Maybe that's why I never saw any difference between the way he treated us or felt about us."

"How did you leave things with your mother?"

He huffed out a breath. "Not good. She needs me to forgive her. I'm not feeling it."

"Do you have to feel it?"

He stopped walking, challenged by her soft question. "No. Forgiveness is a decision, not a feeling." He looked up at the sky through the tall pines, the treetops swaying gently in an indiscernible breeze. "It's an act of obedience."

"Then you'll find a way to forgive her."

He met her gaze. "I'm not so sure. The more I think about it, the less able I feel to do . . . what's right."

"Liam." She touched his arm with her fingertips. "You can. I know you can. God will help you."

Nobody except Jacob would have understood all that he felt, all that he wrestled with and why. Nobody except Jacob . . . until now. Chelsea understood without him explaining. Most of the people he'd hung out with during his years in LA wouldn't understand. Oh, they might say the right things, but they wouldn't understand the part his faith played in the way he wanted to live his life. Chelsea did.

Throat tight with emotion, he managed to say, "Thanks."

She took a step closer, moving into an embrace he didn't know he needed. Her cheek rested against his chest, her head fitting nicely beneath his chin. He closed his eyes and drew in the faint scent of her shampoo. Fruity. Watermelon? He wasn't sure. Didn't matter. His arms tightened around her, pulling her even closer, until he couldn't tell where he left off and she began.

I can't believe I found you. He didn't so much think the words in his mind as he felt them in his heart, and he knew in that moment that he didn't want to go through anything in life without Chelsea by his side.

Never before had Chelsea felt as safe and secure as she felt in that moment. She had embraced Liam because she wanted to encourage him, to offer him hope. But in his arms, she discovered he'd done as much for her. Her emotions soared. Miraculously, her heart was in tune with his. She couldn't say how she knew this. Only that she did.

"We ought to start back," he said, his breath tickling her scalp.

She drew her head back so she could look into his eyes. "Yes. I suppose we should."

He took a step away, his hands sliding from her back to lightly grip her upper arms. "Chipper," he called. "Come on, boy."

It took a minute or so, but finally the dog bounded out of the forest. His black nose was covered with dirt, and a pine cone clung to the long hairs of his tail. But if a dog could smile, that's what he did.

Liam and Chelsea laughed in unison, and as they turned to follow the trail back toward town, they joined hands, as naturally as if they'd been doing it all of their lives.

"I'll call Mom when I get home," Liam said after a lengthy silence. "And Dad too."

She squeezed his hand.

They strolled onward, his stride shortening to match hers. Another thing to love about him. From childhood on, she'd felt it was her duty to keep up. And when she failed, was it any wonder she was punished for it?

She remembered, after she became a Christian, reading a verse in Ephesians about husbands loving their wives as much as Christ loved the church. Loving their wives so much they would die for them. Impossible, she'd thought. No man loved a woman enough to do that. But in this moment, she started to believe it might be possible after all.

Suddenly, Chipper tore away from them, barking not in play but as if in anger or warning. Liam stopped to stare up the hillside where the dog had disappeared through the trees.

"Chipper, get back here."

"What do you suppose he heard?"

"I don't know. I hope it isn't a bear. Not sure Chipper would have enough sense to keep away from it."

"A bear?" She inched a little closer to him.

"Or a skunk," Liam added, a hint of laughter in his voice.

She wrinkled her nose at the mere suggestion. Then, from a distance, she heard a man's voice shout something. Seconds later, the sound of an engine reached them. A cloud of dust rose from the ridge as the unseen vehicle drove away.

Liam began to scramble up the hillside. "Chipper." He stopped when the dog came into view. "Come here, boy. Come on." He turned and came down the short distance, Chipper at his heels. "I guess whoever it was didn't like dogs."

"And the dog didn't like him." She glanced toward the ridge line, familiar anxiety winding through her. "Someone was watching us."

"Maybe a miner wannabe. The road up there dead-ends at the location of the old dredger."

She wanted his words to soothe her jangled nerves. She hated the idea of being spied upon.

"At least I don't have to worry about paparazzi out here."

"Paparazzi?" The idea of who might see such a picture of her with Liam poured ice into her veins and brought fear roaring to the surface.

"Relax. Nobody knows I'm here."

"They might. Your agent's been up to Chickadee Creek twice already." The words tumbled from her mouth, her voice rising with anxiety. "And . . . your new director flew up to Idaho last week. Somebody knows where they came."

A picture of her with Liam. In a newspaper. In a fan magazine. Would they know her name or call her a mystery woman? Would the photo be clear or grainy? What would Tom do if he saw it?

Liam gave her a confused look. The last thing she wanted to do was admit the direction of her thoughts. But she didn't have to. Understanding suddenly filled his eyes.

He took hold of her hand again. "Nobody knows I'm in Chickadee Creek, and nobody knows you're here either. You're safe with me." He drew her close and embraced her. "I'll keep you safe always."

She wanted to believe him, but something in her heart remained on alert.

"Come on," he said. "I'd better get you home."

She drew back from him, determined to sound normal and happy. "I almost forgot. Aunt Rosemary said she was going to make a breakfast casserole while we took our walk. She's hoping you'll come in and have some when we get back."

He leaned forward and kissed her on the lips. Drawing back, grinning widely, he said, "Well, let's not keep her waiting any longer."

As they set off again, Chelsea's gaze went to the ridge one last time, and she prayed that no paparazzi had followed Liam to Chickadee Creek. Both for his sake and for hers.

I've discovered something. Who Jacob's natural father was means nothing to me. He wasn't my half brother. He was my brother. Fully. To the core. My whole brother. Shared DNA. Shared hearts. We were the real deal, no matter what any kind of blood test would tell you.

As for Mom and Dad, there's a lot I've got to work through in my head. It'll take more than one conversation with each of them to get their relationship with me back where it ought to be. I don't think it'll be easy, but I have faith that we'll get there, in time. I've got to have faith, and I'm willing to do the work.

As for what happens between the two of them, that's not up to me. I'll have to leave it in God's hands.

I can't help but think what Jacob would say about all of this. He'd tell me that God still formed him and knew him from the very start. He'd say that Mom might have been surprised by the pregnancy, but God wasn't. I'm sure he'd have to work through his emotions, like I'm having to do, but he always seemed to do a better job of it. He always seemed to know who he was: a man made in the image of God.

Can't decide if I'm glad Jacob never knew about Mom's affair. And I wonder if we find out stuff like that once we're in heaven. The

Bible says there aren't any tears or sorrow there. Would knowing Dad wasn't his dad make Jacob sad?

I guess saying "dysfunctional family" is actually redundant. Isn't every family dysfunctional in its own way?

Liam's Journal

My character's name is Rafe Jones, husband to Maggie and father to Jimmy and Laurel. The film isn't titled yet. They're still deciding. While inspired by a book, it doesn't follow the same story, so it's unlikely they'll want to use that title.

They'll have a finished script any day now. I'm eager to get my hands on it. I'm more excited about this than any movie I've done before.

Jacob was right. Again.

Chapter 22

*L*iam sat in a row of seats in the Boise airport, iPhone in hand. He'd checked both messages and e-mails already, but there hadn't been anything needing his attention. He could send a text to Chelsea, asking how Chipper was doing without him, but he knew his dog was fine. Chipper loved Chelsea.

For the past week, Liam, accompanied by his dog, had spent many hours every day with her. They'd taken more walks. They'd sorted through stacks of books and old papers, looking for more history about Chickadee Creek and the Chandler family. Liam had a growing interest in the dredge mining Preston Chandler had pursued before the turn of the century, while Chelsea only seemed to care about Cora and her music. They'd talked about many things—important things and inconsequential things. They'd covered favorite books, favorite music, and favorite movies. They'd talked more about their families. They'd talked about his upcoming role. He already knew Chelsea Spencer better than he knew anyone other than his brother.

He smiled, remembering last night. He'd gone to her great-aunt's house for dinner, and then he and Chelsea had settled onto the sofa to watch a DVD. Since they were alone—Rosemary had said she wanted an early night—they'd done more kissing than watching, truth be told.

Intruding on that pleasant memory, the announcement came for first-class boarding to begin. Liam hoped his stupid grin didn't give away his thoughts as he rose to join the other passengers.

The nonstop flight to LAX would take just over two hours. Kurt had said he would meet Liam at the airport, and they would go together to the offices of Grayson Wentworth. The contract would be signed, then they would have lunch, discuss more details for the shoot that would begin at the end of September. After that, Kurt would drop Liam at the airport for his return flight. By the time he drove to Chickadee Creek, it would be late. But not so late he couldn't stop to get his dog and kiss his girl.

His grin widened at that thought.

On the plane, he shoved his carry-on into the overhead compartment, then stepped into his seat next to the window. He fastened his safety belt before popping his AirPods into his ears. With his phone set to airplane mode, he hit Play on some music and closed his eyes. With any luck, he would think about Chelsea all the way to Los Angeles.

Laughter erupted upstairs where several teenage girls perused books on the shelves.

"Do you need any help up there?" Chelsea called to them in a slightly raised voice.

All three turned to look over the railing.

"No, thanks," one of them answered.

"They're not buyers," Aunt Rosemary said softly. "They're just looking for entertainment before they go back to school next week."

"Hmm."

"Why don't you take Chipper for a walk?" her great-aunt suggested.

"But you might need—"

"Go on. You need to stretch your legs, and so does the dog. Besides, it'll burn up some time before Liam gets back."

Aunt Rosemary knew her much too well.

Chelsea looked at the clock on the wall of the antique store. Liam must be eating lunch with his director and agent about now. Strange how much she missed him. Perhaps it was knowing he was in another state that made it feel like ages since they'd been together. Or perhaps it was knowing he was in Los Angeles where he'd lived for many years and still owned a house. Would he suddenly realize that he wanted to live there again?

She smiled. No, he wouldn't.

Her confidence brought with it a burst of joy. For too much of her life, she'd acted out of insecurity and uncertainty. But the past week with Liam had given her a new confidence in every area of her life.

"I'm not afraid," she whispered to herself.

She thought of the cellar in the shed on the old mansion property. She'd refused to go near it not that long ago. Today she felt brave enough. If Liam were with her now, she would have gone down those concrete steps and looked inside, just to prove it.

At the door to the shop, Chelsea looked back at her great-aunt. "We won't be long."

"Take your time, dear. I can handle this rush of customers." As she said it, she glanced toward the girls on the floor above.

Chelsea laughed as she closed the door behind her. Chipper walked at her side, head tipped up, watching for a command. Chelsea didn't set him free until they were across the bridge on Chandler Road.

Watching the dog run from one side of the road to the other, she took several deep breaths of air, enjoying the milder weather that had arrived this week. While still August, the temperature that morning had been in the low fifties. The cooler air promised the coming of fall, although the next season was still a full month away.

Up ahead, a deer with two fawns darted across the trail. Chipper was about to give chase but stopped when Chelsea spoke his name in a firm tone. The dog looked back at her with pleading eyes.

"No. You leave the deer alone."

Chipper hung his head, and his tail drooped too.

Chelsea laughed. "Did you take acting lessons from Liam?"

The dog's ears perked up, as if recognizing his master's name.

Smiling as she imagined Liam training the dog to look disappointed, Chelsea walked on. Her thoughts drifted to other walks along this trail. Walks with Liam by her side. Walks when he'd held her hand, and she'd known how deeply he cared for her. There was an honesty about him. There was—

"Hello, Chelsea."

Startled from her reverie, she whirled toward the voice.

There stood Tom Goodson, his expression grim, his eyes hard.

"What . . . What are you doing here?"

"What do you think? I came looking for you. You should know you can't hide from me."

She drew a breath, trying to steady her nerves. "I wasn't hiding." Not entirely the truth. "And there is nothing more that we have to say to each other."

"You're wrong about that. I have plenty to say to you, you cheating little—"

Unexpectedly, Chipper lunged at Tom, but Tom was ready for him. He had a tire iron in his right hand—something Chelsea hadn't noticed before—and he swung it at the dog. Chipper's yelp split the air as he was knocked off the trail and down a hillside.

"Chipper!" she cried.

But before she could run after the dog, Tom grabbed her by the arm and yanked her close to him. "You're coming with me."

"No, I'm not. Let me go. You've hurt him. He needs me."

But his grip only tightened, and he began to drag her up toward the ridge. "Chelsea, I've had enough of this. You're my girl. We had a few fights. So get over it."

"Tom," she said, trying to sound calm, "it was more than a few fights. We don't belong together. We aren't *right* together. You know it's true."

"You belong to me."

She pulled back, digging her heels into the loose earth. "I don't *belong* to anybody."

He called her a foul name as he dragged her—fighting him the whole way—over the edge of the ridge. His car was parked not far away. His green car. She hadn't been wrong. She'd seen it driving down Alexander Road on Saturday. But how had he stayed hidden for nearly a week? Where had he been? A stranger in a small town, and nobody mentioned it to her or Aunt Rosemary? What was wrong with the gossip mill in Chickadee Creek?

The thought would have made her laugh at another time. At the moment, it wasn't funny.

"Get in the car." Tom shoved her toward the rear passenger door.

"No. I'm not going anywhere with you." She tried again to wrench herself from his grip.

He dropped the tire iron, then slapped her. Her head snapped to the side, hitting the roof of the car. She cried out as the world began to spin.

"I said get in."

"Tom, you can't—"

He hit her again. She tasted blood.

"You'll be surprised what I can do," he growled, his mouth close to her ear.

She shivered. No, she wouldn't be surprised.

God, help me!

Liam checked his phone for messages as he walked through the Boise air terminal and headed outside to the short-term parking lot. Kurt was supposed to send him a few more details about the location shoot. There wasn't a message from his agent, but there was one from Rosemary & Time. He grinned as he touched Play and listened for Chelsea's voice.

Only the message wasn't from Chelsea. It was from Rosemary.

"Liam, I don't want to alarm you, but Chelsea went for a

walk with Chipper not long after lunch, and they still haven't returned. It's been four hours. I'm worried. Has she called you? I don't know if she had her cell phone with her since coverage is sketchy. But you young people seem to carry them all the time anyway. Do call me if you've heard from her."

Not waiting until he got to his truck, Liam dropped his carry-on to the ground and punched the button for a return call. When he got the answering machine, he hung up and called Rosemary's house. She answered on the first ring.

"Chelsea?"

"No. Rosemary, it's Liam."

"Oh, Liam. Thank goodness. Have you talked to her?"

"No. She still isn't back?" He didn't wait for an answer since it was obvious. "I landed about ten minutes ago. I'm about to get in my truck and head for home."

"Liam, I'm worried. Friends are out looking for her. The sheriff too. But no one has seen her since she left the shop a little after one o'clock."

He looked at his watch. He and Chelsea had taken some long walks together, but they'd never been gone for that many hours. Something was wrong. But what? Had she fallen? Chipper probably wouldn't leave her if she was injured. He would stay close to guard her.

But what if the dog had stumbled upon a bear? Chipper could be the one that was injured, and Chelsea wouldn't be strong enough to carry him back to town. She wouldn't want to leave him either.

Abruptly, he shut off the scenarios playing in his mind. "Rosemary, I'm on my way. I'll get there as fast as I can."

"Drive safe, but hurry."

"Will do. And Rosemary? Keep praying for her."

"I will, dear. I most certainly will."

He pressed End, slid the phone into his pocket, then picked up his carry-on and sprinted for his truck.

APRIL 1897

As he'd done every day since his wedding, Preston rushed home from the mining offices, eager to see his bride of one week. If he weren't in negotiations for the purchase of a sawmill, he wouldn't bother going to the offices at all. It wasn't as if Ethan Sooner couldn't manage whatever had to be done. In fact, the mine foreman told him that at least once each day.

Entering the house, he removed his hat and tossed it onto a table in the entry hall. He was about to call out Cora's name when he heard voices coming from the parlor. He walked swiftly in that direction. But he stopped abruptly when his new father-in-law came into view.

Both Aaron and Cora looked at him, but it was only Cora he cared about. He studied her expression. He saw no distress, much to his relief. Only confidence.

"Darling." He crossed the parlor to kiss her cheek, then placed a hand on her shoulder as he stood by her side and turned his gaze once more upon their visitor. "Mr. Anderson."

His father-in-law cleared his throat. "I've come to talk some sense into my daughter."

Preston raised an eyebrow but remained silent.

"If I'd learned about that blasted newspaper article sooner, perhaps I could have averted your . . . association with this man." Aaron Anderson tossed a dismissive glance in Preston's direction. "But with some care, there could be a quiet divorce. No one back East need know. Your reputation could be salvaged. You could still find a respectable match."

Anger rose in Preston's chest.

"Father." Cora's voice remained soft but firm. "For once in your life, please hear me. I'm sorry your detective saw that article from Christmas, because it gave you hope for something that cannot be. I'm sorry that you wasted your valuable time traveling across the country. I'm truly sorry you've inconvenienced yourself with not one but two trips up to our little town. But nothing you say or do will induce me to return to New York. I won't leave my husband. I certainly won't divorce him."

Her father sputtered his frustration.

She leaned forward on her chair. "All of my life, I was nothing more to you than a pawn to be played in order to better your standing in society. I wanted your approval, your love. I wanted it so badly that I allowed you to arrange and control my life for far too long." She reached out and briefly touched her father's knee, then withdrew her hand and straightened again. "But I am not that girl any longer, and I am not your property. I left New York because I didn't want to be trapped in a loveless marriage. And I found so much more than mere freedom. I found myself. I found a deeper faith in the God who loves me, even though I'm not perfect." She turned and looked up at Preston, offering a quick smile. "And I found love with a man who doesn't want to control me but wishes me to go through life beside him. As his equal."

"Rubbish!" her father exclaimed. "He's a nobody. He didn't

even make his fortune. He'll likely lose it all. Well, don't come crying to me when that happens."

Preston took a small step forward. "You are quite right about one thing, sir. I am not your daughter's equal. And she is wrong about one thing. She *is* perfect. At least she's perfect for me."

Aaron Anderson rose to his feet. "I could destroy you."

"Perhaps."

Cora stood and took hold of Preston's hand. "I have prayed for you, Father. I will go on doing so. And for Mother. I hope you can be set free too."

The man looked as if he would say something more, but instead, he pressed his lips together, set his hat on his head, and left the parlor. Moments later, the front door slammed behind him.

Preston turned to Cora and drew her into his arms. "Your father is right. I'm not your equal." He kissed her forehead. "But I promise you we'll go through life side by side, and I'll do my best to make sure you're never sorry."

"And I promise you"—she drew her head back to look into his eyes—"that our lives will be rich with meaning and full of joy, even if sorrow comes."

Chapter 23

C helsea awakened on hard, uneven ground. She remembered little after Tom shoved her into his car. Nothing except for an odd smell as he'd put something over her face. She'd seen enough detective shows on television to suspect he'd used ether or chloroform to knock her out. She was thankful he hadn't beaten her senseless instead.

With a groan, she sat up. Wherever she was, it was dark. Too dark to see her own hand in front of her face. Panic threatened to rise within.

"No," she said, the word echoing around her. "I won't be afraid. What can mere man do to me?"

It might not be an exact quote, but it reminded her that God was bigger than her present circumstances.

"It's okay to be scared, but I won't panic."

She pushed up to her feet.

She hated to think what small creatures might be in this dark place with her, but she couldn't stand there, helpless. She didn't know where she was or if Tom might come back soon. She didn't doubt he would come back. He'd put her in this dark place to punish her, and he would want to see the results.

Stretching out her arms, she felt around. She expected to find the rocky side of a cave. Instead, she touched a metal wall. Not exactly smooth. Perhaps rusty? So she was inside some kind of metal room. There had to be a door.

With one hand still on the wall, she stepped forward, moving her other hand through the air in front of her. Even so, she managed to smack her shin into something hard. A large wooden crate, she decided after a brief exploration. And heavy. She inched around it and continued on.

A short while later, her heart quickened. Off to her left glimmered a sliver of light. So faint it was almost indiscernible. But it was there, and it gave her hope. She needed hope.

At least Tom hadn't bound her. He must have thought she would remain unconscious long enough that he could leave for a time. But for how long? How long had she been in this room? How far from Chickadee Creek had he driven before dumping her here?

She left the relative safety of the wall and moved toward the pale light, crossing the black expanse with both arms swaying back and forth before her, feeling for any obstruction. The closer she got, the more certain she was that it was a way out. When she reached her destination, she felt around until she located a large metal latch. She jiggled it, but nothing happened.

Should she try harder? What kind of noise would it make? If Tom was beyond this door, it would anger him that she even tried. But not trying felt worse.

She tried pulling on the latch again. She put everything she had into it. At first, it seemed frozen, but finally, she felt something give. A little at first. Then a snap. The door flew toward her, knocking her back onto the floor. She scrambled to her feet.

It was later than she'd thought. Gloaming blanketed the earth. A few stars could be seen overhead. But that also meant others must be looking for her. Liam would be looking for her. That thought brought a fleeting smile with it.

A second one stole it away. What about Chipper? Had Tom killed Liam's dog?

She stepped into the doorway of her rusted-out prison. She didn't recognize the small clearing, didn't know what this place had been. Mounds of rocks were everywhere, the natural terrain disturbed long ago, judging by the overgrowth.

The sounds of a car carried to her through the forest. Her heart quickening once again, she sprinted for the mountainside, disappearing into the trees, not worrying about any sounds she made. Not yet. Not while the car was still in motion. For now, she had to get as far away as possible.

"You okay, boy?" Liam knelt on the ground and looked into his dog's eyes. There was dried blood near Chipper's right ear.

"We found him up the trail thataway." Fred Bishop pointed to the west. "He didn't cotton much to comin' with us, so I put that baling twine around his neck. I think he's still hurtin', or twine wouldn't've held him."

Liam stood. "What about Chelsea?"

"No sign of her. Folks're still back there, lookin' all over the area where your dog was. Sheriff's out there too. 'Course, we don't know how far your dog'd come on the trail from wherever he got hurt."

It would be dark soon. Too dark to keep searching. Liam

hated to think of Chelsea out there after the sun set. She hated the dark, and he didn't want her to be scared. Although he didn't think she could be more scared than he was for her.

A car came along the road behind him, and he turned around. Even with the headlights shining in his direction, there was enough daylight that he could tell it was Rosemary's vehicle. As she slowed to a stop, he went to meet her.

"Grace Witherstone said there was a stranger in the store earlier. A man about your age. She said there was something about him that didn't set right with her. But that was late this afternoon, after everyone was already looking for Chelsea, so it might be nothing. Still, Grace told the sheriff about the stranger, and she wanted you to know about him too. She said he drove a light-green car. An older model with Washington plates."

Liam frowned. Light-green. Washington plates. He remembered a light-green car going by Rosemary's house earlier in the week while he waited for Chelsea. But he hadn't noticed the plates. Was it the same car? Strangers didn't stay strangers long in a place like Chickadee Creek. But that meant the man had been seen twice in five days. So where was he staying? Who was he?

Liam turned to look toward the trail. That same day he'd seen the green car, that had been the day Chipper chased after somebody on the road that led to the old dredging site. He remembered the angry shout, the dog's barks, the quick departure of the car that left a dust cloud behind it.

Rosemary leaned a little farther out the car window. "Liam, you don't suppose this has anything to do with . . . with that old boyfriend of hers, do you? His car would have Washington plates."

"Fred!" Liam spun on his heel. "Has anybody checked out

the dredger location? It might not be anything, but earlier this week, Chelsea and I heard a car up on that road leading to it. If a person wanted to stay hidden, that would be a good place for it."

"I reckon," Fred answered.

"Let's check it out. We'll take my truck." He turned toward Rosemary again. "I'm going to find her."

Rosemary's eyes widened. "You think he found her, don't you? That man she's afraid of."

"I don't know. It's a guess. That's all. But a stranger with Washington plates on his car . . ." He let his words trail into silence.

"I'll keep praying."

He spun on his heel and took off toward his truck, Chipper right beside him.

On the winding highway up from Boise, Liam hadn't allowed himself to go more than ten miles above the speed limit. Now he drove his truck like a maniac. The way Fred Bishop clung to the door would have been funny in other circumstances. Fortunately, it wasn't that far to the site. Only about five miles.

But it seemed farther.

Daylight was completely gone by the time the truck rounded the last curve. Evidence of the old dredger remained not far from the creek. Nearby, a wooden shack tilted precariously to one side, slats missing here and there. A shipping container, brought there in the later twentieth century by persons unknown, rested against a rock wall.

But this time, there was something else in the center of the clearing. A pale-green sedan with Washington plates.

Liam slammed on the brakes. He couldn't go back and stealthily make his way here. His presence must be known by now.

"Check over there, Fred." He pointed, then opened the truck door, flashlight in hand. "And be careful. We don't know what to expect from this guy." Then he took off toward the container. He was halfway there when he heard a man's voice.

"Chelsea!"

Liam stopped.

"You can't hide from me forever, sweetheart. Come on now. Quit wasting time."

Liam's chest thrummed as he turned toward the heavily treed mountainside rising on his right. Those few words told him Chelsea had escaped. They also told him she was still in danger.

"You know I never meant to hurt you." Tom Goodson's voice was loud enough to be heard, but also sounded gentle and concerned.

Concern and gentleness that Liam knew to be false.

"Quit hiding and let's go home. I came all this way. Don't disappoint me."

Chipper growled. In the glow of the flashlight, Liam saw the dog's head was lowered, the hackles on his neck raised. "Easy, boy. No going without me this time."

From a short distance away, Fred said softly, "They're up there. Now what?"

"Take my truck. Go for help. The guy must know we're here. He'll be feeling desperate."

"You sure?"

"I'm sure. Maybe he'll see you go and think he's got more time to find her." He hoped he was right.

"Chelsea, love, I'm running out of patience."

"Go, Fred. And hurry."

The older man headed for the truck as Liam moved up the mountainside, Chipper close beside him. He didn't dare use the flashlight now. He didn't want Chelsea's abductor to know where he was. For now he would have to rely on what moonlight there was and on his own instincts.

And God. He would rely on God.

APRIL 1922

Violin music wafted from an upstairs bedchamber, filling the entire house. Preston stood at the bottom of the stairs and looked up. He didn't have to join his wife to know how she looked, standing near a window, the instrument braced beneath her chin. After twenty-five years of marriage, he knew everything there was to know about her.

Almost, he thought with a smile. Almost everything. There would always be some mystery about his beautiful Cora, some secret in her woman's heart.

The music stopped abruptly. It always stopped at this exact same spot.

With a sigh, he climbed the stairs, making his way to the chamber that overlooked the gardens.

At one time, he and Cora had hoped to fill all of the chambers with children. Their son, Robert, was born less than three years after their wedding day, and they'd thought that was the beginning of their soon-to-be large family. But one year passed without a second pregnancy. And then another and another and another until it became clear Robert was destined to be an only child, like his father before him.

But what a fine son he was. In another month, Robert would graduate with honors from the university, ready to launch into a career of his own choosing. Of course, Preston hoped he would choose to come back to Chickadee Creek to help run Chandler Enterprises.

Preston had almost reached the bedchamber when the music started again. It wasn't the unfinished melody he'd heard earlier—the one Cora had been writing, off and on, for a number of years. This time it was Tchaikovsky. One of his favorite pieces. He listened for a while, then opened the door. The music stopped when she saw him, and she smiled.

"Our guests will arrive in a couple of hours," he told her as he crossed the room.

"I know. Such a lot of silliness." The look in her eyes belied her words. She was looking forward to the evening.

"Celebrating twenty-five years together is not silly."

"No, it isn't." She leaned forward to kiss his cheek. "How you have put up with me for all this time, heaven only knows." She turned and put the violin in its case.

"Put up with you? You gave me exactly what you promised."

"What I promised?" She faced him again.

Was she teasing him, or did she truly not remember? He reached out and touched her cheek with his fingertips. "You promised that our lives would be rich with meaning and full of joy."

"Even when sorrow comes," she finished in a whisper.

"Yes. Even then."

"And we've gone through it all side by side." Tears shimmered in her eyes as she quoted the promise he had made to her. "And I have never been sorry. Never."

He embraced her then, pressing her cheek tenderly against his chest, love welling up inside of him. Love . . . and thanksgiving to God.

After a while, she drew back. "We mustn't dawdle. We have guests arriving soon. Remember?"

"I know. But I have a surprise for you."

She sent him a small frown. "Promise me it isn't jewelry. I told you I have no need of more necklaces or bracelets."

"It isn't jewelry. It's Robert. He's going to be with us tonight. He should arrive at any time."

"Robert? He was able to get away from school?"

"Only for a short visit. He'll have to head back in the morning."

Cora frowned again, more serious this time. "He isn't driving, is he?"

Preston nodded.

"You should have insisted he take the train."

"He loves that automobile."

"I know he does. But all those hours on those wretched roads. There are so many things that can go wrong."

Preston drew her into another embrace. "He was raised by a strong, adventurous, independent-minded mother. Would you expect him to be different than he is?" He kissed her forehead, still holding her close.

"Mmm."

"I heard you playing your melody." He didn't say more. He didn't need to.

"It's still not right. There's something I'm trying to say with

285

it, but the notes aren't cooperating." She drew back to look him in the eyes. "Perhaps I should be content with playing music written by others. I'm foolish to think I can compose."

"I disagree." He kissed her on the lips. "I believe in you."

Her eyes lit with love, and the look melted his heart, just as it had on their wedding day.

Chapter 24

Chelsea could almost feel how close Tom was to her hiding place. Perhaps within a stone's throw.

Liam was close too. She'd seen the lights from a vehicle flashing through the forest, both when it arrived and when it left. But in her heart, she knew the truck had left without him. He was on this mountainside even now, trying to find her. She wanted to call out but resisted the urge. Desperation wouldn't serve them well. She had to be smart. She had to think through her actions. She wasn't the girl who cowered in the dark any longer. She'd been that girl once but no more.

"Baby, this has gone on long enough." Tom's voice had taken on a new edge. Did he also know that Liam hadn't left in his truck? Or did he think he'd won and his patience had grown thin?

Help me get to Liam, she prayed. *Guide me, Lord.*

Unlike the place where she'd awakened earlier, the forest was not completely dark. She could make out the shadows of trees and brush. She would be able to see movement if Tom came too close. But that meant that he could see movement too.

Hide me in the shadow of Your wings, Lord.

She left her hiding place, moving with great care. Very unlike her mad dash up the mountainside when Tom had returned. Thankfully, Tom wasn't trying to be quiet. He crashed about like a wounded bear. The distance between them grew as she descended the hillside, and she breathed a little easier. But not for long. Movement off to her left startled her. Not Liam. An animal of some kind. A bear? A wolf? A mountain lion?

It came toward her, a darker shadow among dark shadows. She couldn't stop the soft squeal of surprise from escaping her throat as she drew back. A moment later, the creature lunged at her, colliding with her chest. She hit the ground hard an instant before she felt the tongue swipe across her cheek.

"Chipper," she whispered, grabbing his head, breathing in his familiar doggy scent. "You're all right." Then she sat up. "Liam?"

He was there, even more quickly than the dog. His arm reached for her, and his hand pulled her to her feet. His lips found hers in a quick kiss before he whispered, "Are you okay?"

"Yes. But Tom's up there somewhere."

"I know." Restrained anger filled the two words. "Come on. Let's get you out of here." He kept hold of her hand as he led her through the trees.

They were stepping into the clearing when sounds from behind alerted them to Tom's approach. Liam drew her farther from the trees, then moved her to stand behind him. The dog growled and moved toward the trees.

"No, Chipper," Chelsea commanded. She touched Liam's arm. "Call him back. Tom hurt him before."

Liam took a step forward. "Come, Chipper. Stay." When the dog obeyed, Liam took a few steps backward, Chelsea moving with him.

The moon was high in the sky, casting a soft light over the

clearing, making it easier to see Tom when he appeared from beyond the nearest trees. He stopped, his gaze on them. Chelsea sensed his surprise that she wasn't alone.

"You're not welcome here," Tom said as he eased forward.

Icy tentacles tried to wrap around Chelsea's heart.

"You're the one who isn't wanted," Liam replied.

His confident tone warmed her heart, chasing the fear away.

"The sheriff's on his way." Liam turned on the flashlight and aimed its beam toward the car. "If you want a chance to get away, now would be the time." He glanced over his shoulder at Chelsea before passing her the flashlight.

She kept the light on Tom's car, hoping it would encourage him to do what Liam said.

"Liar," Tom growled. "Nobody's coming."

"Do you see my truck anywhere?" Liam's words seemed mocking. "I sent for help."

Tom looked around the clearing. For a moment, he stayed frozen in place. The next, he charged toward Liam, fists clenched. Liam took a moment to give Chelsea a protective push backward, then moved to meet his foe. Chelsea watched, heart in throat, as Tom threw a punch. Liam feinted, ducked, and brought a fist up to catch Tom under the chin. Knocked backward, Tom roared with frustration, then lunged again.

The next moments seemed to happen in slow motion. Chelsea saw each move Liam made. Like watching him in one of his films, more choreography than fight. She could almost hear the score, soaring and swelling at the appropriate times. Only this wasn't a movie. This wasn't pretend. Liam was agile and quick, but Tom had a good fifty or sixty pounds on him. Tom would kill Liam if he could. Her heart raced at the possibility.

The dog whined.

"No, Chipper. Stay." She hoped the words would reinforce Liam's earlier command.

But she wasn't about to do the same. She wouldn't stay. She couldn't stand there and watch. She'd done nothing to protect herself for most of her life. She couldn't do that any longer. Especially not if it meant Liam would get hurt because of her.

As she took a step forward, she remembered the flashlight in her hand. She switched it off and stared down at it. It was long and heavy. If she swung it the same way Tom had swung the tire iron at Chipper, she might do some real damage. But how did she get close enough to hit him? The two men were moving constantly. And what if she hit Liam instead?

Turn it on.

The thought was almost a command.

Turn it on.

She slid the switch, the bright beam hitting the ground in front of her.

For whatever reason, the two men slowed in their fight. Tom looked directly at her. A heartbeat later, she raised the flashlight, shining it directly into his face. His arm came up to shield his eyes, and in that same instant, Liam flew up in the air and kicked out. His right foot caught Tom on the side of the head, knocking him to the ground. It was the exact same move she'd seen him do in *Destination: North Star*. And it had the exact same result.

Breathing heavily, Liam watched his opponent, hoping he wouldn't try to get up again. He'd never been so thankful for anything as the beam of light that had distracted Tom Goodson. Once this was over, he would tell Chelsea she was a genius. He would tell her that and a whole lot more. Like how much he loved her and couldn't imagine life without her.

Chipper entered Liam's field of vision, approaching Tom with a growl, his head low, his muscles tensed.

"Stay, boy," Liam commanded.

Chipper stopped, but his stance said he wouldn't let the man on the ground hurt him again.

Liam took a step forward, then stopped when he heard the sound of a truck engine. Several engines. Before he could glance over his shoulder, headlights lit up the clearing. Moments later, other men were dragging Tom up from the ground.

Liam didn't notice anything else about Tom after that. He was too busy getting to Chelsea, pulling her into his arms, holding her tight against him.

"You're okay," he whispered against her hair. "You're okay."

"I'm okay. Are you?" She drew back, her hands moving up to cup the sides of his face. "You're bleeding."

"Am I?"

She touched a spot below his hairline.

"It's nothing." Now he mirrored her action, holding her face between his hands. "Your lip is swollen. Did he do that?" He felt fury rising in his chest again.

She ignored the question. "I knew you'd come for me." She smiled. "I knew you would. I could feel your love bringing you to me."

He pulled her close again, her cheek against his chest, his cheek resting on the top of her head. "I'll always come for you, Chelsea. No matter where you are, I'll be there."

Liam's Journal

It's over a week since Tom Goodson was carted off to jail. He was charged with kidnapping, theft, and a few other things and is held without bond. It seems he's jumped bail in the past, and the judge isn't taking any chances. Thank God for that.

Chelsea is doing good. In some ways, I think she's doing better than I am. She was like a rock after Tom's arrest. She was interviewed by the police, and I never saw even a glimmer of fear. She just told the facts.

I hired an attorney for her. Not because she's in trouble, of course, but I want to make sure Goodson doesn't get off on a technicality. I want to be sure justice is done.

No, what I really want is for that worthless lump of garbage, who used to be her boyfriend, to rot in prison.

Here's what's crazy: I managed to stay out of the limelight for nine months. No, even longer than that. There were some journalists that came around when <u>Destination: North Star</u> released, but my parents turned them away, and they honored our desire for privacy (that was a surprise) because of Jacob's failing health. Then, after I came up here, the folks in Chickadee Creek never said a word to an outsider about me. It was like they made a pact or something. So again, no word in the press.

But Chelsea's kidnapping and my part in Goodson's capture put an end to that. It feels like there's somebody sniffing around every rock in the area. Now there's talk about the Wentworth movie too.

I didn't realize it at the time, but while I was falling in love with Chelsea, I worried that she would hate that aspect of dating an actor. A relentless press. I can't say she's unfazed by the added attention I've brought to the mix. That wouldn't be true. But she's handling it with humor and style. She really is amazing.

Filming begins next month. I told her if she needed me here, I wouldn't go, even if it meant losing the part. She wouldn't hear of it.

One more reason I know she's special.

Liam's Journal

I fell behind in keeping this journal while I've been in Oklahoma. Been too busy memorizing the script and shooting each day. I talk to Chelsea most every night before I fall into bed. Can't get through a day without FaceTiming her, at least for a minute or two. The movie should wrap in two weeks, and when it does, I'll be on the first flight to Idaho.

I'm going to ask Chelsea to marry me when I get home. Playing this role has made me think a lot about the kind of man I want to be, the kind of husband, the kind of dad. And I know it's Chelsea I want to go through life with. It's her I want at my side. It's time I make sure she knows it too.

I've had a couple of talks with both Mom and Dad while I've been down here. I can't say things are smooth between us yet, but they're better. Mom's gone up to Chickadee Creek to see Rosemary and meet Chelsea. She likes her. "Jacob would love her," Mom said. She's right about that. It's what I've always thought.

One last thing before I close this and turn out the light. One of the guys I've gotten to know pretty well while on this shoot is a Christian, so we've spent time together, talking about the Bible, sharing rides to a church about fifteen miles from our location. There's a chance he might come in with me on the resort. I've decided I want to do it. It would be good for the economy of Chickadee Creek, for one thing. For another, I just like the idea of bringing life to the mansion site again. It seemed kind of a crazy idea at first, but it doesn't seem like it anymore.

Chelsea has talked a lot lately about how God brings beauty from ashes. That's another thing Jacob would like about her. Jacob said the same thing, even while he was dying.

We've come a long way, haven't we, God? The first pages I wrote in here were full of pain and more than a little despair. But You've brought beauty from ashes. Thanks for that.

Cora

Cora stood on the front porch, Preston at her side, waving as Robert, his wife, Rebekah, and their son, Oliver, drove away from the house.

"You've had a good birthday," Preston said.

She cast him a wry look. "When a woman turns sixty, I'm not sure you can say it's a *good* birthday."

"Of course you can." He tightened his arm around her shoulder. "Because it means we are still here together."

"How did we reach this age, Preston?"

"By living our lives one day at a time."

She laughed softly. "You always have an answer, don't you?"

"Yes."

They turned to go inside.

It was true, what Preston said about the passage of time. It did happen one day at a time. But Cora couldn't help wondering where the years had gone. So much had changed since the day she'd caught a train from New York—a train that carried her to Colorado and then another that brought her to Idaho. The Wild West had given way to cities. Horse-drawn carriages had given way to automobiles. The Great War and the Spanish flu had decimated families. The prosperity of the 1920s had given way to what was now called the Great Depression, a far worse financial collapse than the one that happened in the last decade of the previous century. Or perhaps it only seemed that way because she was older and more aware of such matters.

With his arm around her shoulders, Preston guided her slowly toward the parlor, where a fire blazed in the fireplace, chasing the chill of the blustery evening into the far corners of the room.

"I have one more gift for you," he said as they neared the settee.

"Oh, Preston. No. I've told you and told you. There is nothing I need."

"This is different." He drew her down onto the settee, then reached behind it and brought out a thin box with a blue ribbon tied around it. It resembled a box that might hold a handkerchief, only a bit larger. She could forgive him for a handkerchief.

He handed it to her. "Before you open it, I promise you that no one else knows of this. No one else has to know of it unless you decide to share."

What on earth did those cryptic words mean?

She plucked at the knotted bow and let the ribbon fall to the floor before lifting the lid. White tissue paper hid whatever was beneath it. She moved it aside to see her gift.

Sheet music? Why on earth would he—

She saw the title. *Freedom's Sonata.* Her heart quickened. *Freedom's Sonata?*

She looked at Preston. "You had my song published?"

"All those years you worked on it, trying to make it perfect. Trying to make the music say what you wanted it to say. It wasn't right to leave it in a drawer. Cora, when you play this song on your violin, I feel your joy. I feel your love. I understand what your violin is saying."

Tears sprang to her eyes. "You understand it," she managed to whisper around the lump in her throat, "because you understand me."

He'd heard it, of course, this truth that had worked its way into *Freedom's Sonata*. A truth that said real and lasting freedom came from giving herself completely to another person. It came from giving herself to him—one day, one week, one month, one year, and one decade at a time.

Together, they were truly free.

Epilogue

Chelsea stood in a room overlooking the gardens behind the new Chickadee Creek Inn. The grand opening wouldn't take place for another month, but today would be a trial run. Today the inn—built to resemble the original Chandler mansion—was hosting the wedding of Liam Chandler and Chelsea Spencer.

"I have never seen a more beautiful bride," Aunt Rosemary said from the overstuffed chair near the fireplace.

Chelsea looked at the paper taped to the mirror. She'd found a photograph in one of the books at the antique shop and made a photocopy. It was of Cora Anderson on her wedding day. Aunt Rosemary had hired a seamstress to recreate the gown for Chelsea as a special wedding gift.

"I can't believe it's me," she whispered as her gaze returned to the image in the mirror.

The white-satin princesse-style gown had a narrow waist, three-quarter puffed sleeves, and a lengthy train. Although she didn't resemble Cora Anderson in the least, she did look like a bride from the late eighteen hundreds.

Chelsea's mom lifted the bridal veil from the bed, holding the comb in her left hand and draping the silk chiffon fabric over her right forearm. Blinking back tears, she carried it to where Chelsea stood.

"Mom, you've got to stop crying. People will think you don't want me to marry Liam." She was joking, of course. No one would believe that. Debbie Spencer adored the man about to become her son-in-law, and she never hesitated to tell anyone who would listen how wonderful he was to her daughter.

"They're happy tears," her mom said. "Anybody can tell that." She held the comb over Chelsea's head. "Now, turn around. It's nearly time for the ceremony to start."

Nerves exploded in Chelsea's stomach, but like her mom's tears, they were happy ones. She hadn't a single doubt about the life she was about to embark upon.

Once the veil was in place, Aunt Rosemary pushed up from her chair and walked over to Chelsea. After kissing her on the cheek, she said, "'The steps of a man are established by the Lord, and He delights in his way. When he falls, he will not be hurled headlong, because the Lord is the One who holds his hand.'" The older woman touched her forehead to Chelsea's, adding, "God brought you to Chickadee Creek with this moment in mind. I believe that with my whole heart, dear girl." She drew back, her eyes now as misty as Chelsea's mom's were. "Now, I'm going down to find my chair. I've got a front-row seat for this joyous moment. Debbie, I'll look for you soon."

"Relax," Kurt Knight said softly.

Liam looked at his best man. "I'm not nervous."

"You look it."

"I'm eager. Not nervous. It feels like it took forever for this day to come."

Kurt laughed softly. "Between making a movie and building an inn, when exactly did you have time to get married before today?"

The plaintive notes of a violin drew Liam's gaze toward the back of the inn. A moment later, Evelyn Spencer, Chelsea's maid of honor, came down the aisle between the rows of satin-covered chairs. After she arrived at the white gazebo in the middle of the garden, she turned to face all the guests, smiling at Liam as she did so.

Then, to the now familiar strains of Cora Anderson Chandler's *Freedom's Sonata*, Chelsea walked toward him. She looked . . . unbelievably beautiful and completely unafraid.

Chelsea nodded to her many friends and neighbors from Chickadee Creek. She smiled and nodded to Liam's associates from Los Angeles. She nodded to her grandfather, great-aunt, mother, and youngest sister and brother, then did the same to Liam's mother and father on the opposite side of the aisle. And finally her gaze returned to Liam, her smile growing ever brighter.

For a moment Liam wondered if a man could die from pure happiness.

If so, it wouldn't be a bad way to go.

A Note from the Author

Dear friends:

Even after writing over eighty books, I must say that a great deal of how a story comes together in my imagination remains a mystery to me. Some books I know exactly where the idea came from. I can point to a certain moment. For other books, they seem to flower so slowly that I scarcely notice them until suddenly they are in full bloom. Some books begin with a character name or a line of dialogue or even a question in my own life. *Make You Feel My Love* began with a scene, with Chelsea entering the gloomy store filled with shadows while a storm raged outside. I immediately wanted to know who she was and why she was there. And so off I went on a journey of discovery.

As I write this note for *Make You Feel My Love*, I am putting the finishing touches on what will be the book that releases next (summer 2022). The title isn't confirmed yet, so I can't share that. But in case anyone is wondering, I'm not taking readers back to Chickadee Creek. This next story, featuring two sisters, demanded a completely different time and place. I can't wait to share more about it with you.

A NOTE FROM THE AUTHOR

I love to connect with my reader friends. The best way to be in the know about my books (new releases, works in progress, special sales, etc.) is to subscribe to my newsletter. You can do so at robinleehatcher.com/newsletter-sign-up.

And, of course, you can find me on Facebook at facebook.com/robinleehatcher.

Please know that you, my readers, bring great joy to the journey.

In the grip of His grace,
Robin Lee Hatcher

rlh@robinleehatcher.com

Acknowledgments

any thanks to my wonderful editor, Jocelyn Bailey, whose insights always help make my books better.

And thanks to Leslie Peterson, for making sure all those little bad habits of mine don't make it into print.

To the fiction team at HarperCollins Christian Publishing, as well as the sales reps and everyone in the rights department who help my books reach readers. It's a blessing to partner with you.

Thanks to my literary agent of thirty-two years, Natasha Kern. I can't imagine this writing journey without you, and I count you among my blessings.

As always, my deepest love and appreciation to my "plot, play, and pray" sisters in Christ—Tammy, Karen, Brandilyn, Gayle, Sharon, Tricia, Sunni, Francine, Sandy, and Janet—who for the past eighteen years have walked with me through the valleys and mountains of life, building my faith, brainstorming my books, praying with me and for me, both laughing and crying with me, iron sharpening iron, and so much more.

Thanks to my readers for spending some of your precious entertainment hours with the characters who fill my stories. You make the long months of writing a book so worthwhile. I love connecting with you through your emails and online.

To all of the above, I thank my God in all my remembrance of you (Philippians 1:3).

And finally, my eternal thanks to Jesus, my Lord, for His daily presence. I am so grateful that, through the power of God's written word, I can walk in the dust and sit at the feet of the Living Word, Yeshua the Messiah, the King of kings and Lord of lords.

Discussion Questions

1. Who was your favorite character in *Make You Feel My Love*? Why?
2. Did you have a favorite scene in the book? If so, what was it and why?
3. Both Cora and Chelsea suffered abusive relationships in the past. What similarities and differences were there in the way they dealt with their situations? What other characters made a difference in their lives?
4. Chelsea is a new follower of Christ. How did her faith make a difference in the way she found healing from her fears? Can you trace healing in your own life as your faith has deepened?
5. Liam is healing from the death of his brother but also recognized that his faith has only been skin deep in many ways. How does he grow in his faith over the course of the story? Do you keep the God-talk (as Kurt puts it) to yourself?
6. Liam keeps a journal to work through his memories and

emotions. Do you keep a journal? Why or why not? If so, has it strengthened your faith?

7. Both Cora and Chelsea had mentors who made a great difference in their lives. Do you have or have you had mentors who have helped you in your life and/or in your faith?

8. Cora composes a song she calls *Freedom's Sonata*. But freedom is so much more than an escape from bad circumstances. The Bible tells us: "So if the Son makes you free, you will be free indeed" (John 8:36). How has that truth impacted your life?

About the Author

Robin Lee Hatcher is the author of over eighty novels and novellas with over six million copies of her books in print. She is known for her heartwarming and emotionally charged stories of faith, courage, and love. Her numerous awards include the RITA Award, the Carol Award, the Christy Award, the HOLT Medallion, the National Reader's Choice Award, and the Faith, Hope & Love Reader's Choice Award. Robin is also the recipient of prestigious Lifetime Achievement Awards from both American Christian Fiction Writers and Romance Writers of America. When not writing, she enjoys being with her family, spending time in the beautiful Idaho outdoors, Bible art journaling, reading books that make her cry, watching romantic movies, and decorative planning. Robin makes her home on the outskirts of Boise, sharing it with a demanding papillon dog and a persnickety tuxedo cat.